2207
SOUTH
GREEN
ROAD

2207 SOUTH GREEN ROAD

a novel of love and dysfunction

Janice C. Spector

TWO
BAIRNS
PRESS

ISBN: 978-1-7367064-1-1

Published by Two Bairns Press
Lewes, Delaware 19958
Inquiries: JaniceSpector.com

To Barry, Michael, Elise, Luke, and Joely

———

For my cousin Elliot

You all show me every day that anything is possible if it's held together with love

2207 SOUTH GREEN ROAD

Chapter 1

EDNA SETTLED INTO THE CUBBYHOLE IN HER NARROW bedroom closet—her favorite hiding place. She had gathered more supplies than usual this morning, including an extra package of Hostess cupcakes she'd been saving. Her Debbie Reynolds paper dolls were meticulously laid out on the small patch of floor, each matching outfit to the right of the cut-out to avoid cupcake crumbs or chocolate stains.

When she'd asked her Grandma Becky why there were only paper replicas of certain people, she'd explained "You have to be famous, Edna. You have to be a movie star."

That made sense. As Edna dressed Debbie, she impulsively took a small pair of scissors to slightly reshape the hair. *Will I ever be famous? And if I am, will I be a movie star?* She could not imagine a paper reproduction of herself. Who would want a figure of a short fat person who had trouble finding clothes that fit?

She downed the second cupcake and stared at its companion—a package of Twinkies. Not really hungry, she ate the cream-filled sponge cakes anyway, pausing to wipe the residue from her hands.

Although the closet door was shut, she heard her father shouting at her mother. It would not be long before one of her parents stormed into the room.

It was Friday and most children viewed the upcoming weekend as a reprieve from school, but not Edna. At least tonight would be special. She'd be able to lose herself in the mayhem downstairs on the first floor of the house. She'd recently realized that the type of party that was to occur tonight wasn't really what most people considered a *party*, still she was the only family member excited that it was her grandfather Morris Katofsky's sixty-third birthday. The event would be the highlight of the week for the secretive child, who awoke gleeful about spending the evening with the birthday guests—her grandmother Becky's brothers and sisters and their spouses—Edna's great-aunts and uncles.

She knew any party hosted in Becky and Morris's tiny first-floor apartment had the potential to explode like a powder keg. The family rarely disappointed, always flaunting their best indecorous behavior. They were still talking about "the incident"—when Uncle Izzie's *Playboy* magazine fell out of the folds of the *Cleveland Plain Dealer* during Yom Kippur.

Their redemption was in their humor. Edna could count on her family to be funny, outrageous, even nonsensical. Like the time Aunt Millie had them all searching frantically for a string of lost pearls only to find they had fallen into her bra. The aunts were also highly judgmental, so much so that almost any innocent remark might be met with a caustic or even cruel retort. Edna viewed this as an odd form of affection because at least, unlike her father, they cared enough to reply.

Edna wondered if the party, as many were, would be cancelled. Maybe Grandma Becky would be sick again. Although Edna considered herself an excellent detective, as good as Nancy Drew, no matter how much snooping she did around the apartments in the two-family house at 2207 South Green Road, she still had no idea what was wrong with her grandmother. She tried, unsuccessfully, to decipher the hints and whisperings of the aunts and uncles whenever they were talking about Becky, but as soon as the adults noticed her, they always stopped the conversation.

"Well, Edna. What can we do for you? What do you need?" That was how they deflected when they caught her spying. The only answer she ever gave was that she was hungry—and even though the questions sometimes came soon after a full meal had been served, her aunts, uncles, and grandparents always accommodated her with a cookie. Or two. Or three.

Still in her pajamas, her parents unaware that she was awake, Edna dusted away the remaining pastry crumbs and crept downstairs. She pressed her ear to her grandparents' kitchen door and heard Becky hang up the phone, followed by the clatter of pots and pans. Edna detected a familiar aroma...brisket. She never understood why it was served on every holiday and special occasion, but the comforting scent was a sign that things were on track for the celebration.

At the sound of her mother's voice, Edna scurried back upstairs. She squeezed into her closet crawl space to wait for the commotion to stop, resigning herself to being late for school again. She regularly missed the bus, her departure dependent on how long her father spent raging around the second floor. She often arrived at her classroom in crumpled clothes with a hastily scrawled note pinned to her blouse that read "Family Emergency." She listened now as Esther flitted nervously around the apartment and her father raced from room to room, slamming each door with a thud.

The aunts and uncles seldom agreed on anything, but "beyond hatred" was how Edna heard them describe their singular attitude toward Edna's father, Harold. They constantly changed their opinions about what was wrong with her mother, Esther, Becky and Morris's only child, but they were unified in their fondness for their great-niece.

Edna was a smart girl, plagued throughout childhood with illness. She had chronic ear infections that caused her to miss most of the second grade, but she advanced nonetheless because scholastic testing indicated she was the brightest child at Belvoir Elementary School. The family, except for Becky's youngest sister, Aunt Ceal, stayed focused on Edna's academic potential and discounted her emotional difficulties. They saw nothing wrong with the girl being thirty pounds overweight by the time she was in the fifth grade.

To keep Edna engaged, Ceal crafted extraordinary plans. Responding to a newspaper ad, she'd arranged for Edna to audition for the role of one of the Polynesian children in a production of *South Pacific* at the Hanna Theatre in downtown Cleveland. After all, Ceal reasoned, Edna was learning French in school. When Edna, the only non-Asian child there, sang "Dites-moi pourquoi" in full force, Ceal shouted, "Louder, Edna!" ignoring the wincing producers. When Edna was rejected, Ceal consoled her with a huge ice cream sundae at the Old Mill Restaurant, explaining to her great-niece they had wanted "someone more French and less Jewish."

Had the family understood that Edna's emotional issues rivaled those of her mother, they would have been perplexed. They were sympathetic to the strange behavior of Esther, who, although they believed her to be a "nice girl," seemed oddly agitated and occasionally disconnected from ongoing conversations. Yet, they had grown accustomed to their niece's peculiarities, ignoring Morris Katofsky's concerns about his daughter's welfare, presented to them in a sometimes hard-to-follow combination of Yiddish and English. Harold was another case. If blame was to be cast, it would most certainly rest with Edna's disagreeable father. To discourage him from attending family functions, the aunts and uncles displayed open hostility toward him whenever he entered the room.

As the target of their animosity, Harold Kotkin viewed himself as a proud warrior—and even at her age, Edna understood he was an exceedingly narcissistic man who battled life daily. He reveled in the family's open rejection of him and retaliated by escalating his verbal abuse of Esther and constant tirade against Edna. When Harold agreed to move into the apartment upstairs from his in-laws, he had viewed it as hitching a ride on the "gravy train" and was shocked and belligerent when Morris insisted he pay rent. Harold had counted on a subsidized place to live, freeing his money for numerous get-rich-quick schemes. "It's costing me an arm and a leg," he complained to Esther on a regular basis—and emphasized his displeasure by always forgetting Edna at birthdays and holidays.

The only visitor to the house at 2207 South Green Road whom Harold liked was the maid. Harold adored Lurlene, who addressed

5

him as "Mr. Harold," which he deemed appropriate. Lurlene often helped clean the apartment, working around "Mr. Harold" and never asking him to move, no matter how difficult it became to maneuver through the piles of newspapers and toys. Harold so enjoyed Lurlene's deferential treatment, he intentionally turned the upstairs of the house into a pigpen, increasing the anxiety of the obsessively clean Esther. Becky struck back by threatening to charge Harold for the overtime she had to pay, while Lurlene attempted to calm the family by lavishing extra attention on "Mrs. K."

Becky's sisters also liked Lurlene but considered her an unnecessary luxury. They viewed Becky as living an extravagant lifestyle because she was the only one of them who did not work, even though she occupied much of her time keeping the books for Morris's floor-scraping business. "Writing out checks to the *goyim*, you call that working?" Ceal often complained to their middle sister, Libby, using the Yiddish word for all non-Jews.

The aunts and uncles assumed that when Becky was not on the telephone connecting with the rest of the family, she was either eating, cooking, or both. The phone, which hung on the bright yellow wall of the Katofskys' kitchen, began ringing at seven every morning, including weekends. The aunts and even the uncles—Izzie and Arthur—discussed their schedules, peppered with all sorts of unimportant information. Edna never questioned any of this behavior.

———

In a few hours, the guests coming to Morris's birthday party would cram into the living and dining rooms. The house on South Green Road was far too small to host everyone comfortably. It was one in a row of seven identical, brick, two-family dwellings. Morris and Becky had been eager to flee the cramped inner city of Cleveland, where segregated tenements evoked painful memories of their childhoods in Kiev and Latvia. Morris chose the location in University Heights at the urging of one of his fellow Jews from Eastern Europe, his lantsman, developer Sy Koppelman, who lived next door. When Morris broke ground in 1950, the lot sat directly opposite a golf course. Over the years, as the Jewish community flourished, the golf course was sold, becoming the Green Road Synagogue, and the traffic from the congregation became a major irritant to the Katofskys.

At first, South Green Road had seemed perfect to Becky. Idyllic. One block from 2207 was a small group of retail establishments—Weintraub's Grocery, the New York Bakery, Heights Pharmacy (where Harold worked), and Edelman's Kosher Butcher. Becky ordered all her groceries by phone and had them delivered. She liked dealing with the Weintraubs because the husband-and-wife team ran the store the same way she ran Morris's floor-scraping business—employing only blue-collar non-Jews whom they assumed would work more cheaply.

All the architectural details of the Katofskys' house were out of proportion. A huge wrought iron "K" adorned the front door of 2207. With Becky's approval, Morris fashioned an elaborate yard for the tiny dwelling. Evergreens flourished in the front, offset by eight randomly placed, bright-pink plastic flamingoes. The side of the house was bordered by huge blue and white peony bushes. The flowers targeted the back door of Morris's cherished Chrysler DeSoto in the summer, leaving a film of sticky pollen as he barreled in and out of the driveway.

7

A granite path led from the screened-in porch to the backyard. Edna numbered each flagstone in colored chalk, ready for a game of hopscotch. The child had her own swing set, positioned squarely in front of the two cherry trees. Birds plagued these trees as soon as they bore fruit, and Edna often joined her grandfather as he shouted obscenities in Russian and waved away the invaders with a broomstick. A large garden, nestled at one side of the house, displayed more gorgeous pink and yellow roses, always victim to Japanese beetles. The only flowers Becky permitted Edna to pick and bring indoors were on the far side of the garage, bordering the Koppelmans' property. There, wild bright-orange tiger lilies grew uncontrollably and overflowed into the neighbor's backyard. Sy Koppelman, his always-present cigarette dangling from his mouth, would curse under his breath as he hacked them away.

Visible through the trees at the back of the Katofsky property were undeveloped lots where Edna and Esther spent summer days picking huge baskets of wild raspberries and blackberries, which Becky would make into jam. In the middle of the yard was a circular bed, which served as a platform for a small concrete column adorned by a bright, silver-blue glass orb about the size of a basketball. Everyone admired it, although no one was quite sure what it was. Edna told her few friends it was a magic crystal ball.

The tiny house was designed for efficiency—milk boxes at the side door for the daily dairy delivery, built-in mail receptacles in the front of the house, and laundry chutes in each of the two apartment bathrooms to send wadded clothes—and sometimes toys, rocks, and whatever else Edna could find—to the concrete basement floor.

Becky furnished her apartment on the main level in metallic colors and leather. An enormous brocade couch, covered in plastic, ran against the back wall of the living room, giving the appearance of a mantle for the copper and silver wall-clock, designed to look like a sunburst. Although the clock never told the correct time, the Katofskys refused to repair or replace it. A huge leather chair and ottoman sat next to the prized Motorola phonograph. The curtains—a heavy green satin trimmed in gold—had begun to sag and Morris promised to rehang them.

Behind the television was a cabinet where Becky kept garish painted china objects. Edna's favorite was a replica of a seventeenth-century carriage, drawn by two horses led by a man with a pompadour. Stepping out of the vehicle was a woman in a blue-and-white ball gown, her hair fashioned in the same manner as the coachman's. If Edna pushed a button on the base of the piece, it lit up. It was in this living room—with her grandparents and away from her parents—that she tried to spend most of her time.

Gold wall-to-wall carpet connected the living room and dining room where the extended family always gathered. The white leather chairs were lined up like an expectant audience. There was a huge mahogany buffet with solid brass handles where Becky displayed desserts across from built-in cabinets housing her good Noritake china, stamped "Made in Occupied Japan." When held to the light, the base of her wine goblets revealed an etched Star of David.

———

As afternoon approached, Becky arranged those goblets on the table. She did her best to ignore the number of times the doors upstairs slammed. Anxious about tonight's party, her thoughts darted from one family member to another. *Would her prying sisters, eager to glean any information they could about the Katofskys' finances, begin to suspect how successful she and Morris truly were? Would Harold make a scene?* Her son-in-law still owed them this month's rent, complaining bitterly that Becky had raised the payment by ten dollars. And Morris had been babbling for the past few days about some man named Larsh. *Who was this Larsh—this Pole who had befriended her husband? Would Morris mention this mysterious new friend and business advisor to her brothers Izzie and Arthur?*

Eager to rid her mind of these concerns, she rummaged through the kitchen cabinets, searching the contents of several pill bottles for the familiar gray-and-red capsules. In her haste, two receptacles fell, one spilling as it landed in the sink. Not able to remember what the medication was, she pushed the soggy mess down the drain. She found the bottle she had been searching for, swallowed three capsules, and went back to cooking.

The screen door creaked open and a familiar voice called, "I'm here, Mrs. K. Don't go touching those dirty pots and pans—Lurlene will gets them for you." Standing in the kitchen entranceway, her wide, six-foot frame towering over Becky, Lurlene inhaled the familiar kitchen aromas and with "Mrs. K." smiling her approval, began to help with the preparations.

The thumping on the second floor continued, distracting Lurlene. She wondered if the upstairs occupants would join the party tonight. *They sound upset already, and the day not even begun.* She fastened an apron around her waist. *The child is bound to come down for sure.* As for Edna's parents, she was not as certain.

Chapter 2

MORRIS KATOFSKY WAS TIRED. HE STARED AT HIS TWO heavy steel sanding machines and decided he would have to ask George and Willie to help him load the equipment into the trunk of his car. The two men had grown accustomed to seeing "old man Katofsky" (the only proper name they used in referring to Morris) lift the massive machinery by himself at the end of each workday. It had been years since they had offered "the Russki" or "cranky old Jew" any help with the equipment.

Both men detected unusual irritability in Katofsky this Friday and obediently grabbed the sander as soon as Morris asked. As the three of them struggled with the second piece of floor-scraping equipment, Willie lost his grip, and the machine slid toward the pavement, denting the trunk of Morris's red-and-white DeSoto. Willie nervously eyed Morris to see if the boss was angry. He was indeed annoyed but, succumbing to his exhaustion, only muttered something indecipherable in Yiddish. Willie regained his grip on the second sander as he and Katofsky pushed it into the DeSoto, slamming the trunk closed.

Willie and George had remained silent today when Morris decided to sit on the opposite side of the hotel ballroom as they ate lunch. The routine the three men followed always found them side by side during their break, with George doing most of the talking. Occasionally, and today was one of those days, George would insist on plugging in his black, sorely battered, Motorola clock radio and blasting pop music during the entire lunch hour. The throbbing cacophony was so disconcerting to Morris that he spilled the entire jar of red horseradish Becky had packed with his lunch all over the front of his already filthy overalls. George and Willie kept eating, but Willie's eyes stayed focused on Morris, who attempted to mop up the beet-red splotches with the rag usually reserved for wiping sawdust off the machines. Muttering in Yiddish, Katofsky unexpectedly got up and took his crumpled paper lunch bag to the other side of the room.

George and Willie were unaware Morris had been badly bruised in a fall at home the previous week. To save money (at least that is how Katofsky told the story), he had attempted to take one of the sanding machines down into the basement for a minor repair. According to Katofsky's version of the tale, he and the machine landed side by side on the concrete basement floor.

"The sander suffered only a slight dent, thank God," his wife Becky told her siblings in the daily "What's new?" report. Becky neglected to mention that Morris had black-and-blue marks down the entire length of his right leg.

That was ten days ago, and Morris's leg still ached. The many untold truths regarding the accident that he played over and over in his mind distracted him. The first was his indignation that no one asked him about what he decided, in retrospect, should have been apparent to most people. Why would he, Morris, usually a sensible man, attempt to drag a three-hundred-pound sanding machine which was in no need of repair to the basement? Certainly, he reasoned, someone must have asked Becky that question during the "What's new?" report. He was convinced that at least one of the aunts must have suspected the truth: There was nothing wrong with the machine. The basement was one of the few places he could escape Becky, and he had been hiding down there, on and off, for at least twenty years.

But—and perhaps the saddest of the untold truths—he was convinced no one stopped to think about Morris at all. And, since they never thought about him, it was unlikely it ever crossed their minds, even in his presence, what he might be thinking. To most people, he decided, he appeared to be a very uncomplicated man.

So today, lost in thought in the cold, empty ballroom where the three men were working, he seemed like the "usual Katofsky" to George and Willie. That was, in a way, comfortable for Morris. The workday would soon end, and the only thing Morris, Willie, and George would agree on was that they were headed home.

At five o'clock George offered, as he did daily, to drive; and as he did every day, Morris declined. With everyone in their usual seats in the DeSoto, George reached into the pocket of his overalls to pull out his second pack of Lucky Strikes for the day. From the back seat of the car, he passed a cigarette to Willie, sitting comfortably in the front passenger seat, who accepted and pulled out a pocket lighter. The two men began puffing eagerly.

Morris, as always, declined the Lucky Strike. Katofsky wondered why George tried to give him a cigarette every day. George had worked for him for ten years and knew Katofsky did not smoke. Why, he wondered, didn't Willie say anything to George? Willie knew the old man had no discernable vices. And why did Becky, in the telling and retelling of the dropped sanding machine story, begin with how fortunate they were that the machinery was not damaged (thank God) and only casually mention that Morris had been hurt? It was this constant dismissal by his wife, he decided, that put him in this foul mood and certainly in no mood for the party tonight. But it was far too late to come to that conclusion, and he knew that even if he had told Becky a week ago "No party," she would have had the party without him. He was too many years down the road with her, forty to be exact, to be upset that his wife would celebrate his sixty-third birthday even if he refused to attend.

The constant invitation from George to smoke, Morris decided, must be the cumulative effect of the alcohol. While Morris enjoyed an occasional glass of *schnapps*, he was still amazed every time he saw George finish his daily six-pack of beer. He could only remember a single occasion when he, Morris Katofsky, was *shicker*. He did notice, however, that George had not taken a single drink today. This fascinated him.

The goyim. Of course they drank, Becky would constantly remind him. "And why does this surprise you, Moshe?" She would, however, have no ready response to explain why George had not started the day by ripping off the cap of a beer bottle. And she would never detect the slight twinkle in Morris's eye when, in relating this salacious detail, he was able to catch her momentarily off guard.

Instead, he knew, Becky would reiterate her belief that the drinking was just one more example of how they could never really depend on the goyim. As Becky was fond of saying, even if they were occasionally dependable, it would be a mistake to trust *them*.

———

The trio drove to the Katofsky house on South Green Road, the wheels of the DeSoto creaking from the weight of the machines. George spread out in the back seat of the car and finally popped open his first beer bottle of the day. He tucked the cap in his pocket, resisting the urge to flip it into the front seat.

George had tousled red hair that was always dirty and a patchy, red-faced complexion. Although he had crystal blue eyes, massive creases carved lines across his forehead and cheeks. Two of his front teeth were missing, and the remaining ones had a sickly yellow hue. Becky was convinced the teeth had permanent beer stains and he never brushed them, because George's breath had a constant stale foul odor.

George, now on his second beer, offered the more affable Willie a bottle—Willie declined as usual. George viewed this as "rejection" and taunted Willie: "*You'se* so much better than me, *ain't* you? Don't go to no bars. Don't spend money on cigarettes and liquor!" Willie never took the bait, and Morris sensed the two workers were often a remark away from a fistfight. He was convinced Willie never took the challenge because George, who towered over Willie, could easily beat Willie into the ground.

Morris spoke broken English at best and cringed every time George put more than two sentences together. Katofsky resented the fact that George was lucky enough to be born here, in the United States of America. Morris could never reconcile the choices George made—he saw a man who grew up with the opportunity to get an education but was seemingly content to babble inanely and make swilling more beer his life's ambition.

Even though Morris had lived in Ohio for almost forty years, each attempt to improve his English had been unsuccessful. It was not a problem within the family, because they all spoke Yiddish. But Becky found it necessary, depending on the job, to instruct Willie carefully how to speak on behalf of the boss. The frustration with English led Morris to memorize many of the phrases he heard on radio and television and incorporate them into his daily speech. Sometimes he would shout, "Hey, Mabel! Black Label!" when George opened a bottle of beer. George and Willie would snicker, and a defiant Morris would shout even louder, drowning out the sound of the heavy sanders.

Sometimes George and Willie, cigarettes dangling from their mouths, would shout back in unison: "Carling Black Label Beer!" Morris would smile, a gesture George and Willie interpreted as a good sign from the boss. But Katofsky was silently thinking "The *goyim*. Only the goyim would choose a life of empty beer bottles." At least, that is the way it seemed to Katofsky, who limited his contact with anyone outside the family.

Becky tolerated George. She would say nothing as he sat at the Katofsky kitchen table after work, still drinking, while Becky remained in the dining room with her huge green accounting ledger, making out the paychecks. Willie, however, was a mystery to both Katofskys. Becky genuinely liked Willie, and Morris decided it was because she knew Willie had a five-year-old son.

There was always a fresh piece of cake or an assortment of cookies in the Katofsky kitchen, and Becky appreciated the way Willie would say, "Thank you, Mrs. Katofsky. Thank you very much," as she served him and he graciously accepted a package of treats for his boy.

Neither Katofsky knew much about Willie. He would artfully avoid most of the inquiries Becky made into his personal life. Although Willie was friendly and could spend a good hour engrossed in conversation, there was never any mention of the boy's mother. Unable to extract any information, Becky assumed Willie was the lone parent. She nagged Morris to procure more details when he first hired Willie. Unable to satisfy Becky's curiosity, and having none of his own, Morris simply said, "The man works hard, Becky. The child is his business, not ours." But even though she liked Willie, Becky could not suppress a general feeling of suspicion. For a workman, he was fairly well-groomed. And well-spoken. Too well-groomed and too well-spoken, she decided. With no explanation offered about Willie's life, it became, as most things did, another pronouncement about the goyim. "They are not like us. They are different," Becky said. Morris never uttered a word, but silently agreed.

It was just past five thirty, and the DeSoto was only twenty minutes away from the Katofsky house. The stench from the cigarette smoke was beginning to make Morris sick to his stomach and irritate his eyes, but he said nothing. Willie began fumbling with the dial on the car radio, as he always did. Every day for the past two months, it had been the same. Willie would go from station to station hoping he could catch some DJ playing "Hit the Road, Jack."

Once Willie found the song, George popped open another beer bottle, and, waving it in the air before beginning to drink, said, "Here's to you, Ray." The two workers sang along with the radio, with George singing and laughing extra loudly as he parroted the words, *"And don't you come back no more!"* Often by the time they arrived at the house, Morris had heard the rendition three or four times. Today was one of those days.

Morris finally turned the car into the driveway, stopping by the screen door at the side of the house. He yelled, "Hit the road!" and motioned his passengers to get out of the car. The two men lumbered into the kitchen, George squashing his last Lucky on the doorstep.

Becky wanted to be quick about writing George and Willie's checks tonight. Her sharp eyes on the clock, she paid the men and firmly told Morris he had to shower and change his clothes immediately. George headed out to his favorite haunt, The Family Trio Bar and Restaurant. Morris would have been amused to know George would spend the evening eating steak, cheese, and grilled onion sandwiches, telling the bartender about his workday for the "crazy old Jew."

Becky suspected that this is what George did with his paycheck—headed to a bar, never saving a penny. *What else could you expect from them? Not very smart.* But Rebecca Katofsky was a shrewd and devious woman. Taking the advice of her two brothers, who were very successful in business, she would lure the goyim into working for less-than-average pay by writing them daily instead of weekly checks. This, she was told by her brothers, applied to the Blacks as well. Everyone who serviced the Katofsky household left with a paycheck for the day's work firmly in hand, and the balance in the small blue Katofsky savings bankbook benefited from this system.

George and Willie treated Becky with a detached form of respect. George, although he would never admit it, was afraid of Becky. He did not allow himself to think of her as "The Old Woman"—even in his private thoughts she was "Mrs. Katofsky." He suspected if she played poker (she did), she was an excellent card player (she was).

As Morris showered for the party, he chuckled about his routine decline of George's offer to take the driver's seat. George never knew why, but it was because of George's drinking. Instead of muttering his usual "No *denk* you," Morris sometimes shouted, "No cowabunga!" a phrase he adopted by watching the *Howdy Doody Show* with his granddaughter, Edna.

Never suspecting Morris's real concerns, George would laugh and say, "Okay, boss. No cowabunga." The rejection of this offer to drive the boss home would fuel his hatred of the "crazy old Jew." Morris's belief, however, was that Becky was right about the goyim. They were not very smart.

Chapter 3

ARTHUR AND IZZIE SHAFRON WERE SUCCESSFUL BUSI-
ness partners, envied by Becky and their sisters Ceal
and Libby. Lacking formal educations, the men built a
successful wholesale fruit and vegetable business, allowing their
wives to enjoy lavish homes, expensive clothing, and leisurely lives.
In contrast, Ceal and Libby worked dismal jobs and had husbands
with meager incomes. Ceal suspected Becky and Morris might be
as well off as Arthur and Izzie, although she was never able to confirm if her suspicions were true.

Izzie's wife, Ethel, was well liked and the sisters welcomed her
into their inner circle. But Arthur's wife, Millie, was detested by
all the women. This puzzled Arthur, who ruled out jealousy as the
motive. After all, he reasoned, it could not be about the money—he
and Izzie had the same income. And Millie was a warm woman—a
devout woman—always cordial to her sisters-in-law, no matter how
badly they treated her.

Edna may have been excited about the party, but the aunts and
uncles knew that it would not necessarily be an enjoyable occa-

sion. While they were resigned to Becky's status as the matriarch, and always adhered to whatever social schedule she set, some of them fantasized about going an entire year without attending these family functions. They had their own children and grandchildren, but Becky corralled everyone at *her* home, and because Edna and her parents lived above them, unlike her cousins, she saw her great-aunts and uncles all the time.

As the party preparations continued, afternoon dissolved into evening, Becky ingesting varied and assorted pills throughout the day. At just past five thirty, Edna ran into the downstairs living room, where Morris, home from work, greeted her with his wide smile and daily proclamation of endearment, *"Mir fir ir."* Esther followed and haltingly entered the kitchen, asking Becky—who was seated at the table—if she needed any help.

"No," Becky replied indifferently, never looking at Esther, "Lurlene will do it." Then Becky, fatigued from cooking all day, placed her hand solidly on her chest and informed her daughter, "I'm not feeling good."

This remark sent Esther dashing through the small downstairs apartment to find Lurlene, who had spent the past few hours polishing silver, lining up wine glasses, and carefully displaying the good china. The dutiful housekeeper tended to her employer. Becky pointed to the stove, instructing Lurlene to lower the flame under the soup. Becky took one last taste of everything and thanked Lurlene while Morris reclined, Edna in his lap, in the large brown leather chair in the living room.

The tumult began, as always, with the arrival of Ceal and her husband, Al. Ceal flew up the front steps, leaving Al still sitting in the car in the driveway. Unlike Becky, who was heavyset, Ceal, although not slim, displayed her average figure with great care. She preserved her short, dark "permed" hair, slightly streaked with gray, with an inordinate amount of Aqua Net. Longing to show some sense of style, she wore a green dress copied from one she had seen in *McCall's* magazine, made in an inexpensive material that imitated the costlier tweed.

Before she entered the house, Ceal paused to open the two milk chutes. It was imperative she confirm that Lurlene had removed whatever the milkman had delivered that morning. Ceal was still fuming about last week, when she had stopped by on her way home from work to see Becky and found the milk boxes at the front door still filled with fresh milk, sour cream, and butter. The butter was like putty, the milk bottle warm and sweaty, and the carton of sour cream separated. When Ceal demanded to know why the dairy products were outside all day, Becky explained, without looking Ceal directly in the eye, that she had had severe chest pains and spent the entire morning and afternoon in bed.

"Lurlene was off," Becky had told her sister in a lethargic voice, with her hand squarely on her chest, and emphasized, in a matter-of-fact manner, that they could throw away the spoiled products because she had placed a double order for the next delivery. This was upsetting to Ceal, who counted every penny. She had *kvetched* about the incident to Al the entire week.

"There are much bigger problems in that house than sour milk," Al reminded her, and Ceal knew he was right.

After confirming the milk boxes were empty, Ceal joined Becky at the kitchen table and went down her mental checklist for the party.

"Do you have plenty of Alka-Seltzer for tonight?" Ceal quizzed. "Libby called me and said Joe's stomach is bothering him again."

"*Meine* heart," Becky replied. "I don't feel good again tonight—it's *meine* heart."

Before Ceal could continue, Libby swept into the living room. Morris turned up the volume on the phonograph. Following Libby was her husband, Joe, intentionally walking several steps behind his wife. Joe, who understood his role was to appear to be absent, deposited himself in one of the blue-and-gold side chairs next to the coffee table, the protective plastic covering popping as he sat down. For some reason, Al was still in the car, rummaging through the glove compartment.

The popular Jewish comedian and singer, Mickey Katz, was now crooning Morris's favorite song, "Borscht Riders in the Sky." Surreptitiously, Edna, who had eased off Morris's lap, positioned herself in the corner—the best place to observe the performances staged by her great-aunts and uncles.

Libby shouted, "Ceal, are you here?" as she collided with her in the dining room, knocking her sister to the floor. Edna had once made the mistake of asking Aunt Libby, "Why do you shout from room to room? The house isn't really that big."

Lurlene, who was standing right behind Ceal as Libby ran into her, lifted the woman up and helped her smooth her hair and brush the creases from her dress. Lurlene had fashioned a lovely spread, the buffet and main table covered with discreetly patterned, well-pressed white damask tablecloths. The sisters turned to Lurlene and proclaimed as if in unison, "The dining room looks beautiful." Lurlene headed back to the kitchen as Al meandered in from the driveway toward the living room.

Edna, who had taken a pear from the ample fruit bowl, sat riveted as her great-aunts began dismantling the buffet. Ceal, with the flair of a magician, removed the cloth from the table, and handed the vase of flowers to Libby. Libby deposited the flowers on an end table, and the sisters began rearranging the silverware. Lost in conversation, they were unaware they were removing, repositioning, and returning each item back to Lurlene's original location.

In a low voice, as she ran a clean dishcloth over each utensil, Ceal told Libby, "Becky's complaining of chest pains again."

Libby was infuriated. "I'm telling you, Ceal, one of us has got to get on the phone with Dr. Gold. How many pills has she taken since this morning? Did she tell you?"

"No, she won't tell me anymore," Ceal replied, "but I know she had the prescription filled again yesterday. You stay here—I'm going to see if I can find the bottle."

Leaving Libby in the dining room, Ceal slipped into Becky's back bedroom. She closed the door behind her, not making a sound. She slipped off her shoes lest the floorboards compromise her mission. Her gaze went immediately toward the bed, where she was unprepared for what she saw.

Everyone knew Becky and Morris had occupied separate rooms since they moved into the house in 1950. Becky's was the larger, with an enormous bed. At one side was a night table, on the other a huge green oxygen tank with a plastic facemask. Ceal was accustomed to the tank, but was startled that the mask, which she assumed had never left its position in ten years because Becky never used the tank, was draped casually on the bedpost. Ceal put on her glasses and studied the gauge—the tank was only half full.

She rummaged through the medication-laden night table looking for Becky's nitroglycerin tablets. She sorted through bottles of aspirin, Pepto-Bismol, and paregoric. There were several unmarked bottles of liquid, including half a bottle of rubbing alcohol. Ceal took the cap off one and frowned when she could not determine its contents. Pouring a small amount on her finger, she tasted it and concluded it must be some sort of antacid. She found the red, foil-wrapped nitroglycerin tablets and hastily began counting the pills to see how many remained.

Becky had been taking the nitroglycerin for over a year, and the pills always seemed to ease her chronic chest pain. *Angina*— that was what the doctor called it. However, Becky said the discomfort was getting worse, and no one kept track of how many pills she was taking. Not even Becky.

Setting the nitroglycerin aside, Ceal opened the paregoric. She inhaled deeply—she loved the smell and toyed with the idea of taking a small swig of the medication, telling herself she could feel the onset of an upset stomach. The taste reminded her of licorice. The idea of taking the opiate was intoxicating. The warm, bitter liquid would not only ease any stomach pain, but relax her entire body. She inhaled again. *How could anyone not love paregoric?* She paused as she heard faint sounds from the dining room, the voices of Izzie and Ethel. *What would be the harm in taking a small swig?*

With the bottle perched at her lips, Ceal stopped when she heard Lurlene's knock at the bedroom door announcing the arrival of the brothers and their wives. "Coming, I'm coming." Flustered, Ceal closed the lid, almost spilling paregoric down the front of her green dress. For some reason, she stuffed the large bottle of nitroglycerin tablets sideways in her bra. She repositioned the oxygen mask at its proper place on the tank, then changed her mind, leaving it where she had found it. She smoothed her tight, curly hair and returned to the dining room.

Izzie was the first to greet her but stopped mid-sentence. Pointing to the bulge in Ceal's bosom, he asked, "What is that?" Ceal fished the nitroglycerin out and handed the bottle to her brother. "Put this in your pocket," she instructed. Izzie reluctantly obeyed, glancing at the label. As Ceal walked past him into the kitchen, he gave the bottle to his wife, Ethel, and told her to hide it. The ever-obedient Ethel slinked through the living room, her eyes darting to see if she was being followed. Edna, who had overheard Izzie and was monitoring the entire drama, saw her great-aunt headed to the milk boxes at the side of the house.

Having fulfilled her errand, Ethel returned to the party. It was precisely 7:10 p.m. Arthur and Millie, who never arrived on time, had joined everyone in the living room. Becky heaved herself up from the kitchen table, yelled at Morris to turn off the phonograph, and told Lurlene to start serving dinner. The birthday celebration was about to begin.

Chapter 4

BECAUSE IT WAS FRIDAY NIGHT, THE JEWISH SABBATH, Arthur's wife, Millie, made her "usual annoying request" to light Shabbat candles. None of the aunts and uncles were observant—everyone wanted to eat. Becky, speaking on behalf of all the sisters, replied curtly, "*Zaide* isn't coming tonight."

Their father, Ben, who lived with Ceal, was not attending. What the family did not know was that since the death of his wife, Ben Shafron—*Zaide*—had not been observant either. He had no idea why his children assumed he was. In fact, he was puzzled by most things his children did. He was satisfied that his sons and daughters were reasonably deferential. Their spouses were not that interesting to him—especially Morris, whom he privately referred to as "the greenhorn."

Close to his eighty-sixth birthday, Ben kept an active schedule playing cards and kibitzing with his friends at the Hebrew Home. The master of the "Shafron poker face," he concealed from his five children the truth of how little he enjoyed their company—found it irritating and overbearing. Ben often challenged his *lantsmen* at

2207 South Green Road

the home to devise various excuses to avoid family gatherings. As for tonight's party, he had told Ceal he was visiting a sick friend.

Ceal was secretly relieved that her father was not coming—she was preoccupied with the milk boxes and Becky's unrelenting chest pains. With Libby now in tow, the sisters, unable to agree on how to re-set the dinner table, decided to have a buffet.

"Becky made soup," Arthur kvetched to his sisters. "How am I supposed to balance a soup bowl on my lap!" He added, "Why is there a buffet if there aren't enough TV trays for everyone?"

Libby responded by handing one of the trays to Edna, saying, "Go share this with your Uncle Arthur."

Oversized platters laden with paprika chicken, roasted carrots, and *kasha varnishkes* (kasha with bow-tie noodles) followed the soup. Becky had peeled dozens and dozens of new potatoes (Edna's estimate was about two hundred) and fried them in butter and *shmaltz* (rendered chicken fat) until their crisp outer shells were a nice golden brown. There was potato kugel and fresh challah and Kaiser rolls (some poppy seed, some plain). A huge crystal bowl held cantaloupe and strawberries. No one thought it odd—except Edna, who had learned about such things in school—that there were no green vegetables.

All this commotion left Morris feeling overwhelmed. It was not until halfway through dinner he realized his brother was not there. Morris had asked Becky to invite Abe, his sister Lena, and Lena's daughter, Frances, to the party. Not sure what Becky's response would be, he had been surprised when she agreed to invite his brother, but not at all surprised she excluded Lena and Frances.

Morris went to the kitchen to telephone Abe, but Becky's hollers interrupted him. His wife, sprawled on the living room couch, had finished her second plate of food. In Yiddish, she called, "Moshe, bring me some more *flanken*, without the soup, but with some of the red horseradish. And more kugel—not too much—maybe two pieces." The ever-obedient Morris filled her plate. Then he asked Becky if he should call Abe.

"Forget about Abe," she chided. "He will probably call later. Or maybe he will wait until Sunday to come. Or maybe he went to see Lena." Morris understood that as far as Becky was concerned, the subject of his brother was closed for the evening.

As soon as they cleared the dinner dishes, it was time for dessert. Becky lit the candles on Morris's cake and Millie nudged her husband, Arthur, who went outside to his car and brought in a pair of large silver candlesticks and two tall slim tapers. Becky carried the glowing cake into the dining room, but before anyone could sing "Happy Birthday," Millie blew out the candles and proclaimed it was *now* time to light Sabbath candles. The aunts remained silent, Lurlene murmured *"Oy! Gevalt!"* under her breath, and Arthur began contemplating how to orchestrate an early exit from the festivities. The aunts, their arms crossed in a unified display of annoyance, glowered as Millie recited the Sabbath blessings, "Baruch Atah Adonai, Eloheinu Melech Ha'Olam..." Libby tapped her foot. Only Edna noticed that Esther was running up the stairs to bring Harold more food.

The dining room fell silent as Millie finished chanting. Becky, with a massive knife firmly in her grip, moved toward the birthday cake. Edna had a momentary flash of Becky stabbing Aunt Millie. Izzie pulled one of his notorious cigars out of his shirt pocket and began fumbling with his lighter—a sure sign that Millie and Arthur were in trouble. Millie was oblivious to the disdain of her in-laws and stared at Becky, a vacant smile overtaking her face, then became preoccupied with smoothing the creases out of her expensive dress. Her heavy gold charm bracelet caught the end of the tablecloth, and Arthur dutifully rushed to his wife's side to free her wrist. Ceal viewed this ridiculous display of devotion with narrowed eyes, fixated on Millie's diamond-and-ruby-encrusted charms. Turning her own wedding band around and around, she lamented what a mistake her brother had made—marrying this brainless, superstitious woman.

Libby slipped toward the rear of the house to complete the investigation Ceal had started. Watching her leave, Edna considered volunteering to help her two great-aunts find whatever they were looking for. *After all, that's what they must be doing—searching Grandma's room for something.* Edna knew she could be a tremendous help. Whenever she noticed Grandma was preoccupied—which, frankly, was most of the time—she took the opportunity to inspect as many drawers and closets in the downstairs apartment as she could. She was surprised by her confidence when she scoured the dining room last week—after all, Grandma was sitting right there in the kitchen. *How could she not see what I was doing?* Edna had called out to her, but Grandma had not answered; she kept staring into space. *Anyway, I could tell the aunts where everything was.* Suddenly, Edna felt a tightness in her chest—she hoped they didn't look in Grandma's hatboxes in the closet. *No, that wouldn't happen. Grandma had not worn hats for a very long time.*

32

In the back bedroom, Libby recognized she could not be absent from the festivities for much longer and began straightening the medication bottles on Becky's nightstand. There was no time to go through all the dresser drawers, but Libby knew the lower bottom drawer of Becky's walnut dresser was actually a cedar chest, a good hiding place. Libby chose to look there.

She grabbed the small brass ring and pulled the lid open. The smell of cedar was overwhelming, although pleasant, and Libby recognized the gray wool blanket with satin trim neatly lying across the top of the chest—it had belonged to their mother. When she pulled it back, what she discovered startled her. Not wanting to be caught, she smoothed the blanket in place, and closed the chest and the drawer. *What could this mean?* She couldn't wait to tell Ceal.

There would be no opportunity that evening for Libby and Ceal to have a private conversation. Libby fashioned all kinds of sinister scenarios as to why Becky had hidden *so much cash* in her bedroom. Ceal, Libby knew, would try to find a harmless explanation. Libby was determined to meet Ceal's optimism with skepticism and eventually convince her younger sister that a family crisis was evolving. Managing a crisis was one of Libby's many talents—even if said crisis did not exist.

After the cake was cut, Edna and Millie went into the living room to watch television. The aunts and Esther took their coffee into the kitchen, while the uncles remained in the dining room. The uncles talked business while the aunts talked about Millie.

"You heard the latest with Millie?" Ceal began. "Richard calls her from medical school and says he just found out he needs glasses. So, what does she do? She tells Arthur they need to send him bottles of carrot juice."

The aunts cackled.

"Millie is such a stupid woman," continued Libby. "I don't know what Arthur sees in her. I'm out last Saturday to pick up some bagels and I stop at Mawby's for a cup of coffee. Who do I see sitting at the counter? *Arthur*."

Ethel gasped.

"I said, 'Arthur, what are you doing here so early in the morning?' And he said, 'Millie had a headache last night and is sleeping late—I didn't want to wake her.'"

The aunts shook their heads in disapproval and hushed as Millie entered the kitchen. "Edna wants one more piece of cake," Millie told her sisters-in-law, holding out an empty plate. Becky filled the plate with cake, a few cookies, and some apple strudel, and Millie hastily left.

The aunts sat silently until they were sure she was out of earshot.

Libby continued the disparaging remarks. "I once asked Ma, 'Ma, why is Arthur happy with such a stupid woman? How could a man as smart as my brother marry such a *schmoe*?' Ma shrugs her shoulders and says, 'She must be good in bed.'"

The sisters stopped talking—and even stopped eating—after this comment.

Becky changed the subject. "Millie called me yesterday to tell me she was making gefilte fish for Arthur because Arthur loves gefilte fish. He's my brother, so I don't know he likes gefilte fish?"

She continued in muted tones. "Millie tells me how she's making the fish. She tells me every ingredient, how long it takes..." Becky paused for the intended theatrical effect, as the aunts leaned hunched together, forming a semicircle around the yellow Formica kitchen table.

"For twenty years, she has called me once a month to tell me how she makes gefilte fish. And each time she calls me, she tells me how she is making it differently." The aunts, although not surprised, shook their heads again in displeasure. Ceal and Libby wondered the same thing: *Why are we being given this information for the first time after twenty years?*

"So," Becky continued, "at the last poker game, Arthur turns to me and says, 'Millie makes the best gefilte fish in the world—even better than Ma's.'"

The aunts recoiled.

"What did you say to him?" hissed Libby.

"I said, 'Arthur, how can it be the best gefilte fish in the world—even better than Ma's—when Millie makes it differently every time?'

"Arthur looked surprised," Becky continued, "and he said to me, 'She makes it differently every time?'"

Becky positioned her bulky body in an upright pose. "I tell him, 'See, Arthur, there's a lot you don't know about Millie.'" The aunts all nodded in agreement.

Ceal was about to begin a tirade about how, if a wife lies to her husband about how she makes gefilte fish, who knows what else she lies about, but was preempted by Libby, who turned to the frazzled Esther and asked, "So, Esther, when are you going to lose some weight?" Esther, self-conscious about her more than plump frame, shifted in the kitchen chair.

Before she could reply, Ceal interjected, "Leave her alone, Libby. She eats because she's nervous. Harold makes her nervous, so she eats."

The aunts nodded in agreement. Esther, always ready to leave a family gathering, told her mother it was late, she needed to take Edna upstairs. Edna, always reluctant to leave a family gathering, made sure to give each aunt and uncle a kiss. She saved her grandfather for last. With her eyes closed and her head resting on his chest, Edna whispered, "Goodnight, Grandpa."

Ceal, who had found a few minutes between dinner and dessert to run her fingers across the furniture searching for even a speck of dust, said to Becky, "Lurlene, she does a nice job. How much are you paying her now?"

"I give her ten dollars a day—and all of Edna's old clothes for her daughter's child," Becky answered.

Libby was about to ask Becky a question, but Millie walked into the kitchen, and they all fell silent. Taking a seat at the table, Millie turned to Ceal and asked, "How is Rosalie?"

At the mention of Rosalie's name, the aunts riveted their eyes on Millie. Rosalie was Ceal's only child, hopelessly brain-damaged after contracting encephalitis at the age of four. Ceal was inconsolable for many years. It was the primary reason she doted on Edna, her substitute child.

When Rosalie first became ill, the family had mixed responses. Becky and Esther were the most responsive, often taking care of Rosalie when Ceal could not find a babysitter. Edna played gently with Rosalie and asked few questions. Libby, although uncomfortable, was dutiful, and Ceal could rely on her in an emergency. The brothers, however, were superstitious and kept their distance, although Izzie's wife, Ethel, was appropriately attentive when Ceal would call to lament her "poor baby girl."

The real problem was Millie. She had told Ceal that Rosalie's condition was an "evil eye" that had befallen the family, potentially bringing all of them bad luck. Arthur had to stop Millie from verbalizing her fears and coax her into being around Rosalie when Ceal brought her to family gatherings.

The sisters had not noticed when Arthur whispered a prompt into Millie's ear to ask about Rosalie, assuming they would view it as a positive gesture after the candle-lighting debacle. What Arthur never understood was that, for the aunts, there would never be a way Millie could redeem herself.

Surprised to hear Millie even speak Rosalie's name, Ceal waited a few minutes, and then left the table. The other women followed, leaving Millie alone in the kitchen to clear the dessert plates, coffee cups, and saucers. After placing them in the kitchen sink, she took a long pair of yellow rubber gloves out of her purse and began washing the dishes. Lurlene came in, and, alarmed to see Millie doing the dishes, stepped in front of her and told her she would do the cleaning.

As everyone was saying their goodbyes, Morris, who was a bit unsettled, asked Becky again, in Yiddish, if he should call his brother. Becky firmly repeated "No!" before retreating to her bedroom and disrobing, leaving her clothes on the floor. She reached for the nitroglycerin tablets on the table, but they were not there.

Opening the right bottom drawer of one of her massive dressers, she took out another bottle of nitroglycerin, swallowed two, and went to sleep.

It was now eleven o'clock. Morris was exhausted but decided to call Abe anyway. *Odd...there was no answer.* He would try again tomorrow. It was not like Abe to miss a party.

Chapter 5

EDNA WOKE UP PLOTTING HOW TO RETRIEVE THE PILL bottle she deduced Aunt Ethel had put in the milk chute. She went downstairs to her grandparents' apartment, pressed her ear to the door, and was satisfied this was the right moment—Becky was on the phone.

"Yes, Ceal, yes," she heard her grandmother say. "She left what? Where? You don't know? Okay, I will look."

What Edna admired most about the milk chute was that it could be accessed from both inside and outside the house. *Ingenious.* As she opened the inside door, her pudgy little hands grabbed the bottle of nitroglycerin tablets and she put it into her pocket.

Her grandmother's medication delighted Edna. The week, as always, had been tense. Edna failed in her two attempts to avoid going to school, her father giving her a teaspoon of paregoric each time to calm her allegedly upset stomach. Edna never told anyone her school phobia stemmed from one simple thing she knew to be true—if she went, there was no guarantee that when she returned in the late afternoon, everyone would still be there. *What would happen to her then?* She understood she could not live on her own, and, while she did not particularly like life at 2207 South Green Road, being at home gave her a certain sense of comfort, calming the anxiety she experienced everywhere else. In many ways, the house made her feel safe.

As she crept up the stairs to the second floor, the kitchen door opened behind her and Grandma Becky called, "Look in the milk boxes, Edna. Aunt Ceal thinks there is something there."

Edna reported back that the boxes were empty and bolted up the stairs before Becky could make any more inquiries. *Mission accomplished.* A reward was certainly now appropriate. Edna spied two Danish pastries in the refrigerator and ate both of them.

As Edna retreated to her bedroom, a weary Morris trudged up from the basement in his work clothes. He had slept fitfully, unable to understand why his brother missed the party. *It was unlike Abe not to call.* Morris stared at his floor-scraping equipment. *Why did I agree to take this job on a Saturday? For the money, of course.* As Becky was fond of saying, "We can never have too much money, Moshe." And although Morris didn't pay the bills, he knew there was nothing they wanted—at least nothing he wanted—they could not afford.

He paused on the landing and called for Edna to come down. There was no reply. Maybe he would see her later. And maybe Abe would return his call.

When Willie and George arrived at the house, Willie knew immediately something was wrong. He motioned to George to grab one of the sanders, navigated the heavy machine to the driveway alongside the DeSoto, and dropped it before getting it into the trunk, denting the DeSoto once again. The three men stared at each other. Morris motioned to them to lift the sander together. The equipment was now secure in the trunk. Again, without speaking, everyone got into the car. Morris bolted out of the driveway and headed to downtown Cleveland.

Why was Edna the only family member who had asked him about the injury to his leg? Edna had seen the black-and-blue marks and become concerned. The child, the light of his life, was the only one to say, "Did you hurt yourself, Grandpa? Do you need a doctor, Grandpa?"

Was he really unimportant to everyone except his granddaughter? Was he really such a nonentity? And then he remembered Larsh.

Joseph Larsh was a tall gaunt Polish Catholic immigrant who wore wire-rimmed eyeglasses and sported a wide-brimmed Panama hat. He was a general contractor who befriended Morris after his neighbor, Koppelman, introduced them. A "big deal," he heard people say about Larsh. But more important to Morris, Larsh was a friend. A friend Becky knew very little about. He had his own little secret, the wonderful Joseph Larsh. And he had Edna.

He was certain Abe would return his call today. He turned on the car radio and began humming along as Willie and George sang. George let out a huge laugh as the old man joined the chorus. *"Don't you come back no more!"*

Willie wondered what was going on with the old man.

Chapter 6

ARTHUR WAS THE SENIOR OF BECKY'S TWO BROTHERS. Arthur and Izzie were only two years apart. Of all Ben Shafron's children, Arthur had been the one who everyone agreed was handsome. Yet he had been uninterested in his physical appearance, dismissing it and never acknowledging references to what Ceal called his "incredible good looks." Although his sisters had constantly teased Arthur for his lack of interest in women, his brother Izzie, who was homely, secretly envied him. Unlike the handsome Arthur, Izzie resembled his sister Becky—short and heavyset, with a large nose and generally unattractive features. When they were boys, Izzie constantly tried to distract his brother's female admirers, hoping he could convince them to pay attention to him.

As Izzie spent his teenage years desperately attempting to find a girlfriend, Arthur concentrated his efforts on one thing—escaping the poverty of his youth. While their mother, Bessie Shafron, worked as a caterer, the Shafron boys took any odd jobs they could to supplement the family's income. They worked as errand runners, newspaper boys, underage truck drivers, even babysitters for the other neighborhood children. The brothers avoided the local gangs, but Arthur occasionally found himself defending Izzie from various ruffians who would grab his eyeglasses and push him to the sidewalk. Izzie came to view Arthur as his protector, and always deferred to his judgment, even though Izzie was the brighter brother.

The times they had bagged fruits and vegetables at various local markets gave the boys the idea that the wholesale produce business could someday make them rich men. Jealously guarding every penny, they opened their first market by the time Arthur was nineteen. They watched the business expand more rapidly than even they had anticipated. Arthur became quite content, but Izzie wanted more and quietly made other successful investments that he did not disclose. This left Izzie with a sense of guilt, knowing that, although Arthur would never want for money, he had become substantially wealthier than the brother who had always looked out for him.

Izzie's real name was Sanford Isadore Shafron. But the bullying he had endured as a child led him to cast aside the burdensome moniker of "Sanford," adopting instead a nickname he thought would set him apart from his detractors. Arthur, the shyer of the two, avoided all neighborhood parties, mixers, and dances, but Izzie was eager to marry. Nothing held him back, not even that he had only one leg. Too embarrassed by the truth—that he had lost the leg to the diabetes he had suffered since childhood—Izzie gained sympathy by telling outlandish stories that always culminated in a bizarre accident involving a daring rescue (with Izzie as the hero), leading to the tragic loss of the limb. No one believed him, but the tales were so entertaining they became the highlight of warm summer evenings on the stoops in front of tenement apartments in inner-city Cleveland.

As an adult, when he told what became his signature rescue fable, Izzie, for effect, puffing away at a cigar and flicking the ashes rapidly, often removed his prosthetic leg and set it squarely next to him, no matter where he was. People came to expect that when he displayed the false limb, the tragic details of the loss would soon follow. His brother, when present, said nothing, but Libby would roll her eyes as Ceal whispered to whoever was nearest, "None of this is true."

While the family had known Izzie was eager to marry, they had not understood his choice of Ethel. Ethel Schwartz had always been a tall, thin, homely woman who exuded nervousness in every possible way. She had curly, unmanageable, prematurely gray hair and tortoiseshell-rimmed glasses. She spoke in short, breathless sentences and laughed inappropriately during conversations. Although well-groomed, she constantly checked her appearance in any mirror she could find, and she could spend an hour repositioning a single stray hair. She had difficulty paying attention to conversations for any length of time, but always feigned interest in anything her three sisters-in-law, Becky, Ceal, and Libby, had to say. They never asked her opinion, and she never disagreed with them. They doted on her. "A nice woman, Ethel is," the aunts would say. And Ethel doted on Izzie.

Nobody, not even her husband, was privy to the oddest things about Ethel. Often, when she appeared to be engrossed in the aunts' conversation, Ethel was listening to music in her head. Mostly

Strauss waltzes and symphonies, occasionally some show tunes. She never told anyone, because she found the distraction pleasant, and she was concerned that the family would view this trait as peculiar. The hardest thing was resisting the urge to hum along. Instead, she kept a smile frozen on her face and a ready reply, "Oh nothing, nothing," if someone asked her what she found so amusing.

In her purse, Ethel always carried several boxes of Luden's cherry-flavored cough drops which she ate like candy. She was exceedingly uncomfortable without them, and no one knew that she had a box in every one of the twenty-two pocketbooks she owned. She purchased only brand-name products, convinced that anything else would be inferior. Although Izzie brought home massive quantities of fresh fruit and vegetables from the market, Ethel threw them away after a few days. Izzie never inquired why, but Ethel was convinced the produce harbored germs from the "people" that stocked the bins at the Shafron brothers' market. Instead, Ethel instructed her maid—who came three times a week to do the cleaning and grocery shopping because Ethel did not drive—to buy frozen vegetables. She thought frozen and canned foods were wonderful conveniences and loved making lunchtime sandwiches out of Spam and Velveeta.

Izzie demanded a large breakfast which Ethel prepared every morning. She was a mediocre cook (dreadful, if you asked the aunts), but Izzie never complained. While he sat and ate several eggs, bacon, and bagels with cream cheese, Ethel consumed Cap'n Crunch cereal out of the box. Izzie never noticed.

Early in their marriage, Ethel spent much of her time racing back and forth to the elementary school where their son Larry and daughter Lois were always having some sort of difficulty. At the principal's office, when dealing with Larry's problems, Ethel would release her high-pitched, nervous laugh, and say, "Boys will be boys." Izzie had no time or patience for Larry. Ethel, however, characterized everything he did as arising from her son's "nervous condition." As Larry became more difficult, Izzie and Ethel surprised the family by sending him to a private school—an academy. (*"Whatever that is," Ethel wondered.*) Arthur offered his brother no opinion about this, but the aunts, unsuccessfully, tried to convince Izzie that they should keep Larry at home and make him "shape up" and get a job on weekends. Maybe if Ethel were a *real* mother, Larry's life would have been less problematic.

The aunts privately decided that the attention Ethel paid Izzie was even more important to him than the money he made. "Well, of course he is happy with Ethel. After all, the man only has one leg," Libby concluded. *And how many women want an invalid for a husband? Still, our brother is a rich invalid.* Ceal disagreed. She believed the money was important to Izzie, but unimportant to Ethel. She even believed that Ethel would have gone to work if it had been necessary. Becky held no opinion, other than that she was expected to pay respect to anyone who was her brother's wife—at least to her face. She kept to herself how unsettling she found Ethel's flightiness, and took comfort in Ethel's unobtrusiveness. (She also found Izzie's leg unsettling—she tried to leave the room whenever he removed it. The sight of the prosthetic frightened her.)

For all the odd traits Izzie's family had, the real mystery was Arthur's choice of Millie. Although loathe to admit it, the aunts recognized she was a beautiful woman. She had a gorgeous shade of red hair and deep green eyes, and always dressed in the latest style, with lots of jewelry and carefully applied makeup. Ceal and Libby maintained that Millie must go to the hairdresser every day. (*Of course, with Arthur's money, why not?* Libby would muse.) Millie spent most of her time in the kitchen after doing her own marketing. She watched television, attempting to find recipes that were "healthy" for Arthur, who had the same bad habit of smoking as his father—*Zaide*. Depending on when you asked them, the aunts had different responses to Millie's most annoying characteristic.

"It's the way she asks every day, 'What are you making for dinner?'" Ceal said. "I don't think the woman has ever asked me anything other than that."

"She is just plain stupid, stupid I tell you," Libby would add.

Of all the aunts and uncles, Millie had the largest and most lavish home, even surpassing that of the ostentatious Katofskys. The house was ranch style, with four large bedrooms, a huge kitchen, a family room, and a backyard. Every room had at least two plants—one real and one made of wax. Millie often could not tell the difference and watered both out of a sense of caution.

She spent an inordinate amount of time concentrating on her attire. She never greeted Arthur in a plain housedress. She always gave the appearance, Becky would say, "of someone going out to dinner." Wearing her yellow Playtex gloves, Millie took the fruits and vegetables that Arthur brought home and washed them in hot soapy water. She had two basement freezers, always stocked with expensive meats. When she visited, she brought gifts of homemade soups, which she put in small mayonnaise jars that she collected for that purpose.

48

She never read a newspaper, enjoying game shows on television. She had no real interests. Her entire world was Arthur, her children, and the family. She thought nothing of asking the aunts, when they gathered, "What did you pay for this?" or "Did you get this on sale?" and always responded with a blank look when Ceal or Libby confronted or insulted her. Yet, she would greet each of her sisters-in-law with a wide, bright (Libby called it "insipid") grin whenever she saw them, announcing, "You all look gorgeous!"

Her son, Richard, was the doctor in the family. When he was accepted to Harvard Medical School, the aunts remarked, "He took after his father." When he became a surgeon, Ceal said, "He always liked taking things apart and putting them back together." The aunts viewed his sister, Shirley, as a clone of her mother—a nice girl, perhaps, but no brains.

The quality most of the family particularly noticed about Millie was how superstitious she was. Aside from her aversion to Rosalie, Millie was always warding off the *Kinahora*—the evil eye—and wore her charm bracelet for good luck. And then there were the dreams...Millie believed she had visions. At first the family found it amusing, but they became hostile when the daily phone calls came, instructing them where to go or not to go, what to do or not to do, depending on her visions the night before. That her premonitions, as far as anyone could tell, never came true did not deter Millie. She would tell herself there must have been some part of the psychic message she did not remember, or that Arthur had rolled over in his sleep, awakening her too soon.

Arthur ignored his wife's forewarnings. Except for one. If she told him that she "saw" a certain number was either lucky or unlucky, Arthur made business decisions that day based on her advice. If the number was eight and she said it was unlucky, Arthur made sure his orders from his wholesalers reflected the warning, avoiding eight of anything. If the number was nine and she said it was lucky, Arthur would factor nine into his investments that day.

In all things, Arthur considered his marriage a happy one, and he tried to ignore the sniping of his sisters and the sarcasm of his brother. The brothers never discussed their spouses. And they tried not to focus on the misfortunes of their sisters, Ceal and Libby. Only once did Arthur suggest to Izzie that they pull together—all the aunts and uncles—to figure out what was wrong with Becky. But, consumed with their own families and thriving business, it stayed an afterthought. Both brothers assumed that one of the aunts would step in and straighten things out.

Izzie and Arthur admired Morris, although they never told him so. For all the scrimping and saving to build their fruit and vegetable business, they were awed that this immigrant man—who could barely put together two consecutive English words—had grown as successful as he had. In their office late in the evening, sometimes over a glass of *schnapps*, the brothers talked about Morris, both smiling.

"There is no explaining it, really," Arthur said on one occasion. "Who would have thought?"

Izzie, flicking the ashes from his cigar, spoke of Morris's physical prowess—how he had once seen him lift three or four sanding machines in a hotel ballroom. "He has the strength of men half his age."

"Remember the time we had that wedding in Cincinnati?" Arthur asked Izzie, pouring his brother another drink.

Izzie laughed. "And no one knew where Becky and Morris were." The two men guffawed. "They pull into the hotel at three o'clock in the morning because Moshe went to Pittsburgh instead!"

Tears ran down Arthur and Izzie's cheeks. They clicked glasses and said, in unison, what they always said as their tribute to Morris: "No cowabunga!"

Chapter 7

EDNA KNEW SHE ONLY HAD A FEW HOURS BEFORE THE Sunday afternoon guests arrived. Propped comfortably in bed, she pulled out the bottle of nitroglycerin tablets she had taken from the milk chutes the morning after the party and hidden under her pillow. She opened the large Merriam-Webster dictionary she kept in her room. Edna had two dictionaries, one on her dresser and another small pocket edition that she carried with her wherever she could. She consumed half a Snickers bar as she thumbed through the huge book.

According to the dictionary, nitroglycerin was "a colorless thick oily flammable and explosive liquid. Use: manufacture of explosives, treatment of angina."

Angina, what's that?

She inadvertently bit her lip from the excitement and was headed to her dresser to retrieve another candy bar when her mother's furious knock at her bedroom door announced the arrival of Aunt Lena and Frances. Slamming the huge book shut, Edna bolted downstairs to her grandparents' apartment, grabbed a cookie as she passed the dining room table, and settled herself in the living room.

The Sunday visitors were always the same: Aunt Lena; her only daughter, cousin Frances; and Uncle Abe. These were the few members of her grandfather's family she saw. Sunday was the day, Becky told her, set aside for Morris's family. She suspected her grandmother disliked them, because the Sunday food offerings were always leftovers.

Aunt Lena was short and rotund, with no perceptible separation between her chin and her chest. Edna thought she looked like a bowling ball. She often schlepped into the Katofsky living room carrying a full bag of cheap gumdrops from one of the candy stores Abe owned. Like Morris, Lena spoke little English, and uttered only a few words in Yiddish during the Sunday visits. She refused any food Becky offered, choosing instead to dip into the bag of candy she brought, leaving the crumpled cellophane wrappers on the coffee table. Always dressed in the same drab, unattractive clothing (which Becky maintained Lena never washed), her only accessory was a thin black hairnet pulled tightly across her head.

Morris did not notice the odd look on people's faces when he matter-of-factly told the story of Lena's husband, Lipka, who had been dead for many years. When Edna first asked Morris why no one ever talked about Uncle Lipka, he told her that Lena and Lipka had never gotten along and there was nothing nice to be said about her deceased uncle. In fact, Morris had told Edna, for the entire thirty years they lived together, Lena and Lipka divided their tiny, three-room apartment in half, using masking tape for the demarcation lines. Frances lived on Lena's side.

Lena's daughter, Frances, was a perpetually unhappy woman with an abrasive manner who worked as a court stenographer to support herself and her mother. Frances was beyond homely, her black hair the consistency of steel wool, and her bushy eyebrows framed by thick glasses. Edna insisted Frances never shaved her legs and maintained that if you studied her upper lip closely, you would detect a mustache. She occasionally felt frightened by Frances—there was something about this maiden cousin that told Edna she did not want to see her angry.

Morris was the only one who liked her. He approved of her devotion to Lena. He quietly admired what he interpreted as Frances's selflessness when it came to his aging sister. Morris admitted only to himself that Frances was unpleasant, and he promised he would never repeat to anyone what Edna had told him—a conversation she heard between her parents about Frances having an affair with one of the judges at the courthouse, *a married judge.* Morris had overheard a similar conversation.

"What if she gets caught, Harold? What will the family do?" Morris heard his daughter worry.

Harold, sneering, said, "If the truth be told, your cousin Frances is so ugly, I'm surprised anyone would sleep with her." And before Esther could reply, he added, "And who the hell cares what happens to her, anyway? She will run to your father for help—where everyone in the family goes, *if* you know what I mean."

Morris had replied, *"Shah shah shah"* to Edna's question about what an affair was—and had been surprised Harold understood that if Frances were in trouble, he—Uncle Moshe—would help her.

Although Lena and Frances arrived promptly for the Sunday

visit, Abe never showed up, and Frances told Morris that neither she nor her mother had heard from him. Morris was alarmed. For the first time, he realized he had no idea what his brother did when he was not with the family.

Chapter 8

O N MONDAY MORNING, GEORGE ARRIVED AT THE Katofskys'. As he had promised the boss, he brought names and numbers of a few friends who needed work. This surprised Becky. Morris still had not told her that the list was in anticipation of a meeting he had scheduled with his newfound friend, Larsh. Becky appeared to be extremely annoyed today—about what, Morris did not know.

Morris was convinced that, as soon as Becky spent some time with the Pole, any reservations she had about Joseph Larsh would be dispelled. Larsh was jovial and outgoing, and exuded a manner of Old-World charm that would disarm even the unforgiving Becky. Morris suspected Larsh could flatter, out of necessity, anyone who crossed his path. Morris would tell her about his meeting with the man when he came home from work that night.

Unaccustomed to and unskilled at lying, Morris was relieved that so far Becky had not asked how he met Larsh. He was prepared to tell his wife some version of the truth—that their neighbor, Sy Koppelman, had introduced the two men. It was *where* the introduction took place that would be problematic. Surprised several months ago when he came home early and Becky was out, he had gone next door to the Koppelmans. Sy drove the two of them to a bar. It was three o'clock in the afternoon, and this was not typical behavior for Morris. At the bar, there he was: this tall, congenial man regaling the bartender with stories of—well, Morris really did not know what Larsh was talking about, but as soon as Larsh spotted Koppelman, he came over, eagerly pumped his hand, and told Morris how glad he was to finally meet him. Koppelman had spoken so highly of him.

Few people—maybe no one—had ever been this enthusiastic about making Morris's acquaintance. They talked and laughed, and Larsh won Morris over. He pressed a roll of mint Lifesavers into Morris's hand so "Mrs. Katofsky will not know you were out drinking."

———

Just past 5:30, after another long workday, Morris pulled into the driveway of 2207. He failed to notice the car in front of the house. Edna came running out the screen door, calling "Grandpa! Uncle Abe is waiting inside and staying for dinner. Grandma made salmon patties and *lochen kugel*."

Morris's first thought was that Harold would be in a foul mood if Becky was cooking salmon. The aroma of the frying fish, which filled both floors of the house, nauseated his son-in-law. Once, in the middle of a salmon patties cooking production, Harold had confronted Becky, demanding she "cease frying immediately." Becky made it clear she was not going to stop preparing one of Morris's favorite dishes. "After all," Becky had told Harold, "What does my Morris have to look forward to at the end of his day except a good dinner and spending time with Edna?" Becky, in a somewhat ceremonial way, had offered Harold a plate of the patties. They were perfect ovals, the crisp crust enveloping the rosy colored fish underneath. Holding his nose, Harold had replied, "I eat nothing that swims."

Edna's announcement of Abe's visit surprised Morris, but he was relieved that his brother was at the house. Morris greeted his sibling in the kitchen, where Abe was engrossed in an animated conversation, half English, half Yiddish, with Becky.

Morris and Abe, side by side, would never be taken for brothers. Both men were short, but Abe was thin and wiry, wore heavy glasses, and had a protruding chin and balding head. Edna had once seen a picture of a pelican and thought it looked like Uncle Abe.

Dinner went well, with Abe apologizing profusely to Becky and Morris for missing the birthday party. No one paid any attention to Edna as she consumed three times the appropriate amount of food for a child her age. After dinner, Edna reluctantly went upstairs to her parents' apartment, Becky began to wash the dishes, and Morris and Abe settled into the living room, each with a small shot glass of *schnapps*. Abe offered an apology once again for missing Morris's birthday, and Morris assured him it was okay.

When Abe was convinced Becky was fully preoccupied in the kitchen, he leaned close to Morris and said, "Well, Moshe, you must wonder why I'm here. But first, a drink!"

What on earth was Abe talking about?

The men clicked their glasses, murmured the obligatory "*l'chaim,*" and then Abe, inching so close that Morris could smell the alcohol on his brother's breath, said, "Moshe, I need a thousand dollars."

A look of bafflement froze solidly on Morris's face. He was loyal to Abe and Lena, and, until this unexpected appeal from his brother, had believed neither of them had difficulties. But this request startled Morris. Whenever he thought about money, it was for only one purpose—Edna. He was determined his granddaughter would be able to afford any college she chose. She could pursue any profession she liked. He would buy her a house—a big house, not like the crowded one they all occupied. That was the single reason it was important to go into business with Larsh. Becky would understand that.

He reached for the bottle of *schnapps*, refilled both glasses to the brim, and leaned back in his chair. *A thousand dollars?* Morris gazed into Abe's face, which was still set with a broad smile, as Abe downed the second glass of whiskey. *A hundred dollars. A hundred he could explain to Becky. But a thousand? Abe might as well have said a million.*

Morris was not a poor man. He had a bank account of about $20,000. At least, that is what he believed. However, Becky ran the business, Becky did the accounting, Becky had sole possession of the bankbooks, and Becky kept the large green check ledger locked in the top drawer of the dining room buffet. He suspected there might be more money—how much, he did not know. *But did that even matter?* After all, Becky never went anywhere or did anything. Maybe, on rare occasions, she called a taxicab to take Edna to the movies and out to lunch at The Tasty Shop, where Edna would always order an ice cream sundae and bring Morris the paper parasol inserted in the treat.

Morris knew Becky had some amount of affection for Abe, even though Becky's relationship with the Katofsky family over the years had not been a good one. Morris also knew she would never agree to give his brother the money.

"Why so much money, Abe, why?"

Abe had anticipated this question, but he had not adequately prepared an answer. In halting Yiddish, he replied, "It's the business, Moshe. The business. I'm having some trouble with the stores."

Morris knew at once he was lying. Abe, after a few failed business ventures, now owned two small candy stores. As far as Morris had discerned, he was more than able to make a living. He understood Abe to be frugal, so much so that he believed he even charged Lena for the bags of candy she brought over on Sundays.

Pausing for only a moment, Morris said, "But savings, Abe, you must have some savings?"

Abe, not having predicted he would face reluctance from his brother, became agitated, and jumping to his feet, said in a voice that frightened Morris, "No savings, Moshe, nothing. I have nothing! So, it is done? So, you won't loan your own brother any money?" Before Morris could utter another word, Abe walked through the kitchen to say goodbye to Becky, and left the house, slamming the side door.

Morris was bewildered. Abe was in trouble—that he was sure of. *But what could this be about?* He walked over to the phonograph on the other side of the living room, and pulled out one of his favorite records, *Connie Francis Sings Jewish Favorites*. With the record still in his hand, he thought about calling up to the second floor for Edna to come downstairs. He decided, however, he wanted to be alone. Becky, who had finished the dishes, was settled in her bedroom, watching television, and 2207 was quiet.

Keeping the volume low so he would not disturb his wife, Morris played the phonograph. He sank into his favorite seat, the large, brown leather chair next to the record player. Somewhere between Connie Francis singing "My Yiddishe Momme" and "Shein Vi de Levone," he began to cry.

How can I help Abe? And, most upsetting, why hadn't Abe told me the truth? Morris closed his eyes, the tears still running down his cheeks. Before the record was over, he had fallen asleep.

Chapter 9

CEAL CHANNELED HER ANXIETY ABOUT BECKY'S HEALTH by instructing Lurlene to call her if she noticed more contents of the milk boxes being thrown away. By Thursday, Lurlene reported the demise of two cartons of cottage cheese and two containers of sour cream. Becky had said the cottage cheese was rancid and instructed Lurlene to toss it without any explanation. A seething Ceal stopped by South Green Road on the way to work Friday morning to chastise Becky, who remained stoic and unresponsive.

Although Ceal and Libby were desperate to share what they discovered in Becky's bedroom on the night of Morris's birthday party, they kept missing each other's calls. Rosalie had been sick; Libby was having trouble at work. When the sisters finally spoke, they were so pressed for time, they reluctantly agreed to talk later. They arranged to connect Saturday night when the aunts and uncles gathered for their regular poker game at Becky's house.

On the morning before this particular poker game, the awning man was scheduled to come to 2207. The hanging of the awnings was a yearly event Edna eagerly anticipated. Becky told Edna the awnings would arrive by ten o'clock, but Edna decided to start waiting by the front window of the downstairs apartment much earlier just in case.

Edna passed the time watching cartoons—*Top Cat, Yogi Bear,* and *Huckleberry Hound.* She was nervous. She bristled every time the phone rang, convinced it was the drugstore manager calling to tell her parents he had caught her stealing a Milky Way bar. The manager had warned her she could go to jail. She assumed that was true and knew she could depend only on Morris or Aunt Ceal to save her. She feared if she were sent to jail, she'd need a lawyer. The only lawyer she had ever heard of was Perry Mason, and she could not think of anyone in the family like that. She had refused to eat dinner, telling Esther she had a horrible stomachache. Harold poured out a hefty portion of paregoric, which Edna drank rapidly, holding her nose to avoid the vapors before succumbing to the warm, soothing liquid.

Edna fidgeted and waited for the awning delivery, oblivious to what was going on with her grandmother. Becky had begun the day with the usual "What's new?" report but had been in a hurry to focus on her real business at hand. Barricaded in her back bedroom, she had placed six phone calls to the same number by 9:30 a.m. Although complacent when she left the first message at 8:00, she was now agitated, waiting for a reply.

Between calls, Becky chewed nitroglycerin tablets, swigged paregoric, and kept checking—and rechecking—the valves on the oxygen tank. Although she insisted Morris replace the tank yearly, she was convinced that it would malfunction. Morris wearily went through this annual routine, reduced to shrugging his shoulders when the medical supply house insisted there was no need to purchase a new tank.

It was 9:31 a.m. when Becky placed her seventh call, again to the same number. A beleaguered receptionist answered, "Mrs. Katofsky, he's on his way." Becky slammed the receiver down, sank into the three pillows cushioning her head, and rearranged the bedcovers.

Edna, still in the living room, was startled when the dark blue sedan roared into the Katofsky driveway. A deep frown crossed her face. *Dr. Gold.* Edna could not remember the last time the doctor had been to the house but was certain it had not been too long ago. *I should have guessed he was coming. That's why Grandma hasn't been out of her bedroom all morning.* Edna knew instinctively that Gold's arrival was not a good thing.

The blue sedan, the engine still sputtering after the doctor turned off the ignition, sounded like someone with a bad cough. The driver's door swung open, and the doctor emerged. Martin Gold was a heavyset man in his early sixties, with a broad mustache and stooped shoulders. Edna had been told he had been Becky's physician for twenty years. None of the other aunts or uncles used him. In fact, they disliked Gold, and urged Becky to change doctors. It was more than a curiosity to the aunts and uncles—but especially to Ceal—that Becky insisted no one else could treat her.

Tightly clutching his black bag, Gold hurried up the cement front steps. When Edna answered the door, he told her, "I'm here for your grandmother." Only Becky knew it was the fourth time this week the doctor had made a house call.

Abandoning a passing thought to not let the man into the house, Edna pulled open the screen door. Gold brushed the leery child aside and walked straight back to where Becky was sequestered. The doctor, without knocking, entered the bedroom, slamming the door behind him.

Edna was nervous. She had turned the tank on the night before Morris's birthday party while her grandparents were watching television and had panicked because she could not turn the tank off right away. Even if her grandmother had not noticed it was half full, she was convinced Dr. Gold would detect it. Although she had planned an elaborate story about why she was playing with the tank, she was now concerned that Becky had discovered what she had done, and that was why Dr. Gold was at the house. Between the tank and the candy bar, Edna believed she was in a dire situation.

Edna knew Grandma was sick most of the time, but she did not know what was wrong. The discovery of the nitroglycerin tablets only confused her. As soon as Edna had become aware of her grandmother's large, green oxygen tank, she'd asked her mother what it was. Esther explained it was there to help Grandma in case she had trouble breathing. Edna could not figure out why, if this were the case, she had never seen Becky use it.

Edna went to the dining room and looked down the short hallway that led to the two bedrooms in the back of the house. She stared for what seemed like a long time, then decided to continue waiting for the awning man.

She was strategizing. It made sense to tell the truth when they asked her, as she was certain they would, about the tank. *After all, the truth wasn't stranger than anything else that went on in the*

2207 South Green Road

house. But the candy bar...she would have to lie about that. With a firm plan in place, she was calm, and began mimicking Huckleberry Hound's "A hound-dog howdy to you" under her breath.

––––––––

Martin Gold deemed Becky a nuisance with which he had come to terms in his own way. For an obese woman, she enjoyed relatively good health. She ignored his advice to lose weight and Gold came to realize she cared nothing about her own appearance—he assumed it never crossed her mind.

As far as Gold knew, Becky had only experienced one serious health issue in her life. A few months after her thirty-fifth birthday, she complained of severe abdominal pain, and tests revealed a massive uterine tumor. The tumor was benign, but her hysterectomy was complicated, and Arthur and Izzie had to donate blood. Although she recovered, the surgery became a focal point for Becky.

Although she and Gold never discussed it, aside from the angina pain and her constant fear of dying, Becky relived, every day, the death of her first child, a stillborn boy. They had buried the baby, unnamed, in a simple grave marked "Katofsky Child." Morris grieved, but Becky never told anyone what she thought happened—that the doctors killed the baby by crushing his skull with forceps.

Daily, morbid fantasies about dying consumed her. The small aches and pains she felt became monumental. A mere headache was a brain tumor. She became convinced that her chronic chest pain—indigestion from overeating—was a sure sign of severe cardiac distress. Becky's imagined heart condition caused her to place frequent phone calls to Gold.

Unable to convince her that she was not in any jeopardy, Gold began dispensing nitroglycerin tablets on a regular basis, but Becky became increasingly demanding about her condition—the calls came four or five times daily. Out of concern for his own well-being, he reached a solution that was beneficial to him and became a permanent way to quell Becky's fears. Since she always paid cash, he now came to the house whenever she summoned. His visits—and the drugs—seemed to quiet her down.

Edna knew none of this, but she did know that Dr. Gold would not stay for long. Whatever he did, it usually only took a few minutes. Edna often considered pressing her ear to the bedroom door but did not want to risk Gold catching her. She sometimes entertained the thought of protecting her grandmother from Gold by not letting him into the house. Whatever went on in that back bedroom, it frightened her, and she was terrified of incurring the wrath of the mysterious doctor.

The rattle of a full vehicle announced a large truck was attempting to pull into the driveway. The awning man had arrived! The driver began honking at Dr. Gold's car, and Edna wondered how long it would take for Grandma's door to open.

Gold came hurrying out of Becky's room, his black bag wide open and a large wad of cotton still in his hand. He hustled through the front door, dumped the cotton in his bag, and snapped it shut. The truck retreated, allowing Gold to back out and drive away. Edna divided her attention between the awning man and the emergence of her grandmother from the back room as Becky moved slowly and motioned Edna to come to her.

"Grandma, why was Dr. Gold here again today?"

Edna did not expect an answer to her question. She had grown accustomed to the hazy look Becky had in her eyes whenever Dr. Gold left. She stood silently as her grandmother proceeded toward her. Ignoring Edna's question about Gold, Becky draped herself across the living room couch and instructed Edna to go into the kitchen and get her a glass of water. Edna hurried to retrieve the drink while the awnings were unloaded from the truck.

The awning men had reached the second floor of the house when Morris pulled into the driveway. He was having a bad day. He had accepted a last-minute job, but both sanding machines had broken down. He was unable to reach Larsh to procure replacement equipment. Larsh would have helped him out—he was his friend—and Morris was in no mood for any other difficulty.

Edna greeted him at the door, saying, "Grandpa, Dr. Gold was here again today to see Grandma. Is she sick?"

Any good humor left in Morris evaporated with the news that the doctor had once again been to the house. He headed for the living room, and, lapsing into Yiddish so Edna could not understand, turned sternly to his wife. "Becky, this has got to come to an end. The child. What about the..."

Becky raised her hand to silence Morris. Her eyes narrowed, frightening her husband, as an expression that was becoming increasingly familiar crossed her face.

Just then, Esther, who had been visiting a neighbor down the street, walked into the room. Taking a brief look at Becky's glassy blank stare, she turned to her father and fantasized saying, "*So, Pa...Gold has been here again today. It's six months now—the man should have his license taken away. And you, Pa, you do nothing...*

69

nothing!" Esther imagined her voice hitting a shrill crescendo, and her father immediately agreeing to take charge. But instead, as usual, Esther turned to him and said, "Pa, what are you doing home so early?"

Morris, unable to deal with either his wife or his daughter, lifted Edna in his arms and said, "Come, *sheine kop,* outside with me and we'll watch them put up the awnings together."

Becky had forbidden Morris to talk to Gold, and Esther's constant, agitated state made him feel helpless. He was sure Ceal was beginning to suspect something about Becky and the visits from the doctor. Maybe Libby, too. *The person who should do something was that worm of a son-in-law, Harold. After all, he wasn't exactly a doctor like Gold, but he was a pharmacist—maybe he could tell Gold no more house calls. Maybe Gold would listen to Harold.*

Morris knew Harold cared little about what happened to his mother-in-law. Last summer, when Becky had gotten her finger tangled in the mixer while baking a cake, Harold wrapped the almost severed digit and her hand tightly in a towel and drove Becky to the emergency room, not speaking one word the whole way. The following morning, Morris found a gasoline bill from Harold for the trip to the hospital on the Katofsky kitchen table.

With the awnings almost up, Morris asked Edna to go to the drugstore to buy him a copy of *The Forward.* Edna instead slid off her grandfather's lap, announced she had a headache, and ran upstairs. Morris discarded his work clothes for Lurlene to wash, took a shower, and went to sit on the glider on the downstairs back porch.

Maybe things were not so bad. At least Becky could still cook.

Chapter 10

Accoring to Izzie, Ceal had no problems. She did not share the stigma of being an immigrant, had a formal education, and, unlike her siblings, although she spoke Yiddish, considered English her first language. She adapted eagerly to American customs and disengaged herself from what she viewed as the Old-World mannerisms of their parents.

The youngest of the aunts and uncles, Ceal rivaled Becky for the role of matriarch in the family because she was a schoolteacher. Their parents often turned to her for advice because she "understood things about living here" that her siblings did not. This rankled Arthur, concerned Izzie not the least, and caused Becky to keep a watchful eye on her younger sister, determined that Ceal would not usurp her position in the family. In order to compensate for the formal education she lacked, Becky attempted to keep pace with Ceal by becoming a voracious reader and watching television, yet still she found herself belittled by Ceal, who would casually pick up the latest mystery Becky was reading and say, "I can't believe you waste your time on this trash."

Ceal was unconventional in almost every way. Her marriage to Al Kirstein, a man twenty years her senior, had surprised them all. Introduced by a family friend, Ceal and Al described their first meeting as "instantaneous adoration." She told people she'd never met a man "so kind and openhearted." Al described Ceal as "the love of my life," and he was responsible for her adopting the trendier moniker of "Ceal" instead of Celia.

She loved going to the movies. And to the theater. Musical theater. She bought every show album she could and amused Al by singing along with the songs she memorized. *Someday I will no longer have to wait until the road company comes to the Hanna Theatre. I'll see one of these shows in New York.* She was every heroine in every Rodgers and Hammerstein show she saw. She was adventurous, like Anna in *The King and I*. Al was her "wonderful guy."

Al Kirstein was born in Brooklyn. He entertained family members with stories of how he attended the same elementary school as Danny Kaye. Al's father remarried shortly after the death of his mother, and his stepmother occupied most of his father's time, leaving Al and his three sisters essentially parentless. By the time he met Ceal, his sisters had all succumbed to cancer. With no family, he was initially reluctant to leave New York. He'd opened an ice cream parlor in Brooklyn, which went bankrupt in less than a year. ("That's because I ate all the profits," the ever-joking Al would tell people.) An unexpected contact from a distant cousin in Ohio intrigued Al, and eventually brought him to Cleveland Heights. A new start. A fresh beginning.

When Al first met Ceal, he worked in a kosher butcher shop. It was the only way he could get a job. "Didn't even own the butcher shop, just worked there," Izzie and Arthur would say privately. But Al looked for every opportunity to find a better livelihood. He wanted to take night classes to get some sort of degree but had no money. Then the "opportunity of a lifetime" came along. Al became an insurance salesman for Prudential Life. As Ceal never hesitated to remind Becky and Libby, he was a "professional."

When Libby complained that Ceal talked too much, Al told her, "Ceal has trouble containing her enthusiasm and excitement. Her thoughts get interrupted by more thoughts." He ignored the scornful reaction he received from Libby, and he always sided with the beleaguered Uncle Joe. He called everyone in the family either "Sweetie" or "Honey." It was impossible to elicit a bad word from Al Kirstein. And although she tried to dislike him, even Libby became fond of her brother-in-law.

While Al was no match for Ceal's wit, his sense of humor made navigating the aunts and uncles easier. The group could depend upon him to interrupt one of Millie's superstitious rants by announcing, "Now Lil, we don't want to agitate that old Hawaiian god *Kinahora*." They could depend upon him to break the tension of any gathering by telling a Henny Youngman joke while keeping a watchful eye on Edna, whom he assumed suffered from some form of childhood depression.

It did not bother either Kirstein that they'd been impoverished in the early years of their marriage, but Ceal had not anticipated that money would become a lifelong problem for the couple. Al never shared the insecurity he'd first felt in the presence of Arthur and Izzie, and, like Ceal, he preferred to view her brothers as having good intentions because they were family.

His cheery demeanor enabled him to remain relatively anxiety-free when he spent time with his daughter. He was fond of taking Rosalie and Edna for long drives from University Heights to Chagrin Falls. Edna called them the "rides to nowhere." Al always found a route with twists and turns and shouted, "Hold on to your hats, coats, and umbrellas! We're going 'round the bend!"

Izzie viewed his sister's situation with Rosalie as "the cards Ceal was dealt." Al, stoic from the beginning, reluctantly accepted his daughter's diagnosis. At first, he said nothing, as Ceal took the tiny, fragile baby from specialist to specialist, hoping to find a miracle treatment that would restore their daughter to health. Eventually, Al convinced Ceal that she needed to save her physical strength for Rosalie's day-to-day care, which was exhausting. Initially, Ceal rejected any suggestion that she could not tend to her own child, but, as Rosalie became older, the stricken girl began suffering tremors. Bathing and dressing her was arduous. The family—at least some of them—was willing to help, but Rosalie needed full-time attention.

Ceal had to abandon teaching—the hours were not conducive to the demands of a handicapped child—and took a job as a bookkeeper. Unsolicited, Millie suggested that Ceal stand by various bus stops in the poorer areas of Cleveland and look for someone to help with Rosalie and also to serve as a cleaning lady.

Ceal did not listen to the family's suggestions, but eventually took advice from a woman who became her best friend, Victoria Masters. Victoria also had a brain-damaged child, Robert, who was the same age as Rosalie. They met at the office of one of the doctors Ceal brought Rosalie to see. Victoria, too, had taken a menial job to be able to stay with Robert, and the two women gave each other the resolve to make the lifelong accommodations they had to face. Neither listened to those who counseled them to place their children in institutional care—even during the day. Finally, Ceal decided a full-time resident aide was the only answer.

She contacted several agencies and was surprised when one got back to her quickly. She took her usual good time in dressing Rosalie on the day the home health aide was due to arrive and made sure the house was in respectable shape. When the doorbell rang, a flushed Ceal opened it to find a slight, bespectacled, Negro girl, holding all her belongings in a large brown paper bag. "My name is Ira. I come to take care of the baby," she told the astonished Ceal.

The agency said Ira was eighteen, but Ceal knew that the child on her doorstep could be no more than thirteen years of age. Ira wore tattered, stained clothing, but a big smile that exuded confidence. She entered the Kirstein domicile with great enthusiasm, although never before having been outside the inner city.

Lacking in amenities, but spacious, the Kirstein house was in one of the older neighborhoods in Cleveland Heights. Ira was fascinated by the space off the living area, with its two heavy, glass-paned doors, shrouded in old-fashioned lace curtains, which led to a small room that Al proudly claimed as his office. The kitchen had no modern appliances and only a miniscule "icebox" refrigerator. Ira asked where she should put her things, and Ceal motioned to the back bedroom.

What on earth am I going to do with this little girl? Slowly, Ceal formed a plan. When Al came home for dinner that night, Ceal told a reluctant Ira to join them and her father Ben at the table. Ira sat

75

nervously as Ceal patiently fed Rosalie. The always-good-natured Al peppered Ira with questions about her family and friends, but Ira was not forthcoming. When dinner was over, Ceal rose from the table and announced, with an approving nod from Al, "Ira is a new member of the family." Turning to the frightened Ira, she told her, "Tomorrow we go down, register for school, and buy you some new clothes." Ira protested, but Al intervened with a huge smile and a wave of his hand. "You are a member of the family now, Ira. You can help with Rosalie, but you live with us."

Ira asked if she could speak with Ceal in the kitchen and began rambling about how she was sent here to do work. Ceal grabbed Ira by both shoulders. "Ira, you are going to school. Otherwise, you will wind up scrubbing floors for the rest of your life."

The Kirstein household now numbered five—*Zaide*, Al, Ceal, Rosalie, *and* Ira. They gave no thought to how the rest of the family would react to Ira. Ceal's brothers did not know what to make of her: Arthur found it strange, but Izzie found it amusing, and even admired Ceal for her guts and innovation. Arthur tried to explain the decision to Millie, although he confided to Izzie that he did not understand it himself. Izzie had to instruct his wife repeatedly that Ira was now a member of the family, not a live-in cleaning lady. Arthur gave up trying to explain that Ira was not related to Lurlene, and he instructed Ira to ignore Aunt Millie. Libby was sardonic; it was irrelevant to her that Ira was a Negro, but she lectured Ceal, "This is not going to help or solve your problem with Rosalie."

Morris, upon meeting Ira for the first time, shrugged his shoulders, and Becky, in the daily "What's New?" report, emphasized that Ceal was always a little *meshugeh*, but Ira seemed like a nice enough young person. The first time Ira was at the Katofskys at the same time as George and Willie, George's "eyes popped out of his head," according to Edna. George, usually not wanting to confide in Willie, said he was astounded that "them Jews seems to like the coloreds better than they like you or me." Willie refused to let George draw him into the Ira debate, but registered that the Katofskys were definitely unpredictable.

Edna was thrilled to have a friend and playmate in Ira, although Ira was reluctant to engage with her. Edna would arrive at Ceal's with every toy imaginable to coax Ira to play, not understanding that their age difference precluded such an arrangement. Now enrolled in school, Ira uncomfortably endured the stares and whispers from her classmates about "the Negro girl" in their midst.

The first parent-teacher conference Ceal attended for Ira was uncomfortable for the teacher, who had trouble concentrating as soon as Ceal entered the room. Unwilling to address the teacher's discomfort, Ceal instead shared that she was once an educator, too, hoping that would put the woman at ease. Ceal was unsuccessful but determined. She and Al attended Parents' Day and every school function they could to help Ira assimilate.

The Kirsteins eventually realized that the only comfort zone they could provide Ira was the family, and content with their decision, they made no extra efforts in the community. Rosalie loved Ira, and Ira was an enormous help to Ceal around the house. Ceal's unexpected ally in the family was Harold, who took pleasure in instructing Ira not to help Lurlene. After all, Harold explained to the often-confused Ira, "Lurlene *works* for my mother-in-law. You—you're a member of the family."

Much to her own surprise, Ira settled into being one of the Kirsteins. She never confided in Ceal about her own family, and Ceal gave up trying to find out anything about Ira's past. The one thing that no one would have ever predicted—even Ira—was that she enjoyed being Jewish. "If only I had anticipated that," Ceal lamented to Al, "I would have sent her to Hebrew school, too."

Chapter 11

I T WAS A WEEK AFTER THE BIRTHDAY PARTY, AND BECKY, obsessed with reaching Dr. Gold on Saturday morning, had told Ceal to place the order from Lefton's Delicatessen for poker that night. All the aunts and uncles played cards, except for Morris and Millie. As Ceal was fond of reminding everyone, "Millie can't even remember how to make gefilte fish, how can she possibly play a game that requires concentration?" Morris typically spent the evening watching wrestling in the living room and ignoring Millie's chatter.

Ceal was annoyed that Becky left the cold cut order entirely up to her, because their brother Arthur complained at the last gathering about the amount of tongue on the platter. Arthur hated tongue—and had asked Becky why no one ever remembered that tongue was the one thing he did not eat. And, he had reasoned, because they were all paying for the trays, one of the aunts should have consulted him before placing the order. Becky dismissed her brother as usual, but the next time this came up, Arthur took the opportunity to confront Ceal.

"So, Arthur, what is the big deal?" she asked on the phone that morning. "There is corned beef and pastrami, too—so what if you don't like tongue? You didn't exactly go hungry."

"I'll tell you what the big deal is," Arthur shot back. "First of all—it's not like I'm going to some stranger's house. And I'll tell you, just last week Izzie and I were invited to have lunch at Leo Berlin's—he wanted to talk a business deal—he wants to start buying from the market. So, this man, who is really a stranger—he says to me, 'Arthur, I'll have Rose buy some cold cuts.'"

"Get to the point," Ceal interrupted.

Pausing for dramatic effect, Arthur continued, "And then Leo says to me—and I remind you, this man is practically a stranger—'Is there anything you and Izzie don't like to eat?' And I say to him—'Izzie eats everything—unless of course his stomach is bothering him, then he doesn't eat too much of anything, but I,'" Arthur emphasized each syllable, "'*don't...eat...tongue.*' So, if a total stranger asks what I eat and don't eat, why do I have to remind my own sisters? Especially when I am paying for the food!"

"Okay, Arthur, we won't order any—"

"And, if you had asked Millie, she would have reminded you that I don't eat tongue."

Ceal lost her patience. "Arthur," she said, "the reason we didn't ask Millie about the tongue," and she weighed her words carefully here, "is because we have been ordering tongue every Saturday night for the last ten years—and this is the first time you have reminded us that you don't eat it."

Arthur had to stop and think. *Was this true, that for ten years he had not told anyone he did not like tongue?* He knew whatever he

80

said next had the potential to haunt him.

Arthur was not a stupid man. No one would ever know how much he privately lamented never having the chance to get a formal education. Still, he and Izzie were wildly successful in their business endeavors. It surprised him that the only aunt who seemed to share their business instinct was Becky. Libby, he assumed, was unable to make more of herself because she was, as she once told him, "saddled with Joe." And Ceal, unfortunately, even with the steady Al at her side, was unable to "get past" the plight of poor Rosalie.

*Ten years of tongue, ten years of tongue...*went around and around in Arthur's head, until he finally said to Ceal, "So, now you tell me that I've been paying—for ten years—my part of the cold cut tray for something I don't eat?"

"But you make it up in potato salad—you eat twice as much potato salad as anyone else, Arthur." And with that pronouncement, she hung up the phone.

Arthur stared at the receiver. He entertained a fleeting thought of never eating potato salad again at the poker game, but immediately realized that would be a tremendous mistake. He put the receiver into its cradle.

The cold cut tray arrived that evening with corned beef, pastrami, turkey (instead of tongue), coleslaw, dill pickles, and—Arthur noticed instantly—twice as much potato salad as ever before. There was always rye bread, and most everyone cringed (although no one kept kosher) when Joe asked for Russian dressing for his corned beef sandwich.

Ceal and Libby never told anyone how the cold cut tray was becoming an unwelcome expense for each of them. *Why didn't Becky offer to pay for the entire meal? Or one of the brothers? Especially one of the brothers.* Arthur and Izzie were not known for being generous—except with their wives.

Along with the cold cuts came an enormous amount of pastry, which Becky had taken out of the freezer in the basement. Libby did not bake, and Millie always brought a cake—even though no one asked her to. The aunts would refuse to eat Millie's cakes and had tried for many years to discourage the uncles from eating them as well, but with no success.

The night of the poker game, Ceal and Libby finally had a chance to talk about what Libby found in Becky's bedroom on Morris's birthday. Libby announced to Ceal that Becky had *a thousand dollars* in cash hidden away under the blanket in the cedar-chest drawer.

Ceal was startled. "What is that all about?"

Libby had tried all week to come up with an answer to this question. The sisters agreed that Morris did not know about the money. *But who was Becky sending to the bank to cash the checks? Becky did not drive and never left the house on her own.*

The sisters knew Becky did not trust Harold, and it was inconceivable she sent Esther on this mission.

"It must be Lurlene," Ceal whispered to Libby. But Ceal did not believe the maid was cashing the checks and not telling her. After all, she and Lurlene were the guardians of the milk boxes. They had a bond—Lurlene had every opportunity to confide in her and had said nothing about this.

Libby was becoming frantic. "If Lurlene is cashing the checks, is she stealing some of the money?"

Ceal realized Libby was trying to make a bad situation worse and had to steer Libby in another direction.

"I should not have said Lurlene is cashing those checks," Ceal replied. *But who was going to the bank? And why so much money?* The sisters agreed to formulate a plan. Libby was convinced that something nefarious was going on; Ceal, who did not disagree with Libby, had a mild wave of anxiety. *Something was terribly wrong.*

———

Arthur and Millie were the last ones to arrive the night of the poker game. Arthur was still upset about a phone conversation that morning with his son, Richard. Richie had called from medical school—*Harvard* Medical School—to tell his parents that he had done it—he had ended his relationship with "that" girl.

Maybe, Arthur wondered, he and Millie had been too severe by threatening to kill themselves if Richie married a gentile? It was what they thought, it was what they believed—but maybe they had been wrong.

Arthur knew Millie had no regrets about the histrionics. But his son's voice had been so sorrowful, so flat. And the truth was he would never kill himself no matter what Richie decided, although he was never quite sure what Millie would do. *Should he tell the rest of the family about this?* Arthur was uncertain. Maybe he should concentrate on playing cards and eating the appropriate amount of the potato salad ordered on his behalf.

The potato salad and Millie's cakes weren't the only reasons the Saturday night poker game was the highlight of Edna's week. Aunt Millie sat quietly in the living room, staring into space. Morris, jabbering in Yiddish, had his club chair pulled close to the television to watch Saturday night wrestling. Sitting on the edge of his seat, Morris would levitate slightly, throw small punches as if he were boxing, and yell in broken English, "Kill him, kill!" as Gorgeous George grabbed his opponent and threw him to the mat.

Meanwhile, in the adjacent dining room, the poker game had begun. Becky won the first two hands, her glare narrowing as she looked at each card with unmistakable determination. Ceal and Libby eyeballed everyone at the table, both wondering if any of them were involved with Becky's secret money and not confiding in them. Edna, who was used to an air of humor and frivolity at every game, detected none at the table this evening, and announced she was leaving the party and going outside to throw her favorite ball against the side of the house.

Edna's Saturday continued in an anxious mode. She had eaten far too much already—most of it pastry. On the weekend, unlike during the week, pastry was available all day. She had spent the afternoon, as she spent most Saturday afternoons, watching old movies. No one ever questioned Edna's choices or found it odd that she glued herself to the television and *Mrs. Miniver* or *A Tale of Two Cities*. She did Greer Garson imitations so well that Ceal made a mental note to revisit stage auditions for her. When Edna told her second-grade teacher, Mrs. Keinz, that her favorite movie was *It Happened One Night* with Clark Gable and Claudette Colbert, she was sent to the guidance counselor's office for evaluation. The counselor found her unusually engaging for a ten-year-old but sent a note home suggesting Edna spend more time playing with friends and doing homework. The note was tossed aside.

The poker game continued, hand after hand, in a tedious, tense manner, everyone at the table preoccupied. Al began to deal when Becky turned to Ceal, who was sitting next to her, and said, "You have been cheating!"

The aunts and uncles were stunned.

Ceal and Libby began perspiring heavily. Arthur and Izzie sat in silence. Becky lifted her bulky frame from the table, looked at Ceal intently, and drew in a heavy breath to begin speaking, when suddenly, everyone turned their heads in response to the high-pitched screams coming from the kitchen.

Edna was holding her arm and wrist, both rapidly oozing blood all over Becky's kitchen floor. Bored with playing ball, she had grabbed the handle of the door at the side of the house, accidentally let go, and put her hand through the glass. Everyone ran to the injured child, except for her grandmother, who moaned wildly and sank back in her chair. Ceal wrapped Edna's hand in a kitchen towel as Libby screamed up the stairs for Harold and Esther to come right away.

Although Esther rushed downstairs, Harold refused to come even when they hollered that Edna was hurt. After all, he reasoned, *it's not like there isn't anyone to take her to the hospital. He was entitled to his relaxation and it was Saturday night.* Bonanza *was on TV—he wasn't going to miss that.*

Ceal grabbed the screaming girl, and everyone—except for Becky—piled into their vehicles, forming a frantic motorcade to Huron Road Hospital. Edna told Ceal she was scared that they would saw off her wrist in the emergency room.

"Where do you get such ideas?"

Edna launched into a lengthy explanation of how she knew about amputations from watching *Gone with the Wind*, and Ceal patiently explained things had changed since the Civil War. Edna sank back into her aunt's arms and thought about her father. *He is the only one missing. Except, of course, for Grandma.* Grandma must be sick. Again. *Grandma was always sick.* At least, that is how it seemed to Edna.

When the last car had left the house, Becky lumbered to her bedroom. Shaking, she felt the pains begin to envelop her chest. She took a few pills—although she was not sure which ones she ingested. She gave no thought to what had transpired. Her screaming grandchild was not even a momentary contemplation. What she knew no one understood was that it was she, Becky, who should be on her way to the emergency room. This was becoming more and more commonplace—that no one understood. She could count only on herself to stay alive. Not caring, or remembering, that Harold was still upstairs, she slid under the bedcovers and placed a call to Martin Gold.

Chapter 12

EDNA RECEIVED SEVEN STITCHES IN HER WRIST AND TWO in the palm of her hand. She started to scream as the emergency room doctor began to probe the cuts for glass fragments, not realizing the anesthetic had not yet taken effect. The clinician withdrew the probe, and, to calm the hysterical child, asked, "How did you miss the door handle and go through the glass panel?"

Tears streaming, nose clogged from crying, Edna told him, "I did it on purpose!"

Ceal blanched, and before the doctor could speak, said, "Really, Edna," then turned to the clinician, "She is hysterical. Can't you give her something for the pain?"

Motioning to the nurse, the physician produced a syringe, and injected more medicine, calming Edna instantly. Her eyelids almost too heavy to keep open, she began to murmur, and Ceal thought she heard the drugged child ask, "Is this nitroglycerin?"

Edna's accident, and especially Harold's dismissive reaction, was the only thing the aunts and uncles talked about for weeks.

Morris stopped speaking to his son-in-law. Esther was unpredictable, often hysterical; Harold told her to "just shut up" when she brought up the incident. Although Becky appeared to be upset by what happened to Edna, both Ceal and Libby were convinced that Becky's concern was minimal. No one mentioned the "cheating" accusation again.

Edna's grandmother had no reaction when Edna thrust her bandaged wrist into her face.

"See what happened to me, Grandma?"

Becky's odd, vacant stare made the child tremble. She retracted her arm at once, as if she were withdrawing a weapon. Upset, she imagined Becky swallowing an entire bottle of the mysterious nitroglycerin pills. *Would it be like a movie? Would the tablets "tick" away, until Grandma exploded?*

For the time being, Ceal and Libby also ignored Edna. Instead, they concocted nefarious, possibly catastrophic, scenarios. *Hidden money, random medication bottles, a half-full oxygen tank—what was going on?*

Equally unhappy about the drama at the Katofsky home was Dr. Gold, who was not pleased to now be getting calls from Becky even on Saturday nights. He concluded what Ceal and Libby suspected—that Becky was unmoved by the traumatic episode her granddaughter experienced. Edna's misfortune was only another opportunity for Becky to have him come racing to South Green Road to "treat" his increasingly difficult patient. He now spent as little time as he possibly could with Becky, and during his most recent visit, bowing to his own irritation, he made a choice.

While everyone was at the emergency room with Edna, Gold

encountered Harold in the driveway. He cornered the disengaged father, who was heading out for ice cream, and as he groped inside his black bag and withdrew a pre-assembled packet, said, "If Becky tries to reach me again, give her this."

Surprised by Gold's overture, Harold examined the package. Not wanting to delay his evening, he watched the physician drive off without telling him he did not intend to get involved in Becky's affairs. He went to the second-floor apartment, hid the package from Gold's bag in the china cabinet, and continued with his Saturday night.

When he got home from Baskin-Robbins ice cream parlor, Harold decided to examine the contents of the package. *Demerol? So that's what the old lady is up to!* But no doctor prescribes this much Demerol for chest pains. Then it all fell into place for Harold—the constant visits, the mood swings. *Becky is a junkie! How about that?* He had the whole night to ponder how he could use this to his advantage.

In the commotion following the trip to the emergency room, none of the adults noticed that Edna saved the blood-soaked towel that cradled her wrist. It was kept tucked neatly in her closet. The towel served as a backdrop for a new game Edna played behind her closed bedroom door. Dolls perched precariously on the edge of her bed, she pushed them one by one onto the bloody tableau laid out below them, then donned her toy stethoscope and declared Raggedy Ann, Barbie, and two stuffed animals officially dead.

Death was something Edna, given the appropriate audience, was happy to talk about. She knew famous people died—when that happened, there was a big story in the newspaper. She once overheard Becky, Ceal, and Libby talking about death. At least that is what she thought they were talking about. She was eavesdropping outside the kitchen, about to enter, when her grandmother murmured, "I'm afraid to die." Aunt Ceal, apparently startled, was silent. Libby blurted, "As if the rest of us are looking forward to it. Stop this *mishigas*, Becky."

This incident had given Edna the courage to ask Becky about dying, but her grandmother, becoming pale and trembly, retreated immediately. So, Edna was left to her own thoughts. *Was heaven an actual place? Was it a sad place or just different? Could it be sadder than the house at 2207?* She doubted that.

Chapter 13

A STUDENT OF EVERYONE'S BEHAVIOR, EDNA DETECTED a definite change in Becky and was certain her grandmother was spending much more time on the phone. A week after the accident, as she saw Ceal and Libby pull into the driveway within minutes of each other, Edna decided to hide in the stairwell between the two floors of the house. Standing outside her grandmother's kitchen door, she overheard Libby say, "We need to say something to her, Ceal, she just can't leave all that cash lying around." Ceal agreed. She told Libby she would call Becky the next morning, reveal that they knew about the money in the cedar chest, and not hang up until Becky gave her a satisfactory explanation.

Unknown to anyone, the morning following Morris's birthday party, after Becky discovered the nitroglycerin tablets missing from her bedside, she increased her doses of other prescription medications. She avoided asking Lurlene if she had seen the missing tablets—Becky assumed the chest pains were now affecting her mind. *Do I need new medication for that, too? Could they even give you something for that?* She didn't know and was becoming anxious about the possibility that her memory, which she had always relied upon, was affected by her heart condition. *Well, if that were the case, it was the fault of that no-good Martin Gold. I'll have to take care of that without delay. Until then—an extra Darvon or two— just until I sort things out.*

———

Several weeks after the drama of Edna's mishap, the day began for Ceal like most others, with the family making their "What's new?" calls, but there was one difference. No one could reach Becky. This had happened on previous occasions, although it was rare. Becky sometimes began the day with a bath, her difficulty maneuvering her large body out of the tub adding extra time to her routine.

But by noon, Ceal was frantic.

Why wasn't Becky answering the phone? Maybe her sister went to have her hair done. But Ceal knew there was no one to take Becky to the hairdresser. Morris was working, Harold would not drive her even if asked, and Esther did not drive. At work, still unable to reach Becky after several more hours, Ceal kept a sharp eye on the time. It was now three o'clock, and Al would not be home until 4:30, so she had no way of getting from work to the house on South Green Road. The bus line went nowhere near 2207. *Maybe I should take a cab? But cabs are expensive, and Al and I count every penny.* She told her boss she needed to make one more call and tried Becky again. Still no answer.

At 3:30, Ceal decided to declare an official state of emergency.

She had to do something, even if it cost her job—*after all, what if Becky were dead?*

———

Ceal, perspiring profusely, threw several bills at the cab driver and leaped into the driveway at 2207. Before leaving work, she had placed several emergency calls, including one to Ira to say she'd be home late. *What would she do without Ira?* Rosalie adored her, and Ceal knew that Ira reciprocated the disabled child's affection.

An ambulance, a fire truck, and a police car were in front of 2207. The official vehicles blocked Harold's access to the driveway—he had decided to leave the pharmacy early and now, muttering obscenities, he parked his car at the curb. The sight of the emergency entourage did not faze him one bit, but Esther, returning from the corner grocery store, dropped her packages. It was now late afternoon and Edna, sauntering home from where the school bus had dropped her, stopped daydreaming as soon as she saw the scene, and rushed after her mother, who was running toward the house.

In the hallway, pounding on the kitchen door that led to the downstairs apartment, were two police officers. Standing directly behind them was Aunt Ceal.

"Mrs. Katofsky, Mrs. Katofsky, are you in there? Open up if you are in there!" shouted one of them.

Ceal had called the police and arrived by taxi at precisely the same time as the patrolmen. She was losing her patience. They, after all, had been there for about three minutes. For some reason, the door to the kitchen was locked.

"Break down the door!" Ceal commanded. "She may be unconscious—she may be dying. Break down the door!"

The University Heights Police Department did not face many emergencies like the one occurring at the Katofsky house. Following Ceal's instructions, the firemen began breaking down the door.

At the sight of them demolishing the entrance to her mother's apartment, Esther went into shock. Her back hugged the wall. She slid to the floor; her legs splayed in two directions.

Edna grew more terrified with each attempt to gain entry to Becky's kitchen. *What if Grandma is dead? What will I do if Grandma is dead?*

Ceal, in the retelling of the incident, would always begin, "It took them hours..." but, in truth, within a few minutes, the kitchen door was shattered enough to be entered. Aunt Ceal, hiking up her skirt to step over the broken wood, pushed the firemen to the side and raced through the apartment, not noticing the perfectly measured cup of flour, chopped nuts, and sugar on the kitchen counter. The police and the ambulance crew, carrying a stretcher, were close behind.

Edna instinctively began to follow them, but a policeman stopped her, saying "This is no place for you, little lady," and deposited her next to Esther, who was still sprawled on the ground, making whiny, whimpering sounds.

While all this was going on, Harold unloaded several cartons of Coke from the trunk of the car, cursing the whole time because he had not planned to carry the heavy glass bottles from the curbside to the house. He walked past everyone in the hallway and headed directly to his apartment. He thought about asking Esther what was for dinner, but instead continued to the upstairs kitchen. He went to the freezer, prepared a bowl of ice cream, and with the group below him frantically searching the downstairs apartment, sat in a living room chair and turned on the television—the volume extra loud to drown out the chaos below.

Edna, waiting until her father was out of sight, got up off the floor and ran into her grandmother's apartment. In less than five minutes, Ceal and the police had searched everywhere—Becky was nowhere to be found.

The perplexed police officer turned to Ceal, saying, "As you can see, Mrs. Kirstein, your sister is not—"

Suddenly Ceal let out a shriek. "The bathtub, maybe she's dead in the bathtub." The officer thought he had looked in the bathroom, but found himself headed in that direction, Ceal dragging him by the arm.

As a practical matter, Edna had decided to watch all of this from the dining room to have the best view. *Of course, that must be it. Why didn't I think of that? Grandma must be dead in the bathtub. I guess she drowned.* As Edna was beginning to picture what it would be like to drown in a bathtub, Ceal ripped the shower curtain from its rings to discover...the bathtub, half-filled with water, a large brown washcloth, and a big bar of Ivory soap.

The immediate crisis was coming to a close—at least for law enforcement—but not for the family. Ceal placed an urgent call to Libby. Edna nudged her way past the entrance to Becky's apartment. She saw the police and Aunt Ceal now filling out some papers. She went into the hallway to tell her mother that Grandma was not dead. Not only was Grandma not dead, she was not even at home. Edna told her mother that wherever Grandma had gone, she had taken a bath first. And Edna reassured her that Aunt Ceal would get to the bottom of this.

With Becky missing, the kitchen door demolished, Esther semiconscious in the hallway, Edna wondering what would happen next, and Harold out of sight, Ceal awaited the arrival of the cavalry: Aunt Libby. Meanwhile, Ceal insisted the police officers fill out a missing-persons report, berating them the entire time, because the question remained: *Where was Becky?*

Chapter 14

NOBODY IN THE FAMILY THRIVED ON BAD NEWS AS much as Libby did. She was a dependable confidante and ally for any real or imagined disaster. With Becky missing, Ceal knew her sister would immediately adopt a catastrophe mentality.

Libby suspected many of the family members found her unusually nasty, and she was comfortable holding that distinction. Libby and Joe worked for Joe's nephew, who owned a burlap sack factory on the west side of Cleveland. Joe oversaw arranging the shipments, which originally sold locally, but were now bought by vendors in Pennsylvania as well. Libby, who, like her husband, had no formal education, was a quasi-bookkeeper, and had carved out a role for herself in the factory that made her indispensable, a sharp contrast to her unambitious husband. She was placed in charge of tracking the shipments and the payroll, and when there was a problem at work, everyone knew you asked Libby what to do.

Izzie and Arthur's evaluation of their sister was simple: Libby should have been a man. Her temper and assertiveness would have done her well in business. They knew there were so many things in the world that few people had the stomach for—firings, disputes with vendors, cracking the whip to assure things were done on time and with precision. The brothers understood Libby filled this role for Joe's nephew at the factory. Arthur suspected it was frustrating for her to have this much "talent" without a salary to match her contributions. Guilt sometimes surfaced in the Shafron brothers because they did not offer their own sister a better job, but they were wary of the consequence of such an offer. *How could we help Libby and not help Ceal at the same time?*

Izzie almost relented once. He had stopped by Libby's house, and as he always did, compared the meager, dismal, ranch home to his fine large, four-bedroom house in Shaker Heights. Libby greeted him warmly—at least what they came to define as "warmly" for Libby. He was overcome with sadness by the peeling Formica kitchen tabletop and the chipped coffee cup. These had belonged to their parents and represented the poverty of his youth. As his sister talked nonstop about what had taken place at the burlap factory that day, Izzie formed the words in his mind: *"Libby, come to work for me and Arthur."* But he never uttered them to his sister. And Libby never knew her brothers entertained the idea of rescuing her.

The family realized that Libby and Joe had a disastrous marriage. Only the aunts knew that Joe had begged Libby for years to give him a divorce. The request to terminate the relationship had come as a surprise to the aunts, who always viewed Joe as responsible for the failure of the relationship. While Ceal and Becky agreed that it was Joe's fault that the marriage did not work, they acknowledged (but only if you asked them privately, never when they were together) that Libby was a difficult woman.

Joe Warhaft was a quiet, mousy man, whom Libby berated all day and all night. He was unusually homely, which made him easy to pick out in a crowd. If you put Joe in a group of the plainest people you could find, you would immediately be attracted to his sorrowful demeanor. A *punim* full of pain, a face you could not imagine sporting even the slightest grin or smile.

Although the Warhafts had two daughters—Roberta, whom the family called Bobbi, and Florence, nicknamed Flossie—they were distant and irresponsible parents. When the girls were seven and eight years old, Joe and Libby shuttled them between Ceal's home and the Katofsky house, as Libby retreated to bed for days, despondent and uncommunicative. Neighbors would ring the Warhafts' doorbell, intending to help. On the rare occasions Libby answered, she greeted them with a slew of obscenities before slamming the door in their faces.

While Becky was frightened of her sister and content to tend to Bobbi and Flossie, Ceal knew she and Becky needed to do something about Libby. And then it happened. Ceal received a call from a frightened Flossie, saying her mother was throwing dishes—breaking everything in the house. Joe Warhaft eagerly signed the papers committing his wife to a local mental institution. Libby was taken away, clawing at the attendants as they tried to sedate her.

It was one of Esther's most vivid childhood memories—living with her two first cousins or visiting them at Ceal's. Flossie read quietly or watched television, but Bobbi and Esther spent hours in the backyard fashioning mud pies and serving them to their imagined gathering of family members.

Libby had the potential, even well into her forties, to be an attractive woman, but her physical appearance over the years adopted the hardness of her personality. Her facial features were always rigid, and the lines on her forehead and through her cheekbones telegraphed her notoriously bad moods. The things that came out of Libby's mouth were legendary. The other aunts and uncles could be acerbic, dismissive, and mean, but everyone agreed they were no match for Libby. Not even Harold, who liked to say to Esther, "Your aunt is a disagreeable individual—if you know what I mean."

One of Esther's more painful memories came long before she made the mistake of marrying Harold. Ceal had taken in a border, a "nice young Jewish man" named Hymie Rosenfeld, who made a decent living as an encyclopedia salesman. Esther was working at her job for the Department of the Navy, what the family had come to call "not an important job, a civil service job." As she walked in the door from work one day, the phone was ringing. It was Aunt Libby. Ceal had told Libby that Esther refused to let her fix her up with Hymie. Libby called her niece to tell her, "You know, Esther, you should not be so particular. After all, you are not very good looking," then hung up the phone.

Always rushing to their own defense, the aunts and uncles rationalized their behavior. They labeled their conduct a "response" to a situation, or "only wanting to help," or claimed, "Of course I put in my own two cents—he was (she was, they were) in need of my advice. We are all family, right?" But not Libby. Libby observed most situations from a distance and then, matter-of-factly, made the most devastating pronouncements, plainly intended to inflict pain on her targets.

It was not unusual, on occasional Sundays when Lena didn't visit, for the Katofskys and the Warhafts to drive to White Castle for hamburgers. Joe loved cheeseburgers, but Libby never permitted him to order one. Along with everyone else, he would tell the waitress what he wanted: a cheeseburger with grilled onions, ketchup, bread-and-butter pickles, French fries, and birch beer. After all the orders had been placed, Libby would inform the server, "We need to make a change. My husband will have a plain hamburger. Nothing on it. No fries. No birch beer. He can have water." Joe Warhaft became a symbol of oppression to the small group of workers at White Castle—the "poor little man" who came in with the wife who wouldn't let him order anything to eat.

Although it was no secret how unhappy Joe was, even Libby would have been surprised to know how much Joe hated her. Through Libby's endless tirades that became the soundtrack for the life of Joe Warhaft, he would daydream that she was dead, and he was heaping huge quantities of dirt over her coffin as rapidly as possible. He would then go to White Castle and order two double cheeseburgers, French fries, onion rings, and a chocolate milkshake. In his fantasy, none of this food made him ill—*the reason for his gastric distress was now six feet underground.* He would spend his days talking to people without the anxiety that someone was listening to his every word, ready to criticize, contradict, or silence him. He would tell everyone at the burlap factory about his loveless marriage—maybe he would even meet some nice woman. And he would never have to speak to any of the aunts or uncles ever again—co-conspirators, every one of them.

Piercing shouts always interrupted these thoughts: "Joe! Joe,

where are you? Joe, what are you doing? Joe, come here immediately!" The incessant summoning by his horrible wife, year after year, produced profound bouts of stomach acid, for which Alka-Seltzer became the steady remedy. Joe, who always responded
to Libby's calls, never confided in anyone that the antacids did not
help, and he grew more despondent year after year.

The most exciting thing that Edna could remember Uncle Joe
ever doing happened during the summer of 1959, when the family
had become convinced there was a rat in the backyard on South
Green Road. Behind the rows of bushes that fashioned a clean
line—like a border fence—along the backs of the houses on the
block, there were several acres of wild blackberry and raspberry
bushes. The land had recently been sold, and new construction
begun for a small group of homes. Disappointed that she could no
longer spend summer mornings picking baskets of berries with her
mother, Edna prowled the construction sites with a metal bucket,
gathering chipped pieces of porcelain to add to the assorted tiles
she kept in a large box in the basement.

It was on one of these tile outings that Edna became convinced
she had seen a huge rat. She dropped the bucket of tile and ran
screaming into the house. Becky had been terrified that the rat
Edna thought she saw (which Edna later realized might have been
a squirrel but was afraid to alter her story) would somehow make
its way through the backyard, up the two steps leading into the
screened-in porch (Morris sometimes left that door slightly open),
and into the back bedroom. Logic dictated that the rat would bite
her and infect her with bubonic plague or whatever disgusting disease these loathsome animals carried.

Libby and Joe were at the Katofsky house that evening for dinner, and Becky and Libby decided they would give Uncle Joe the mission of finding and killing the filthy animal. Joe sat silent as his wife and sister-in-law explained to him that it was his job to solve this problem. Morris tried to interject, in Yiddish, that he could send George and Willie out back to take care of the matter, but the sisters insisted it had to be Joe. And it had to be done that evening—right after dinner.

Joe walked silently down South Green Road to the small shopping center at the end of the street. His first purchase—in the amount of two dollars and eighty-five cents—was at the drugstore. The second purchase was at the grocery store, which was closing. In less than half an hour, he had returned to the Katofsky house.

With a broad smile, Joe Warhaft walked into the living room where his wife and the rest of the family waited. He proudly announced his plan—he was going to slather several pieces of Kraft American cheese with rat poison and leave them in the backyard. Libby started to speak, but unexpectedly held her tongue. With a confidence no one had ever before seen, Joe headed to the backyard for the kill. Libby thought, *maybe there is something Joe can do right,* but quickly refocused her attention elsewhere.

Joe meticulously layered four slices of cheese with the poison and laid them in a row between the cherry trees in the backyard. Convinced he had found a solution to the problem, the Warhafts departed after an otherwise uneventful evening.

The next morning before he left for the day, Morris went out to the backyard to find, much to his surprise, that the poisoned cheese was gone. What Morris failed to notice were the three dead squirrels next to Edna's swing set. Edna's screams when she went into the backyard that afternoon rang throughout the neighborhood. Becky insisted that their next-door neighbor, Sy Koppelman, remove the animals, because Morris was at work.

For her part, Libby interpreted this as one more thing Joe could not do: "You were supposed to be killing rats, Joe—not squirrels." The incident was further proof to Libby that Joe was a miserable failure. She berated him endlessly in front of Edna, who meekly interjected that maybe there wasn't a rat to begin with, only infuriating the unstable Libby more. Edna, who was somewhat sorry she had ever reported the rat to her grandmother in the first place, solemnly announced she was never eating grilled cheese sandwiches again.

Ceal found it fascinating that the whole incident had only been described to her days later—and not by Libby, but by Edna. When Libby finally had gotten around to it, she had grossly exaggerated the events, painting a picture of hordes of rats invading South Green Road. Ceal knew Joe would never dispute his wife. Becky shrugged her shoulders, a noncommittal, bored response, when Ceal asked her what had happened. Edna assured Aunt Ceal that should something like that ever occur again, she was suitably armed with a green plastic water pistol and would handle the matter herself.

Chapter 15

WESTRUCK BY THE DEMOLISHED DOOR, THE POSSE gathering in the driveway at 2207 continued to expand as Morris, George, and Willie arrived at the house. With a stern, "I will be with you in a minute, Morris. Becky is missing!" Ceal dismissed her confused brother-in-law and continued describing Becky to the police. Morris (always a sensible man) turned his attention to the next logical place—the remnants of the door.

The job of fixing the entrance to the Katofskys' apartment fell to Willie. As soon as he heard George assuring Morris that "they" would take care of it, Willie understood the task would be his. Ordinarily Willie would not have minded, but it was late in the day, and he knew Morris—and suspected the same was true for Mrs. Katofsky—would want the new door in place by tomorrow. He considered appealing to what he viewed as the Russki's common sense, explaining to him that this job would take some time. But he realized that Becky's sister was the one who had given the order to the police to take down the door, and besides, there was the unhappy reality that no one seemed to know where Becky was.

Willie did think it was odd that Becky never seemed to leave the house. He knew she didn't drive but assumed she must go out during the day from time to time. With friends. *Everyone has friends, right?* Or with someone from her family. Willie had met only a few of the aunts and uncles, but he got the sense the family was always around.

It made him nervous that Mrs. Katofsky's disappearance led to the authorities being involved. He was reasonably sure the police had no questions for him. Anyway, he had been at work all day. With George and Morris. This was no problem for him—he had not done anything wrong.

But where could Mrs. Katofsky be? Did people kidnap little old ladies like her and ask for money? No, that was his imagination running wild. Totally wild. He was sure there must be a simple explanation—much simpler than having to replace the kitchen door by tomorrow.

Willie asked Morris if he could use the phone before he went to the supply store. Everyone around him seemed preoccupied, and no one would be able to hear what he was saying. (Ceal thought about eavesdropping on his call but was engrossed in giving a description of Becky to a second officer who had arrived.) Before Willie could dial the phone, however, one of the police officers tapped him on the shoulder.

"Could you come outside with me?"

Willie began to perspire heavily and followed the man to the driveway, where George had just finished half a pack of cigarettes. The policeman looked at both men and asked, "What do you know about the people who live here?"

George seemed puzzled, but straight away told the officer, "I—we work for them. Katofsky," and he pointed as best he could through the kitchen window to Morris. "He's our boss?"

"That right?" the man said to Willie.

Willie nodded.

"Do they seem unusual to you?" the officer asked George, who had a quizzical expression on his face. Willie understood the question, but before he could offer an answer, George said, "*You'se* mean 'cause they are Jews—'cause old man Katofsky and Mrs. Katofsky are Jews?"

Willie froze, but George continued, "Nah, they are okay. For Jews, that is. He's a pretty good boss. Makes a lot of money that he *don't* pay me!" George laughed.

The perturbed officer turned in Willie's direction. Willie cleared his throat slightly, and said, "If you are asking if something like this has happened here before, officer, not to the best of my knowledge."

The officer then felt the weight of Ceal's hand on his shoulder, and she ordered him to come back into the house, adding, "There are a few more things you need to know. And Willie, you need to use the phone, right?"

"Right," Willie replied, taking advantage of the officer's confusion, and wanting to leave as soon as possible.

Willie dialed and grew impatient waiting for an answer. What Ceal could hear from his end of the conversation was not particularly telling: "Yes, I know. I'm sorry. I will be as quick as I can. Yes, I understand that. Thank you. Yes, I know."

Morris gave Willie cash and three hours later a new entryway door (unvarnished, but Morris understood) was in place. Willie made his first stop on the way home. Then his second. When he arrived at his destination, he was exhausted. He was accustomed to the walk up to his third-story apartment, although today he would have to make two trips. He never attempted to carry his groceries and his son Dennis at the same time, not since he dropped that entire carton of eggs all over the second-floor landing. Although she had felt sorry for him, Mrs. Winslow, the landlady, had made it perfectly clear that he would have to clean up the oozing mess and shells immediately. She kept a spotless apartment house.

Willie had to pay the babysitter extra today to take Dennis to the doctor. Even though Dennis had no fever, he was ill, and it made Willie nervous to have to wait until Saturday for the doctor to see his son. And, if Morris asked him to work on Saturday, which had happened more and more lately, the truth was he could not afford to turn down the extra paycheck.

Willie's initial disdain for Morris did not match that of his coworker, George. Unlike George, he did not care that the Katofskys were Jewish. From his point of view, nobody seemed to care that he, Willie, was a lapsed Catholic. He knew the Katofskys, but especially Becky, were curious about his private life, but, if he could not bring himself to tell the whole story, why tell them anything? He suspected there would be an inevitable barrage of questions, especially from Becky, and unsatisfying answers, if he divulged even a little bit of his history. That made Willie uneasy.

He was uncomfortable because he did not have ready answers for what he presumed they would ask. *Why did Dennis's mother leave? Did you try to find her, Willie?* (He did not.) *Why didn't you try to find her? After all, a child needs two parents.* (Willie was not convinced that was true.) Willie also did not want to tell anyone that Leona had been reluctant to have the baby. Willie had been shocked when she had raised the possibility of an abortion, and he had been fearful for the child's safety after Dennis was born. Leona's cavalier attitude toward abortion—"Every woman knows where to get one"—had kept him up many nights during her pregnancy. If she got up early to go to work, he fantasized that maybe she had headed to a back-alley doctor to get rid of their baby. When Willie looked at Dennis, he often felt overwhelming sorrow that his mother so reluctantly brought him into this world. Willie's theory that Leona would find happiness being a parent had been mistaken.

He became agile at ducking questions from Becky. *What would either Katofsky say to him if they knew his real story? Would they fire him?* That was his biggest fear—and now, especially because Morris was going into business with Larsh, what a time to lose his job. Larsh seemed to be a real good thing for Katofsky's business, and Willie wanted to be a part of it. He wanted to make a good impression on Larsh. He knew any conversation with Morris was futile, but maybe Larsh would be interested in some of his ideas. He convinced himself that Larsh saw "big things" when he looked at the enterprise Morris had built.

Would whatever was going on with Becky put a damper on those big things? No, there must be a simple explanation for where she was today. But he knew that some explanations were complicated. Even if the explanations were true, it often did not turn out well for whoever was doing the explaining. *That was his experience, wasn't it?*

With Dennis down for the night, Willie sank into the second twin bed across from his son. He closed his eyes but awoke an hour later. *He had to stop worrying. He had no idea where Becky was. He had been at work all day. And no one suspected him of anything. But that's what he'd thought the first time. He had not taken any of the money, and where did the truth get him? Nowhere. Well, nowhere except a jail cell. How could you wind up in jail if you had done nothing wrong?*

He often considered telling both Katofskys how grateful he was for the way they treated him. Morris, he knew, would have no idea what he was talking about. But Mrs. Katofsky, she would appreciate a kind word. Willie wanted to tell both how much he liked Edna but was afraid that would be misunderstood and only invite more questions about his personal life.

He felt sorry for the girl. He had never known a child who spent so much time in the company of adults. He never knew a child this lonely...so lonely. He knew if he was working on a Saturday, Edna would be waiting for him when he arrived at the Katofsky house. "Play a game of catch, Willie?" she'd ask. Or "Play jacks with me, Willie?" And he would shoot a glance toward Mrs. Katofsky, who would give him a slight nod of approval.

And the unexpected things that could come out of that child's mouth! Last month, she wondered what it would be like to be on board a pirate ship, sail around the world, and look for buried treasure. Like the book she read—*Treasure Island.* "What would that be like, Willie?"

He could not tell her.

Or what if the prince had never found Cinderella? What if one of the ugly stepsisters had fooled him? "Would he have married one of them, Willie?" she had asked. Willie said, "I'm not sure, but I don't think so, Edna."

And why is my father the way he is, Willie? What do you think? She never actually asked him that question, but he always sensed it was coming, as Harold would interrupt their game of catch, pulling Edna away. "He works for your grandfather, Edna. Leave the man alone."

Willie never told the Katofskys the things that Edna asked him when she knew they were out of earshot. "Are you married? Why not? Where is Dennis's mother? Can I come to your house one day after school and play with your son?"

He would change the topic, asking Edna instead to get her bucket of tiles so he could see what she had collected. He would admire the odd mix, many of them ragged, chipped pieces, and was somewhat intrigued when she arranged random fragments to form a shape. She made a pink and green replica of 2207. He told her that was a creative use of bathroom tile. She constructed a white model of her vision of Antarctica, with tiny broken pieces for the polar bears. He helped her drag the bucket down the basement stairs and told her to ask Morris for another vessel to store her huge collection. He was amazed at how she, although tiny, could hoist the bucket onto a basement shelf (for safekeeping, she told him).

Edna often lingered as Becky wrote out Willie's paycheck and waved goodbye to him enthusiastically. He wondered if this child would ever find a time and place to be happy. Although he was convinced they would retrieve her grandmother, tonight he had a momentary thought that maybe it would not be such a bad thing if Mrs. Katofsky were gone for good.

Chapter 16

A BE KATOFSKY WAS LATE. IT DIDN'T MATTER, HE DID not have the money to pay them. At least he was clever enough not to divulge any real information like where he lived or what his telephone number was. But that really wasn't all that clever—they could be waiting for him at his candy store. Reluctantly, he picked up the phone and made the call. The low voice that answered told him next week would be okay—this one time. Abe soothed himself with the thought that everything was going to be all right—it was just this single occasion. He had always paid them before. He had been flabbergasted when his brother did not give him the money. One week to get the cash. *How could he accomplish that?*

Maybe he could ask his sister, Lena, but he knew Frances would intercede. Unlike Morris, Abe had only a passing relationship with Lena and Frances, based solely on the fact that they were family. Besides disliking Frances for her sour disposition, Abe was convinced there was something "not right" about his niece. Morris brushed aside Abe's concerns that Frances "can't be trusted" by telling his brother, "There is nothing to have to trust her with, Abe. She makes a good living, she takes care of Lena, and so what is there to worry about?"

Or maybe there would be an opportunity to get back in Morris's good graces? *Could he ask him again?* No, Morris had said no. A quite definite no. His only chance was Lena, which might mean his only chance was Frances.

If he could only get Lena alone, that might work. That had to be the plan—Lena. Had he ever asked Lena for help before? He could not recall a time. Had he ever had a real conversation with Lena about anything? He could not recall that either. There was that peculiar story about her life with her husband. And her bizarre relationship with Frances. Well, Lena liked eating out— that much he knew. He was overjoyed, although surprised, when Frances simply informed him, "I have to work late, just take Ma to dinner. I will see you later."

As he put on his worn suit jacket and tie, he studied his meager apartment. Dilapidated furniture, peeling wallpaper, an icebox that sorely needed replacing. A tenement compared to where his rich brother lived. A tenement compared to where Frances and Lena lived. His face felt flushed. *Was he nervous about seeing Lena tonight? Or was he angry at Morris?*

He arrived at his sister's apartment complex promptly at 5:30. He turned around to get a better view of where she and Frances lived. Depressing. Old. Not that his place was better, but Abe always suspected that between her daughter's income from the courthouse and her late husband, Lipka's, pension, Lena was well taken care of. After all, Lipka had been a union man. There had to be some money. Lena would tell him if he asked, and he had decided to ask.

A child rode past him on a bicycle. Oblivious, Abe thought how dark and dismal this complex really was. Still, it was better than where they had grown up.

The door to the entryway creaked open and a woman close in age and appearance to his sister brushed past. She nodded hello; he nodded back. He adjusted his tie before ringing the bell, and Lena buzzed him up. As he climbed the two flights of stairs, he felt confident about the evening ahead. Lena would at least be honest with him. *Or would she?* He had decided many years ago that the silence between his sister and him stemmed from Lena's inability to let herself bond with anyone. Frances took care of everything. And there did not appear to be very much to take care of—Lena seemed content to live a cloistered and uneventful existence.

He knocked on his sister's apartment door, and she emerged, coat buttoned, purse grasped tightly in her hand. A noticeable stench hit him. *Did she bathe at all?* Her cheerless attire didn't register, as it did with other members of the family, because he could not recall seeing her look any other way.

After proudly announcing he had a reservation, Abe escorted his dowdy sister into Mike's Steak House. Patrons stared at the odd little lady, clutching her faded and stained brocade handbag, her hair held captive in a nylon net. Abe ignored the under-the-breath murmurs but caught the "Would you look at the two of them?" from the next table as he helped Lena into her chair.

He straightened his blue silk tie again—his best tie, chosen instead of his only other one, the yellow silk cravat patterned with green stripes. The brother and sister talked rapidly in Yiddish, evoking even more stares from the other diners. Because nothing was forthcoming from Lena, they spent the meal chatting about whatever Abe could think of.

After the entrée dishes were cleared and they were waiting for their dessert, Abe said, "Lena, I need your help." He launched into a fantastic story about expanding his candy store business, ending with, "And I need to borrow a thousand dollars." There—it was done. He had said it! There was no immediate response—unlike the reaction from his brother.

Lena rummaged through her forlorn bag and pulled out a small blue bank deposit book, and said, still in Yiddish, "Look at this. Look at this and tell Frances what you need." Their hands brushed as the tattered book was passed. Abe rubbed two fingers together and began turning the stained yellow pages. It was a joint account, in the names of both Lena and Frances. He tried not to show his excitement when he got to the balance. He was right! Lena had the money to give him. All he needed was a way to deal with Frances.

As they headed back to the garden apartments, Abe entertained, and dismissed, various strategies for approaching his niece. He knew Frances could not be sweet-talked. She seemed to care only about two things—her mother and her job. Her job? Now, what did Morris tell him about the funny business at her office? She was involved with a—was it a judge Morris had reluctantly told him? As they entered Lena's apartment, Frances emerged from the back bedroom in a floral silk bathrobe, thick layers of cold cream covering her face. Her hair was wrapped around thin, bristly rollers, reminiscent of a porcupine. Abe winced at the sight of his niece, thinking that whoever this judge was, he must be desperate to be canoodling with her.

Lena kissed her daughter and said a quick goodnight to Abe. Frances, in what Abe perceived as an unusually amiable mood, asked him to join her for a cup of tea. As the kettle whistled, Abe became flustered, and he blurted, "So, Frances, Morris tells me you are seeing a nice man at work. A judge."

Frances froze and slammed the kettle back onto the burner. In a menacing voice, she turned to her uncle and said: "What are you talking about, Uncle Abe? I don't know why Uncle Moshe would tell you something like that."

His heart pounding, Abe fiddled with his glasses, removed them, and began wiping the lenses methodically. Then, with his hands outstretched as if to caress and soothe a wounded child—or maybe a wounded animal—Abe said, "*Shah, shah.* I must be mistaken. Please forgive me. Frances. I intended no harm."

What to say next? Well, might as well just ask.

"Frances, I need to borrow some money. I am not sure when I will be able to pay you back."

The homely woman, now seated directly across from her anxious uncle, drew her unpleasant face toward to his. "Whatever you need, Uncle Abe, we will lend it to you. But you must promise you will never talk about this judge business again."

Abe nodded repeatedly, and after a hot cup of tea, bid his niece goodnight. Walking toward his car, he wiped traces of Frances's cold cream off his cheek.

Chapter 17

WHILE HER FAMILY WAS SEARCHING FOR HER, BECKY was draped on a gurney too narrow for her wide frame in the emergency room of Huron Road Hospital. She had admitted herself several hours earlier after arriving by Yellow Cab, complaining of chest pains. She had begun her day in the usual manner, finishing a quick bath, neglecting to drain the tub, then checking the milk boxes and discarding the fresh carton of cottage cheese. She had left an admonishing note for the milkman and intended to start cooking when the chest pains began.

Dr. Gold had gone out of town for three days and his partner, Morton Sass, refused to come to the house to see Becky. Gold's receptionist coolly informed her she would have to make the trip to the office if she was feeling ill.

Come to the office! Was this woman crazy? The next thing, she was sure, would be the *shiksa* telling her to call the emergency telephone operator—which she had no intention of doing. Her anxiety alternated with rage—this was not how it was supposed to work. Becky was supposed to call the office, and Gold was supposed to come to the house. That was the routine; she would call, and Gold would come.

Becky slammed the receiver in the receptionist's ear, and then opened the cedar chest in her dresser. She removed the neatly stacked packet of fifty-dollar bills and stuffed six of them into her purse. She gave a thought, as she often did, to counting the money.

The bank had called her the first time she sent Lurlene to cash a check, which had been somewhat annoying because Morris was in the kitchen when the phone rang. She'd told Lurlene not to tell Mr. Morris she had sent her on the errand, and she knew she could depend on Lurlene to keep a secret.

When Lurlene had returned with the money the first time, Becky became preoccupied with deciding where to hide it. She could not remember how long ago that was. *Six months? Seven months?* And when she did decide to count the money, she was troubled that she could not recall how much she had withdrawn. No matter, there was always plenty, and dealing with her heart issues was far more important than anything else.

Although it may have been a dim memory to Martin Gold, Becky could repeat, precisely, every word the doctor said to her when he tried to convince her the chest pains were imagined and reassure her there was nothing wrong with her heart: *"This is all in your head, Mrs. Katofsky. You should be glad there is nothing wrong with you."* How Gold could have told her those things, when she knew she was in real danger of dying, she could never understand. And he was supposedly a good doctor—a Jew.

The emergency room was much busier than she had antici- pated—she had only planned to be away from the house for two hours. She had set out the ingredients to bake *mandel* bread to-day—not nut horns as she had told Ceal. She was going to make two batches, one with nuts and chocolate, and one plain. But the chest pains began shortly after she entered the kitchen, and she had felt light-headed. So, she measured the flour and sugar and then called a cab to take her to the hospital.

Much to her surprise, the doctor in the emergency room de-cided to run some tests, and the entire afternoon slipped away. Everything in her small cubicle in the emergency room seemed wonderful to Becky. There was an apparatus somewhat like the oxygen tank she kept by her bedside, but much more complicated. Even though she had no idea what it was, she decided that it was a piece of equipment that a woman, especially one in her condition, should have at home. They did not understand—Morris, Esther, Ceal, Libby...none of them understood the jeopardy she was in. No matter what Gold told her, the truth was she could stop breathing at any minute. And then there were the chest pains. She could not begin to convey to anyone their intensity. And Gold—that idiot—to suggest the pains might be imaginary. *How could pains that could stop your heart in an instant not be real?*

The nurse came in to take some blood, and for the third time Becky asked her how many tests they were running. She was hooked up to a heart monitor, and it occurred to her that was something she needed for her bedroom as well. She was, however, getting a little impatient. She made it clear—*absolutely clear*—that she needed something immediately to ease the discomfort in her chest. She assumed it would not be much longer.

Although gratified by the amount of attention she received

when she told them about the pain, she realized that it was unlikely she would be home in time to finish the mandel or make the stuffed cabbage she had promised Morris for dinner. At least, she thought, these people at Huron Road Hospital understood the danger she was in—and she would have some strong words for Gold about his partner when he got back into town.

The intensity of her panic and fear would have startled the aunts and uncles. If Ceal knew, she might have taken a minute or two to listen to Becky. The one characteristic Morris most admired about Ceal, which made her different from all her siblings, was that she was willing to step back from the "attitude" about Becky's situation that he mostly heard from the aunts and uncles: "So, *nu,* what are you going to do, presented with these compelling facts?" Morris did not process it quite this way. If you asked him why Ceal could, at times, seem more reasonable than the others, he would reply in his broken English, "She is the one who *gots* the education!"

The rest of the aunts and uncles held firm ideas as to what was wrong with Becky. Libby, regardless of what she might be told, would never afford Becky what she perceived as "the luxury of understanding." It was widely accepted by the aunts and uncles, except for Libby, that it was their mother, Bessie Shafron, who had determined that, unlike the rest of them, Becky was too frail to work. Both Libby and Becky, as teenagers, had been employed by a local factory to help support the family. On her first day on the job, Becky had shocked Libby by calling a taxicab mid-morning and going home, where she crawled into bed to wait for Ben and Bessie to arrive. Ceal, being the youngest (and, unlike the others, born in the United States), of course had been in school. Libby was sure there would be a price to pay for using precious money to take a cab—and then Becky telling their parents she did not feel well enough to work, but, instead, Bessie Shafron succumbed to Becky. This had disconcerted and angered Libby, but, like her siblings, she dared not question decisions her parents made.

The brothers—Arthur and Izzie—huddled in private and talked about how "Ma and Pa just needed to have a firmer hand with Becky." But the brothers' focus was on starting a business. They were desperate to build a solid path out of poverty—determined not to be relegated to the few choices their parents had. They were relieved when Becky married Morris—although he was uneducated, he was a hard worker like them. He shared their drive—maybe in a quieter way, but it was there. They knew no matter how peculiar Becky was, she would always have a solid roof over her head.

If Becky had ever had the opportunity to receive any kind of counseling, it would have revealed the answer to the question "What exact thoughts go through your mind when the chest pains begin?" She was always fixed at one place in time—her mother's funeral. Bessie died of a heart attack at the age of seventy. At first, Becky had refused to go to the service. Both Ceal and Libby, however, had made it clear to her that she was going even if they had to drag her there.

The casket, in accordance with Jewish custom, had been closed, but the brothers and sisters requested a private viewing the night before the burial. Morris called Ceal late that afternoon to tell her that Becky still insisted she was not going, and Ceal told him that she and Libby were on the way to the house. When Ceal and Libby arrived, Becky was in bed, refusing to get up. Libby marched into the bedroom, yanked the blankets away, and pulled Becky to her feet. Ceal rummaged in the closet for clothes. The sisters dressed Becky, and, each holding onto one of her arms, took her to the car where Morris was waiting.

The four of them sat silently on the way to the funeral home, each lost in private thoughts. Becky, though, was filled with terror about seeing her mother dead.

At the sight of Bessie in the casket the brothers and sisters had wept quietly but Becky gave in to shock and anxiety. They had to escort her, trembling, to view her mother's body. At one point, the sisters realized that, although they were talking to Becky, she was not responding. They were too preoccupied with their own grief to give it much attention.

Becky kept her head low, shaking it from side to side. She began to wail louder and louder, like the sound the wind makes as it whips through the trees right before a thunderstorm. As the bawling intensified, everyone around Becky, including the rabbi, froze. Their attention was no longer on the late Bessie Shafron, but on her out-of-control daughter. Becky's brothers moved toward her, and Ceal made sure they escorted Becky out of the funeral chapel and deposited her in one of the waiting rooms.

Was I frightening them? But if they knew what I know...can't they all see that I'm not well? That I am next?

The hospital gurney was growing uncomfortable for Becky, and she was annoyed at the number of tests they were insisting on running before they would discuss her treatment. *I know what I want, and I won't leave the hospital until I get it.*

Three hours passed, and finally someone drew back the curtain of her small cubicle. The resident on duty, Dr. Gary Brownstein, entered the room. Becky surveyed him suspiciously. He looked far too young to be a doctor and far too young, in her estimation, to understand the treatment she needed. *Well, if I can handle Martin Gold, I can handle this young man.*

With a huge smile that overtook every other feature on his face, Dr. Brownstein said, "Good news, Mrs. Katofsky. There's nothing wrong with you. Your heart is fine. We can send you home."

Becky recoiled upon hearing these words. She studied him for a moment, and then, pressing her hand against her chest, said, "It's *meine* heart. I have pain. I need my medicine. It's *meine* heart."

Becky could not understand why this doctor—this exceedingly young doctor, Dr. Brownstein—was listening so matter-of-factly. *Was this supposed to be some sort of pleasing bedside manner?* She was not amused, but rather incredulous as he continued to address her.

"Well, Mrs. Katofsky," said Brownstein, still smiling, "you may have a little indigestion or gas pains. I guess we can give you something for that. But the good news is that your heart is fine."

Wipe that smile off your face, young man. She tuned out the physician's chatter, far from being relieved. She raised her fist and shook it at the doctor. "*Meine* medicine. I need *meine* medicine."

Brownstein responded, "You seem confused about your medical condition and overly anxious, Mrs. Katofsky. What do they usually give you for indigestion? I'd be glad to give you that."

Becky, without a moment's pause, replied, "Demerol."

There was no immediate response. *Why does he look so confused? Is he hard of hearing?*

The doctor drew a sharp breath before he spoke. "Mrs. Katof-sky, Demerol is a powerful narcotic. A powerful painkiller. Nobody prescribes Demerol for indigestion. I would be happy to give you an appropriate antacid."

In a loud voice that fell just short of a scream, Becky said, "Listen to me, young man! I know my medicine. I want my Demerol—and I want it now!"

"Mrs. Katofsky, I am going to have the nurse bring in an antacid. And I'm going to have another doctor come to see you—a specialist."

Finally, the boy was making sense. *A heart doctor—that is what she needed.*

Dr. Brownstein continued, "I'm going to have Dr. Joshua Cohen come down from the psychiatric floor to spend some time talking to you—we will both be right back."

Within a few minutes, a nurse appeared and presented Becky with a small cup, holding two antacid tablets, and a glass of water. Becky took the two white pills and hurled them across the room. She lifted herself off the gurney, dressed, collected her pocketbook, exited the emergency room, and proceeded to the taxi stand.

She slid her large body into the next available cab. The driver, without glancing back, said, "Where to, lady?"

"The emergency room, Mt. Sinai Hospital," Becky replied.

Chapter 18

GRABBING HER CHEST AND MOANING, BECKY PLODDED into Mt. Sinai Hospital. The emergency room personnel immediately accommodated her, placing her on a stretcher, working rapidly to determine if she was having a heart attack. Just like their counterparts at Huron Road, the physicians discovered there was nothing wrong. While Becky was formulating a protest, the curtain to her cubicle was drawn back, and the resident on call exclaimed, "Aunt Becky, what on earth are you doing here!"

It had not occurred to her when she chose Mt. Sinai as her next stop that her nephew, Richard, would be on call that afternoon. She quickly demurred to avoid her brothers' and sisters' cross-examination when she arrived at what she now begrudgingly knew would be her next destination—home.

Richard called his father, Arthur, who by now had heard three times from an hysterical Ceal. Arthur and his brother headed to the hospital to retrieve their sister. Izzie had no desire to leave work to get Becky, but decided it was easier than remaining at his office, fending off family calls. No one knew why Libby still had not arrived at the house.

Arthur and Izzie had made a pact, confidentially, that they were not going to intercede with anything going on with Becky. The more Ceal tugged at their consciences, the more they retreated. The brothers had watched at a distance as Ben and Bessie indulged their neurotic sister but agreed their parents did the best they could. They knew Becky and Morris did not need money, and they were hesitant to create a situation where either Libby or Ceal would then also feel comfortable coming to them for that kind of help. The agreement the brothers made—to be unavailable—remained rooted in their fear that, if they allowed her, Ceal would ask for financial help for Rosalie. Making an exception could be expensive.

So mostly they avoided the "Becky problem" whenever they could. However, this time Arthur thought retrieving his crazy sister from Huron Road Hospital made sense for all of them.

Becky decided her best ploy was to appear "sheepish" to her brothers, avoiding eye contact when they arrived, while thanking them profusely for coming to get her. Arthur was glad the drama had come to an end so quickly—he had spent enough time dealing with this *mishigas*.

Esther had calmed down; Harold was silently brooding, convinced his wife was not cooking dinner tonight; and Edna took a cookie from the jar, wondering what would happen next. As Becky headed to her bedroom, Ceal sank into an armchair, exhausted.

When Libby finally arrived at the house, she feigned relief that Becky was back, but was silently angry that the situation had been resolved without her participation. Ceal pulled her aside and instructed her to keep Becky company in the back bedroom while she spoke to Morris. Ceal's instinct was to approach Morris in a soothing manner—maybe she could cajole him into dealing with whatever was happening with Becky.

But Morris was preoccupied with another matter—he was going to have to tell Becky what he had done. He had gone behind her back. He had struck out on his own. He had agreed to something that was irreversible. Becky would be furious.

Sensing Morris's tension, Ceal was surprised when he said to her, "This business with the doctor, and the hospital—maybe it is over for now. I have to tell Becky something I have done—she will not be happy with me. But...it is done. And I think someday she will see it is a good thing."

"What is it, Morris?" a surprised Ceal asked.

"I have a new business partner," he replied. "I went into business today with Larsh."

"Joseph Larsh—*the Pole?*"

"Yes," Morris said, nodding, "the Pole."

A slight smile crossed Ceal's lips—she had been listening to Becky complain for weeks about this man Larsh with whom Morris had become friendly. Becky reiterated that no one would keep the books except her: "No Larsh, no one." Ceal instantly decided this could be the thing that might distract Becky from her aches and pains because nobody guarded the Katofsky accounts like Becky.

"Tell her in the morning," Ceal instructed Morris. "I'm going to wait for Al to come and get me."

Ceal felt a headache beginning, so she put the teakettle on and started rummaging through a cabinet for aspirin. She paused when she noticed the two half-empty bottles of paregoric. Pushing the narcotic aside, she found the bottle of Darvon, took two of those tablets instead, and began explaining to Libby what had happened that day.

Chapter 19

A S HER EYES CLOSED, THE DOORBELL RANG. CEAL went to the Katofskys' tiny front-door vestibule, where a petite, immaculately groomed blonde greeted her. The woman had dark sunglasses and polished, long, ruby red finger-nails that seemed to sparkle. She wore a flowered skirt with a flat-tering white blouse, balancing in her hands what appeared to Ceal to be a "bakery-bought" white cake adorned with chopped walnuts.

Removing her glasses, she smiled at Ceal, cleared her throat, and said, "This is for the Katofskys. I hope poor Mrs. Katofsky is okay." Ceal nodded, took the cake, and as the woman began to walk away, said, "Excuse me, whom should I say this is from?"

"I'm Dorothy. Dorothy Frankel."

The newest residents of South Green Road, on the other side of the Katofskys, were Mort and Dorothy Frankel. The Frankels owned the house, lived in the upstairs apartment, and rented out the apartment below. They had two sons, Ricky, who was Ed-na's age, and his older brother, Gary. They had lived there for six months, and this was the first time Dorothy had gone to the Katofsky home, having limited her interaction to the exchange of pleas-antries in the driveway.

Dorothy Frankel was a trim, unattractive blonde, who spent the good weather on a chaise longue, in a bathing suit, in the small backyard. Becky and Morris had a screened-in back porch, which, much to Becky's dismay, gave them an unobstructed view of the sunbathing Dorothy.

"Would you look at that? Lying there like a lox in front of ev-eryone," Becky said to Morris.

Morris pleaded with his wife to stop. "*Shah*, Becky, *shah*, she will hear you."

"So, I don't care if she hears me—she should hear me. What kind of a way is this for a wife and a mother to spend the day? Ricky comes here to play with Edna. You would think he had never seen a cookie or a piece of pie..."

"Becky, *shah*, she isn't bothering anybody."

The day the Frankels moved in, Becky had gone over with a chocolate cake—and was most unhappy that Dorothy took the cake, closed the door, and did not ask her inside to see the apartment. Although Edna and Ricky often played together, it infuriated Becky that no Katofsky had ever been inside the Frankels' home. Ricky had instructed Edna to stand at the side of the house and call upstairs to see if he could come out. However, what no one knew was that Edna had been upstairs at the Frankels—and had taken ten dollars from a small stack of bills Mort had left Dorothy on the kitchen table.

Esther did not talk to Dorothy. She was envious that Dorothy Frankel had a husband who did not care if his wife spent all her time lying around the backyard. And even though Dorothy was not good-looking, Esther was envious of her trim figure.

The downstairs apartment at the Frankels' had been vacant for some time when Morris told Becky matter-of-factly one day that he heard from Sy that Mort had finally found a full-time tenant. That was all he said, so Becky had watched suspiciously while the moving van delivered the furniture of the new South Green Road residents, angry that the Frankels had not thought it necessary to tell her anything about her neighbors.

"I'm going to ask her who she is renting the downstairs apartment to," Becky said. And before Morris could stop her, she shouted out the window to Dorothy, who was reading in the backyard, "Mrs. Frankel, so who is renting the downstairs apartment—who are you renting to?"

Dorothy grudgingly raised her head, removed her sunglasses, and shouted back. "Mort told me it's a family from Toledo—they sent their furniture—they will be here next week."

"What is their name?" Becky demanded.

"I think it's the Christophers—yes, Mort told me their name is Christopher," Dorothy replied.

Becky walked away from the window and sat back down in the kitchen. She nudged Morris and said, "Did you hear what she just told me? The Christophers. *Goyim*. They rented the apartment to goyim." Morris shrugged his shoulders and buried his head in his newspaper.

Ricky and Edna, however, were far more interested. They had been planning for weeks how they could sneak into the unoccupied downstairs apartment while Ricky's mother was sunbathing. Ricky knew where his parents kept the key.

The children found an opportunity one afternoon after school when Dorothy was completely set up in the backyard—she had a small cooler with lemonade and a portable radio (which annoyed Becky even more), and she had told Ricky that's where he could find her for the rest of the day.

When Ricky saw his mother had begun to doze, he cracked open the front door to the tenants' apartment. He slipped inside and Edna followed. The first thing Edna noticed about the living room of the about-to-arrive Christophers was that there was no plastic covering any of the furniture. This seemed strange. As she and Ricky crept through the apartment, she thought how ugly all the furniture seemed—an icky green color—and it was old, with stuffing coming out of some of the pieces.

But the real surprise was in both bedrooms—and that was the reason Ricky wanted to sneak Edna into the house. When they got to the first bedroom, Ricky opened the door, and Edna's eyes grew wide as he opened one of the boxes on the floor. Ricky held up a heavy wooden object that Edna knew immediately would be unwelcome news to her grandparents.

Later that afternoon, sitting at Becky's kitchen table, Edna turned to her grandmother and said, "Grandma, Ricky took me into the downstairs apartment to see the new neighbors' furniture."

Becky immediately stopped chopping onions. "And so, *nu*—what was it like?"

Edna wrinkled her nose. "The furniture was ugly, Grandma. But guess what?"

Edna described the huge box of crucifixes belonging to the new neighbors as Becky muttered, "The goyim. That lousy Mort Frankel and his no-good wife."

———————

Morris assumed Becky would stop speaking to him for at least a week after he told her about his partnership with Larsh. He had carefully rehearsed his speech the night before and startled his wife when, calmly drinking his morning coffee, he announced, "While you were sick yesterday—while you were gone—I made a deal with Larsh. We're partners now—fifty-fifty."

Becky began to talk, but Morris continued, "I would have told you, but I tried calling you all day and no one answered the phone."

Becky recoiled, aghast that Morris would attempt to be clever with her. But she also realized that this was a good distraction, a way to avoid discussing with anyone what had happened yesterday.

Pausing to choose her words carefully, as Morris had done, she replied, "So there will be more money now—with Larsh—more money?"

"Yes, yes, much more money," Morris replied, relieved that this seemed agreeable to her.

"And who will keep the books?" Becky inquired.

"Larsh agreed to let you do that," Morris told her.

"Well then, Moshe," Rebecca said, forcing a smile, "it is okay."

Buoyed by the lack of resistance from Becky, Morris allowed a slight spring into his step as George and Willie arrived at the house. The two workers were thrilled about Larsh, whom they had liked from the moment they met him. He was such a departure from "the boss"—well-dressed, jovial, pumping their hands with both of his, eager to see them.

Ready to pursue the good humor he detected in Morris, George, brushing the cigarette ashes off his overalls, said. "So, how's *you'se* today, boss?"

A giddy Morris turned to his employees and said enthusiastically, "We are the best location in the nation!" from the popular promotional slogan Cleveland created for the city in the 1940s.

"Yeah, yeah, boss, 'The best location in the nation,'" George replied.

Chapter 20

EVERYTHING SEEMED BACK TO NORMAL IN THE KATOFSKY household. Abe finally reappeared, giving no explanation to his brother why he had not returned his calls. Morris anticipated he would ask for money again and was prepared to tell him maybe he could eventually help him now that he was in business with Larsh, but Abe behaved as if nothing was amiss, and Morris was grateful to settle into what he had come to believe was a typical family routine.

Becky was careful not to telephone Dr. Gold on weekends. She was nervous that he might stop coming to the house, and now carefully planned when she informed him that she was having chest pains. She saw nothing wrong with orchestrating Gold's visits for the days when she was feeling fine—after all, the pains came so frequently, it only made sense that Gold should medicate her in advance. Her back began to bother her as well, but Gold was dismissive when she informed him of the new ailment.

"There is nothing wrong with your back, Mrs. Katofsky," he said to her as he filled the hypodermic needle with Demerol. "And, anyway, the Demerol will take care of any pain you are having."

That was true. The Demerol worked...for today. Becky now realized her mistake at Huron Road was asking for Demerol. *Maybe there were other medications that could make the aching stop.* The Darvon wasn't bad. And the one thing the house had plenty of was paregoric—Harold often brought it home from his pharmacy for Esther and Edna, and Becky could rely on her daughter to supply her with extra bottles.

She knew she could not return to Huron Road or Mt. Sinai—but there were lots of other hospitals in the area. So that's what she decided to do—go to another emergency room. She would tell them she needed something for her back.

———

Edna was hard at work writing a play for the Belvoir Elementary School UNICEF/Halloween contest. She desperately wanted to win and had incorporated all her favorite cartoon characters into the plot. *It's genius. Boris Badenov and Natasha Fatale are going to rob the Bedrock Bank of all its UNICEF money. The Flintstones—all of them—and Betty and Barney Rubble will save the day.* She knew she wanted to be a playwright. And an actress. Edna was convinced the play would win. Edna decided she would read the entire opus to the family when they were at the house for the next poker game.

She felt compelled to entertain them, even though her attempt the previous summer had been a failure. It had been a balmy evening—hot, really. After dessert and before the cards were dealt, Edna had summoned everyone into the living room, turned off the lights, and let loose an entire jar of fireflies. Becky began screaming. Aunt Ceal flicked the lights back on right away and took Edna by the hand into the kitchen. As Edna grimaced, Ceal explained that, although the firefly display was "a good idea, Edna, you always have good ideas," her grandmother was a "bit excitable" and it wasn't something Ceal recommended she do in future "shows" (as Edna called them).

The only person outside the family she told about the firefly display incident was Willie. She could tell he was trying to keep from laughing. Now, she sought Willie's advice on what she described to him as "character development" for the UNICEF project. Willie, always amazed by Edna's imagination, patiently listened, responding to each question she posed with, "What do *you* think, Edna? A playwright has to make these decisions on her own."

The play served as a distraction from a day Edna was dreading—she had to have her tonsils out. And her adenoids, too. Constant sore throats and earaches kept her out of school—sometimes for an entire week—and finally the pediatrician had said it was time for a tonsillectomy. Dr. Bloomfield explained to Edna what tonsils were, and Edna understood. Only Harold seemed to know what adenoids were, and although Esther pleaded with Harold to explain this to Edna, Harold had no interest in taking the time to do so.

Everyone in the family was reassuring, which somewhat eased Edna's anxiety about going to the hospital. Grandma seemed to know everything about hospitals, which even Edna found odd. But they all said she would be fine. Everyone, of course, except Harold, who said nothing about it.

The day of the surgery, Esther woke Edna up at 6 a.m. and Harold unceremoniously dropped them off in the lobby of Huron

Road Hospital, where Ceal was waiting. Esther was fidgety and nervous, so Edna had kept silent on the ride to the hospital. The sight of Aunt Ceal, however, calmed her.

"So, Edna," Ceal said, brushing the hair back from her forehead, "we're going to get those tonsils taken out—one, two, three."

Dr. Bloomfield had already told Edna that none of this would hurt, but Edna asked Aunt Ceal again.

"Hurt? No, not at all," answered her aunt. "You will go to sleep, and the next thing you know, you'll be eating ice cream."

Edna's first inclination was to be skeptical, but she decided to take Aunt Ceal at her word. Ceal was all smiles and continued to reassure the child. Esther remained distant and distracted.

After the three of them settled in the waiting room, Aunt Ceal handed a bag to Edna.

"Open it, Edna—open it up!"

Edna reached in and pulled out a redheaded doll dressed in a Scottish kilt. Ceal took it and turned a large, silver key in its back. She placed the doll on the floor, and it began to spin around and around in small circles.

The doll served as a momentary distraction, but Edna had another question for Aunt Ceal. Before she could speak, a nurse appeared and said, "Edna, come with me." Sandwiched between her mother and her aunt, Edna followed the nurse down a long corridor with several twists and turns before they arrived at an elevator. When the group reached the third floor, the nurse took Edna's hand and said, "Tell your mom you will see her later."

Ceal anticipated that Esther would become undone at this point and picked up Edna to give her a big hug and kiss. Still in

Ceal's arms, Edna leaned over and kissed her mother's cheek. Ceal handed Edna over to the nurse, then guided her distraught niece back to the family waiting room.

Ceal told Esther she was going to the cafeteria to get them some coffee. While she was waiting, Esther, who had spied a pay-phone, decided to call Harold at work.

"Leader Drug," he answered.

"Harold—" Esther began, but before she could finish, he said, "I'm backed up here with ten prescriptions, make it fast. What do you want?"

She was silent.

He barked again, "What do you want!"

"I forgot to get Edna something for when she comes home from the hospital. Can you bring her something from the store?"

"I'm not coming home after work," was the reply.

"You're not?" She paused a minute and then asked, "Well, where are you going?"

"I'm picking up my Aunt Rosie—she needs me to take her somewhere."

"Well, where?"

"Somewhere, somewhere," was the sharp reply before he hung up the phone.

Aunt Rosie was the younger sister of Harold's late mother, Sadie Kotkin. Like Sadie, Rosie was a severe, domineering woman who exercised a good deal of control over Harold. She disapproved of Esther and would privately talk about what a strange woman her nephew had married.

Rosie lived in a small apartment that was a ten-minute drive from the house on South Green Road. She was in her late seventies, and she depended on Harold for trips of any distance. Harold was putty in her hands—he would never refuse her any request no matter how much it affected him or his family. Maybe he truly didn't know where he was going. After all, he would take Rosie anywhere she asked him.

Esther returned to her seat in the waiting room. Ceal was there with two cups of coffee. Esther told her about the conversation with Harold. Not wanting to increase her niece's already heightened anxiety, Ceal dismissed the information and reassured her that she and Al would get Edna home from the hospital.

Not coming home after work? What is that all about? And what kind of a man was Esther married to? Ceal did not detect any great affection between Esther and Harold, but that did not trouble her. She viewed her relationship with Al as unique—she believed her marriage was the only happy one in the family. Well, maybe that was not true—Izzie and Ethel, Arthur and Millie seemed content. But love? Only Ceal and Al were in love. She had something special—something she assumed everyone wanted, but only she had. *Is that why she was given the challenge of Rosalie?*

She tried to believe in God—but she did not. And the subject, except on rare occasions, never came up in the family. It was Edna who had surprised and baffled her by asking, "Why is there religion if no one really believes in God, Aunt Ceal?"

"Well, Edna. It's not that they don't believe in God—it's just that maybe they are not sure if there is a God." She paused, seeing the quizzical look on Edna's face. "And if they are not sure, maybe it is better to try and believe just in case it's true." Edna stopped asking questions, and Ceal regretted not having a better answer for the curious child.

After a while, the nurses escorted Esther and Ceal to Edna in the pre-op room. While her mother sat and fretted, Edna remained entirely composed. With all the necessary preparations completed, the staff told Edna it would only be a few more minutes before the doctor was ready for her. Much to their surprise, Edna looked at them and said, "I have to talk to the doctor before he takes my tonsils out."

The surgical team had never had a child ask to speak to the doctor before a procedure. "You will see the doctor soon," a nurse replied.

They were ready for Edna now, and an orderly moved her gurney into the operating theater. Surrounded by masked men and women, Edna tried desperately to determine which one was the doctor. Suddenly, a tall man seemed to appear out of nowhere. He leaned over Edna and said, "Hi, Edna. I'm Doctor Marks. I'm going to take your tonsils out."

Edna had a single, brief response: "I want to save my tonsils. I want to take them home in a jar." Dr. Marks nodded slightly, and then motioned to the anesthetist to put Edna to sleep.

———

Becky had a perfect opportunity. The house was empty and would remain empty for hours. Everyone was accounted for—at Huron Road Hospital with Edna or at work. She was especially relieved she could avoid the prying Ceal.

This was her second trip to the emergency room of South Euclid Hospital. *Why hadn't she thought of this before? All she had to do was tell them she had back pain, and those reasonable doctors would give her Percocet.* In retrospect, it was probably unnecessary to have taken the precautions she now planned.

The first stop the cab made was the bank. She now realized that Lurlene and Ceal had some sort of relationship, and rather than question her faithful maid, Becky would cash the checks herself. She even enjoyed the ride to the ER—maybe if she had more time, she could start going out to lunch after the visits instead of immediately heading back home.

For a moment, she wondered if the receptionist at South Euclid recognized her. It made no sense, but it was the way she asked, "What is your name, please?" that made Becky suspicious. *Was it a mistake to tell this woman she was Ida Koppelman?* Well, her neighbors (if you could call them that) would never find out. They were even less friendly than the Frankels.

She was pleased with herself. She could never have imagined there were so many hospitals in the area to choose from—ready to help her at a moment's notice. She could hardly keep track of how many there were. But she made sure she was organized when it came to this mission. Lurlene had not asked why Becky had requested a small notebook that would fit in her purse. The notebook now contained—in alphabetical order—the names, addresses, and phone numbers of a dozen hospitals.

Relaxed, sitting idly in the emergency room, with an occasional moan for effect, Becky tried to remember how much Darvon and paregoric she had at the house. It didn't matter. These items were easy to obtain, and besides, tomorrow was a "scheduled" Dr. Gold day. She had a fleeting thought of her dead mother. She shivered, then smirked. Whatever happened to Bessie wasn't going to happen to Becky. She had everything under control.

———

When Edna awoke in the recovery room, she was startled by the noise level. Through heavy eyes, she saw Aunt Ceal in the distance engaged in an animated conversation with a lady dressed entirely in white. *That must be a nurse.* When Ceal glanced over her shoulder and realized Edna was awake, she hurried to her bedside, where a nervous Esther sat chewing on her index finger.

Ceal stroked Edna's hair and told her she would be back in a minute with ice cream. Edna surveyed the room filled with dozing and semiconscious children. She saw the lady in white briskly walk past Ceal to another child's bed. Edna closed her eyes, wanting to fall back to sleep. The noise in the recovery room was dissipating.

Esther kept removing her wedding band and placing it on each of her fingers. She was calming down as well. The incident that occurred while Edna was under anesthesia seemed to be over. Esther had been upset when she and Ceal entered the recovery room and saw, on a gurney sandwiched in the room along with the other children, an adult male. The nurse gave Ceal, who demanded to know why this man was here, a plausible explanation. He, too, had his tonsils removed. And although it upset her, Esther was silently proud that Ceal had taken the initiative and wheeled the sleeping man out of the recovery room, into the hallway, and made it clear to the astonished hospital staff that the bed was "not to reenter the room with the children under any circumstances." Now, Esther had time to focus on the question that had been troubling her all day: *Where could Harold possibly be taking Aunt Rosie?*

Chapter 21

CEAL ALWAYS THOUGHT ESTHER'S WAS THE FIRST FACE you were drawn to in any family photograph. Hers was the only face without a smile. A sullen, depressive child, in her youth, Esther had few playmates outside the family. She had lamented that she was an only child, longing for the company of a sibling.

For years Morris and Becky kept secret from her that she was in truth the second Katofsky child to be born. But eventually—after Millie blurted it out at a family gathering—they told Esther she had a brother who was stillborn.

This news had troubled Esther for many years, and, with no outlet to discuss her fears and anxieties, she produced fantastic ruminations about the death of her brother. *Would he have been a good companion, someone she could have trusted and relied upon and someone who could have understood her most basic feeling—that she detested both of her parents? Or would she have been ignored even more by her parents, all the attention diverted to the boy in the family? Did Morris and Becky resent that she wasn't a boy? Or was the reality that*

*they did not want children at all? Did they lament that she had not died
at birth like her brother?*

Maybe that was why they gave her such a peculiar name. She
did not know any other Esthers. And that wasn't even her given
name; only the family called her Esther. Her real name was Estelle. She had navigated her discomfort by telling her classmates
and teachers that Esther "was her Jewish name," and they accommodated her by calling her Estelle. *Her classmates and teachers had
paid more attention to her than her own parents. And why did her
father call her "Estekeh" in his embarrassing broken English?* She
cringed every time he did.

She had never complained about her family's habits, but growing up she knew other children did not live the same way. Her
paternal grandparents had occupied the second bedroom in the
cramped Katofsky tenement apartment on Kinsman Road, and
she had been relegated to a tiny cot in the corner of Morris and
Becky's bedroom. She had loathed her grandparents, especially
her grandfather, who she maintained reeked of the chickens he
slaughtered in the kosher meat market where he worked. She had
vivid memories of her mother fighting—in Yiddish—with Morris's
parents, when they refused to allow Becky to launder their sheets
or clean their room. She had visions of dead chickens stuffed in her
grandparents' closets, and she worried the apartment would be
overrun by some sort of lice or vermin. She refused her grandparents any affection, afraid to let them touch her meticulous clothing when they walked her to school.

As a young girl, Esther's physical appearance had been her
only priority. She insisted on wearing bright satin ribbons in her

hair, wanting to appear fashionable like the other girls in her class, and Becky had obliged. But Esther could never convince her mother to buy her clothing in a more youthful style. Instead, she found herself dressed in drab browns and practical grays. Once she stopped on her way home from school and bought a bright red blouse from one of the lower-end stores that were interspersed among the tenement buildings, but her mother had ordered her to return it. Becky never questioned her about where she got the three dollars (which Esther had artfully slipped out of her father's trouser pocket).

She had been an accomplished student, and, for a time, convinced Becky and Morris to allow her to take cello lessons. She adored classical music and opera. Her favorite was *La Bohème*, and she could often be heard humming "Musetta's Waltz." As a rule, she chose a waltz, and she could name any Strauss, Chopin, or Lanner piece ever written. Her love of music was the one positive quality she successfully imparted to Edna.

Her only childhood wish that had come true was the death of her grandparents. She showed no remorse when the elder Katofsky died, soon followed by the demise of his wife. Esther had insisted their bedroom, which became hers, be sanitized to a point that surprised even Becky, who had a cleanliness obsession.

Finally, at the age of ten, Esther had the comfort and privacy of her own room. She hung posters of Ramon Navarro and Mario Lanza on her bedroom walls. And another one of George Gershwin. She had a wide-frame mirror over her dresser to which she attached leftover golden satin hair ribbon. Morris and Becky had traded in her cot for a bed, where she perched her single stuffed animal, a large Dalmatian, the consolation gift from her parents who had been appalled at her request for a real pet.

The death of Morris's parents had opened new avenues for the Katofskys. To Esther's surprise, her mother and father began returning their next-door neighbors' friendly overtures. Esther had known it was untenable for the Katofskys to associate with gentiles while her grandparents were alive, but afterward, Esther sensed an eagerness on her father's part to shatter the artificial barrier that the elder generation had placed between Jews and gentiles. Their first invitation had come from the Cafferellis. As early as Esther could remember, Becky had been uncomfortable with the Cafferellis, but when the elder Katofskys died, her parents finally returned the approaches from the immigrant Catholic family. Becky would always greet them, "Hello, Mrs. Cafferelli" or "Nice to see you, Mr. Cafferelli." Yet, Becky still turned down numerous invitations to the Cafferelli home. Morris had been disappointed. He did not share Becky's hesitancy and he seemed to long for interactions outside of the family.

And then, with no explanation, after numerous invitations, in 1936 Becky accepted for Christmas Eve. "You mean she relented," Libby had told the other siblings when she heard Becky was going to the Cafferelli home. "It probably has to do with Esther—it's not good having such a difficult child around the house. Becky has to do something to entertain her."

Like everyone else on Kinsman Road, the Cafferellis had a small, cramped living space. Especially for a family with five children. But (*miraculously*, Esther had thought), their tiny living area was overwhelmed by a glistening Christmas tree. Esther's recollection of that Christmas remained with her forever—the angels clinging to the green needles on the boughs, the colored lights flickering. She had read about mistletoe and heard the other children talking about it at school, but she'd never seen it before. Mrs. Cafferelli gave Esther a small bouquet, tied with a red ribbon, which Esther kept under her pillow for weeks.

Although Becky had agreed to attend the party, her participation had been subdued, which confused Esther. Becky seemed to like the Cafferellis. She had admired the large, freshly baked trays of Italian pastries they put out to welcome the Katofskys into their home. And Esther's experience had been that her mother never did anything she did not want to do. *Hadn't she agreed to go?* Morris, she noticed, was far less reserved, eating and drinking freely. He had told her he and the elder Cafferelli were, after all, *lantsmen* of a sort—two immigrant men hoping to build a better life in America.

Although she had remained quiet for most of that evening, Becky gave Esther permission to visit the Cafferelli home whenever she desired, and Esther took swift advantage of this opportunity. Esther now had friends. Playmates. A place she could go after school. Somewhere she was welcomed. Of particular interest to her was Vincent Cafferelli, five years her senior, for whom she developed a secret longing. Vincent had bright blue eyes and thick, wavy black hair, and he sat and talked endlessly to Esther—about the latest music, the latest movies, the latest fads. She did not know how she was going to tell her parents that this was the man she was going to marry—this non-Jew. She knew *his* parents would forgive this one dissimilarity. And she knew it was only a question of time before Vince realized that they were meant to be with each other. Vince played the violin. They traded books, and Vince was even curious about her religion. And, as he said, after a lengthy explanation of Catholicism, one could argue that everyone was a little bit Jewish.

As 1937 rolled in, the future looked bright. "President Roosevelt will take care of everything," Morris had told her. Vince had agreed that Morris was right, FDR was a great man. In February of that year, Esther gained the courage to share a secret with Vince. She heard things. Not voices, she said, but strange whispers during the night, close to her ear, almost a hush. They would "call" to her—always enticing and soothing, even if she could not quite make out what they were saying. At first, Vince seemed puzzled, confused. But eventually he told her that these sounds were part of her "wonderful, creative imagination." He did not find it odd—only marvelous. He told her he hoped the sounds would encourage her to do amazing things, and Esther became convinced that no one in the world would ever understand her like Vince Cafferelli.

1937 also saw a wicked flu season, and Vince became ill, rapidly deteriorated, and died of pneumonia at the age of seventeen. The Cafferellis were inconsolable, as were the Katofskys, although Becky refused to attend the funeral because she "was not setting foot in a church under any circumstances." Esther took the news of Vince's death without affect, not a tear, but she retreated to her room every chance she got. She wrote secret poems about Vince, which she kept between the pages of a book he had given her. She asked Morris to take her to his gravesite a month after the funeral, and, despite Becky's protests, Morris reluctantly conceded. Esther stared at the simple granite headstone, again with no emotion or expression, and left a small, sealed envelope, addressed to Vince, on the grave.

She entered high school not caring much about anything, never knowing she was the envy of many of her classmates. Although the boys did not tell her (nor later did friends of Harold), they all thought she was beautiful. She had auburn hair which casually draped over her shoulders; huge, almond-shaped brown eyes; and a petite figure. They secretly admired her, but never approached.

When the Cafferellis moved to the suburbs, Esther became more reclusive, until one day she came home from school and shared a story with her parents that frightened Becky. "I had a dream last night that this girl in my math class, some girl I don't even know, would not be in school today because her father had died. And when I got to school, I found out it was true. Her father died last night."

Becky had stopped what she was doing and begun to tremble. She had no idea what to make of this premonition by her usually unremarkable daughter. Ceal thought this was all "stuff and nonsense"—Esther was a sullen child who was often confused. Millie was immediately convinced her niece had a special gift and began to call the Katofsky apartment almost daily to ask for advice from Esther.

After high school, Esther's first and only job was with the Department of the Navy, tracking down owners of war bonds. Most of the servicemen resided in either California or Virginia, and although she found the job boring, she often told people she received some very nice thank-you letters. What she never told anyone was that she saved all those letters. After all, they were addressed to her, *Estelle* Katofsky. And, she knew, the thanks were not some sort of meaningless courtesy. It was the way she had spoken to the senders that prompted them. Professional, kind, and courteous, but concerned. Involved. Wanting to know how they were. What they did now that the war was over. Were they married? Did they have a girlfriend? *Was she married? Did she have a boyfriend?*

She always answered untruthfully to that last question—yes, she said, she had a boyfriend. She had almost said no once. His name was Winston Purlee, and he lived in Santa Monica, California. She had heard wonderful things about California—she even met someone who had been there once. It was not that she minded Ohio. It was pretty enough in the spring and fall, and not too hot in the summertime. *But someplace where there was no snow, what would it be like to live someplace like that?*

Winston—yes, she had called him Winston, and he had called her Estelle—had said it was "real nice," and "maybe somehow" he "could get to Ohio" and they could meet. But Esther knew the answer to that was no.

She met Harold at Thanksgiving in 1948 when her cousin Sheldon, the son of Uncle Arthur and Aunt Millie, brought him home from college for the holiday. Sheldon and Harold were roommates at Ohio State—both in pharmacy school. He was skinny, with slicked-down hair and a huge gold-plated *chai* (the Hebrew word for life) pendant, which he wore on a garish chain around his neck. They corresponded for two years, Harold sending her effusive letters that she saved. They always began, "My darling" or "My beloved." She had wanted to love Harold, but she did not. When he proposed, she matter-of-factly accepted.

Her lack of passion ignited Harold's hot temper, and after the birth of Edna, Esther gained weight. Even Esther had been surprised how unrelenting Harold could be when he did not get his way, and she was dismayed that his personal habits rivaled those of her late grandfather. She was particularly disgusted by how he drank milk out of the carton and placed it back into the refrigerator. Soon, having studied the fastidiousness of her mother, she began buying milk in small quantities and throwing it out once Harold contaminated the carton.

Disheveled and overweight and a reluctant attendee at parents' meetings and school open houses, she suspected she embarrassed her daughter. The one day that would remain in her memory—and Edna's—was when Edna was in the second grade. It was a week before Thanksgiving, and Belvoir Elementary had been decorated with autumn leaves and pumpkins for the school's open house. Edna had written a story that earned her five gold stars and a prized place on the bulletin board. It was about a turkey that ran away to avoid being eaten for the holiday. The story had impressed the teacher with its realistic, unchildlike ending: The turkey was caught and eaten anyway. Esther and Harold had been fighting that morning, and Esther had shown up at Belvoir in a sloppy dress and dirty mohair coat, with no makeup and her hair unwashed. Edna had cringed when her mother entered with the other parents, and had tried to keep her distance, hoping none of her classmates would realize they belonged together. Esther knew instinctively how upset Edna had been and resolved never to go to an open house at the school again. Instead, she decided to indulge Edna's every whim and eccentricity. *After all, how else was she to keep happy a child she thought she never should have had?*

Chapter 22

HAROLD KOTKIN WAS FORTUNATE TO HAVE SURVIVED his childhood. On a warm spring day in 1933, his mother Sadie found him hanging from a tree limb not far from their house, his eyes bulging, barely breathing. She frantically cut him down, and after Harold received medical attention and was quietly resting at home, she proceeded to march through the neighborhood armed with a baseball bat seeking the culprits. As if this horror wasn't sobering enough, from then on, Sadie kept an overly watchful eye on him, screaming, "I'm going to murdelize you!" if he wandered too far from home.

He was bullied throughout his childhood, and never thought to connect his early life experiences to the way he treated his wife and daughter. As well as being shunned as a child, his one boyhood friend, a collie he named Sparky, ran away. There was little tolerance in the Kotkin household for tears or complaints. Sadie spent weekends indulging herself, sending Harold to the movies all day with a brown paper bag filled with sandwiches and a nickel for drinks.

He enrolled in the Pharmacy School at Ohio State University, where he excelled academically but was blackballed at the two fraternities he pledged. A smart but lonely man, he had fantasies that someday he would meet the woman of his dreams. But women were not attracted to him. His decidedly plain appearance and off-putting personal habits saw him refused dates time and again.

When Esther Katofsky showed an interest, he was overwhelmed. He wrote her long love letters. He ignored her peculiarities and refused to acknowledge what was only a feigned interest in him—even though she accepted his marriage proposal. His ardor was never returned, prompting anger and bitterness to take hold. Lashing out became his only relief.

Harold's entry into Esther's family—the nuptials—was, as he liked calling it, "a very problematic occasion—if you know what I mean." Both Katofskys badgered him and Esther to include the dour Frances in the wedding party.

The wedding was a grand event at the Tudor Arms Hotel in downtown Cleveland, although Harold became annoyed his new father-in-law could not say anything that evening except to point out to the wedding guests he had refinished the ballroom floors.

The bridesmaids and ushers made handsome pairs. Even the homely Frances looked nice in the fashionable purple satin dress the bridesmaids all wore. As a show of good faith, Harold decided Frances would walk down the aisle with his college roommate, the friend who had introduced him to Esther, her cousin Sheldon.

As the wedding march began to play, Frances stunned the group by announcing, "I'm not walking down the aisle with Sheldon—everyone knows how much younger he is than me. I won't be laughed at for being an old maid. I am walking down the aisle alone."

Harold's first inclination, which he shared eagerly with everyone at the reception, was "to belt her right in the kisser!" Esther became distraught—the wedding she did not want to attend anyway, her own wedding, was ruined. The music continued to play while curious guests wondered why the processional had not begun.

Harold cornered Morris, bellowing, "Fix this right now. You hear me?" Morris tried to cajole Frances for fifteen minutes, to no avail, with everyone finally capitulating to the angry young woman who walked down the aisle unaccompanied.

I should have known then. Crackpots—all of them. What Harold came to view as rejection from everyone became apparent to his wife, who soldiered on no matter how unpleasant a man he was. Esther, fond of watching beauty pageants on TV, realized the depth of his unhappiness when, after three years of marriage, he announced he was no longer going to watch the Miss America contest.

"No use looking at something you can't have," he said to his wife. He waited for her to respond. She never did.

After his marriage to Esther, the one photo he kept on his bedroom dresser was of his mother, who had died of a massive heart attack when Edna was two years old. Sadie had few possessions of value but bequeathed an antique diamond and sapphire ring to Edna, her only grandchild. Harold toyed with the idea of selling the ring—often turning it to the light to see the diamonds shine.

He had trouble holding down a job. He had an aversion to taking orders—only content when "doing it my way." It had been an abnormally hot day in July of 1960 when Harold stormed into the house at 2207 at five o'clock and announced that Hy Zipp, his boss at Heights Pharmacy, had told him to pack up his things and get out. Edna was sent to her room, but she had pressed her ear to the door so she could hear her parents' conversation.

"That bastard, that Zipp, he told me to get out, right away, in the middle of filling prescriptions."

Esther, at once confused and upset, asked, "But why? I don't understand...you've worked for Hy for five years. What could be the problem?"

"He said I was stealing from the store—the son of a bitch, he said I was *stealing*."

"Stealing? But how...why?"

"The *scrips* he had me deliver. I wrote myself checks for the gas and my travel time. Why should that come out of my pocket? And Zipp—Zipp says, 'That's stealing.' The *momser*. The bastard!"

Edna was frightened by what she overheard. *What did that mean, for Daddy to lose his job?* She had stayed in her room until dinnertime. During dinner, Harold wolfed down his food as the three of them sat silently at the kitchen table.

He gave Esther strict orders not to share the information—that he was now out of a job—with Becky or Morris. Becky, he assumed, would not be surprised. It was the way his mother-in-law looked at him, the way she tried to ignore him, that telegraphed to Harold how little she thought of this man who *did her a favor* (in his mind) by marrying her crazy daughter.

Harold was equally convinced that Morris thought him lazy. He secretly shared the rest of the family's admiration for Morris's physical prowess—he often wondered how this short, stocky man never seemed to tire. How did his father-in-law, covered each day in layers upon layers of sawdust, manage to lift *any* of the machinery he depended upon for his trade? Harold knew the Katofskys were annoyed by how he absented himself anytime something around the house needed to be done. He would sneer and remind them, "That is what the two of you pay Lurlene, Willie, and George to do. I pay rent. I am the professional. I went to college. I could have been a doctor if I had wanted but didn't want to take the time or spend the money."

Harold knew he was no help when it came to fixing things. Even the simplest physical task frustrated him—a screwdriver was a limp instrument in his hands. He distinguished this deficit from the role he had played when he was in the Army, stationed as a surgical nurse in a VA hospital in Battle Creek, Michigan. Although he was relieved when he was designated I-B—fit for only limited military service—because of less-than-perfect eyesight, the taunting he took from his fellow draftees at his induction physical embarrassed him. Having worn inch-thick glasses since he was a kid, the shouts of "sissy" and "four-eyes" still resonated.

He was determined to outshine his fellow recruits in the operating room, and even surprised himself when he tolerated the amputation surgical rotation to which they assigned him. Initially queasy as he witnessed the removal of limbs, he eventually came to believe and understand that the doctors were giving these poor souls plucked from the battlefield a second chance at life. He amused Edna with gruesome stories, such as how he "wiped thick blood off the glasses of one surgeon who had just removed a leg." For her seventh birthday, he granted Edna's request for a book (with photos) that he had from college about horrible communicable diseases.

His mother was the real reason Harold never went to medical school. She made it clear when UCLA accepted him that "No son of mine is going that far away from home." It was Harold's job to make sure the Kotkin household had enough money so that Sadie would not have to endure the terrible Cleveland winters. Nothing interrupted Sadie's seasonal plans—spending the cold months shuttling between relatives in Arizona and cousins in Lompoc, California. Pharmacy school was good enough for Harold, Sadie informed him.

And so, he resigned himself to filling "scrips" speedily and precisely. He never made a mistake. He knew people often counted their pills when they got the prescription home—and, under the watchful eye of Hy Zipp, he then had to endure the berating of those *alter cockers* who insisted they were short a pill or two.

Harold left the house only once during the three days after Zipp fired him. Esther's explanation to Edna was that her father was not feeling well and had a doctor's appointment. Then, out of nowhere, Harold announced he was taking a trip. He was going to Miami Beach for a week. Esther told Edna he was suffering from nervous exhaustion. The girl had not understood what that meant but was glad to see her father leave.

The week Harold was gone had been one of the most peaceful weeks Edna could remember. She had not known what to expect when he returned—she had heard her mother telling her grandparents he would have to look for new employment. Harold had not gone job-hunting right away. Instead, he lounged around in a bathrobe, eating and watching television. Edna had been annoyed that she could no longer watch the shows she liked when she came home from school because Harold had made it clear that his preferences came first.

It was on the third day after his return from Miami, while Esther was preparing dinner, that Harold told Edna he had to have a talk with her. Still dressed in only a robe and pajamas, sprawled on the green sofa in the living room, he motioned Edna to come over to the couch. When Edna sat down, Harold removed his gold wedding band.

"See this, Edna? See this wedding ring?" he said, turning the band over in the palm of his hand. "When I was in Miami Beach, I was lying by the pool at the hotel, and one of the cabana boys comes over to me and says, 'Are you here alone? Are you here without your wife?' I told him yes, I was. And then you know what he said to me?"

Edna shook her head no.

Harold continued, "He said, 'If you're here without your wife, you should take off your wedding ring.' But I told him, 'No, I'm not that kind of guy.'"

The child was too confused to ask what a cabana boy was. She waited a minute, and then asked if she could go to her room.

Chapter 23

STHER HAD A PECULIAR LOOK ON HER FACE, AND CEAL, in a loud voice, said, *"Feh,* Edna. These belong in the garbage. *Feh!"* Edna, however, was not to be deterred. Holding the jar close to her chest, she looked at her aunt and her mother and spoke in a hoarse whisper, "No, they're mine. I want to take them to school for show and tell. They're mine, and I'm taking them with me!"

Much to Edna's surprise, Aunt Ceal and her mother relented, and in a few hours, Al picked up the three of them, along with Edna's tonsils, from the hospital. Esther put Edna to bed as soon as they settled back at the house. Grandpa would be up to see her as soon as he got back from work. Later, Grandma would call her on the phone. (Becky never set foot in the upstairs apartment.) Edna asked where her father was and was told he would be arriving late that night.

The next morning, Esther announced that Edna had a visitor—Aunt Libby was there to see her. Libby walked into the bedroom and handed Edna a flat package. She opened it—a new book of

Debbie Reynolds paper dolls! She was surprised anyone as grumpy as Aunt Libby had noticed how much Edna loved the popular actress. Maybe it was because Edna walked around the house singing "Tammy" from her hit movie. But, after she thought about it some more, Edna knew her singing could not have drowned out the chatter of the aunts when they were around. Probably no one knew she sang "Tammy." She did once see Uncle Joe smile as she sat next to him humming the tune, only to be followed by a scary inquiry from Libby: "Joe, what on earth are you smiling about?"

Maybe Aunt Libby simply knew Edna liked paper dolls, all paper dolls. Her most prized set, until today, was the Lennon Sisters, a singing trio of young girls that appeared regularly on the *Lawrence Welk Show,* a TV variety program she watched each week with her grandfather. All in matching dresses. And singing. It was wonderful.

She examined the present, then said, "Thank you, Aunt Libby. But..." she paused, "one of the dolls has been punched out. One of the dolls is missing."

"Don't talk, Edna," Aunt Libby replied. "You'll hurt your throat."

"But—"

"They were on sale, Edna. On sale. That's why one of the dolls is missing." Turning to Esther, Libby said, "Come, Esther. Let's go downstairs and have a cup of coffee."

Edna asked if she could listen to the Indians baseball game. Libby uncharacteristically said she would check. Soon she returned to the bedroom with a small clock radio tuned to the child's favorite station.

Esther told her daughter, "I'll be down at Grandma's—I won't be long."

Edna nodded, and began punching out the single paper doll. To be fair, she admitted to herself, given the chance, she could understand why someone might take out Debbie Reynolds when no one was looking. Maybe some of the extra clothes would fit the Lennon sisters. But no, the Lennon sisters and Debbie were two different sizes.

As evening approached, Esther was back upstairs making dinner. Edna had only gotten out of bed once, to turn on the hall light near her bedroom door. Edna did not particularly like the dark. Now, even from her bedroom in back, she could hear footsteps coming up the stairs. *Probably Dad.* But the footsteps belonged to Morris, who was eager to see his grandchild.

Edna fell asleep early, but Esther stayed awake most of the night waiting for Harold. She finally nodded off around 2 a.m. Harold walked in the door an hour later, trying to decide whether to tell his beleaguered wife the truth about where he had been all night. Lying, however, was so comfortable he decided against being candid. *Besides, it was easier to make up some cock-and-bull story than to tell Esther he had spent most of the night in a police precinct.*

Edna was first aware her father was home when she woke up and saw the hall light had been turned off. Walking past his sleeping wife, Harold had peered into Edna's room. A bleary, half-asleep Edna sat up slowly on her bed.

"So, Edna, how's your throat?" he asked, standing in the doorway. "It's sore, right?"

"Yeah, and it still hurts."

"Here," he said, finally entering the room. "Here."

Harold handed her a bulky paper bag. She had forgotten it was Thursday. Once a week her father brought home all the new comic books that had come into the drugstore. He allowed Edna to keep them until the following Wednesday night when he collected the comics and took them back to be returned to the distributor for credit. If any comics were missing, Edna had to pay for them out of her allowance. Her father referred to the number of comics as "the count." There was always trouble if the count was off. At first, when Edna was told she could not keep a comic she so desperately liked, she would hide it under her mattress. Harold would stomp around the second-floor apartment, agitated, often shouting, "You need to look again, Edna. The count is off!" On one occasion, becoming alarmed at how angry her father was, Edna snuck the hidden comic into the kitchen and casually put it on the Formica table, insisting that it had always been there in the place he now found it. Today, because of the tonsillectomy, Edna was hoping that maybe there was something else coming—a present. There was not.

She wondered if her mother would ask her father where he had been—why he had come home so late. But, like most questions she had concerning her father's behavior, she let it go unresolved.

———————

Edna was out of school for a week. She kept the jar of tonsils on the dresser in her bedroom. After her first day back at school, Edna came home excited—the next day would be show and tell.

The reaction of the fourth-grade class at Belvoir Elementary School to the jar of tonsils was mixed. Miss Goodman, the teacher, was absolutely horrified, but managed to keep her composure so as not to upset the children. Edna's classmates, however, were enthusiastic (except for Janice Giles, who told Miss Goodman she had to go to the bathroom to throw up). Everyone wanted a chance to get a close-up look, so the jar was passed around the room.

When she got home that afternoon, Edna carefully positioned the container on her dresser at an angle so that she could see it when she woke up in the morning. She went to school the next day, as usual, but when she returned, the jar of tonsils was gone! Edna was beside herself. With all the fury a ten-year-old could muster, she stomped into the kitchen and confronted her mother, demanding, "Where are my tonsils?"

"Edna," said Esther quietly, "Edna, sit down." With both situated at the kitchen table, Esther said, "Edna, nice little Jewish girls don't keep their tonsils in a jar on the dresser."

Furious that her tonsils were gone, Edna stormed to her room, slamming the door. She gave a fleeting thought to taking something of her mother's and throwing it away. But she knew her mother had few personal items—and certainly nothing that would be missed. She went to her dresser drawer and pulled out a large hidden box of Good & Plenty candy and consumed the entire thing.

With Edna home from the hospital, Morris felt now was the time for Becky to meet Larsh. Morris had noticed a calm about Becky lately—everything seemed under control. He knew that Larsh wanted to surprise her. This formal, but charming, man would

169

sweep into the Katofsky kitchen and dazzle her—addressing her as Mrs. Katofsky—and dissolve any qualms she had about the new business venture. But surprising Becky was not an option, and he told his wife that Larsh would be coming home with him after work today—just to meet her, just to say hello.

That afternoon, with Morris covered in sawdust and Willie and George waiting for their checks, Joseph Larsh, wearing the large wide-brimmed hat that was his trademark, walked into the Katofsky kitchen. Unlike Morris, Larsh spoke English with only a slight accent, and he always entered a room with outstretched arms and a beaming smile. He was an imposing figure at six feet five. He tipped the brim of his hat directly at Becky and handed her a huge box bound in red velvet ribbon.

Becky seemed surprised when she opened the box but adored the contents instantly. Nestled in red tissue paper was a large, green, Italian ceramic bowl with a pedestal base. It had grapes and leaves, the same color as the bowl, around the entire perimeter. Becky said to Larsh, "I will display this in the middle of the dining room table."

Morris was mostly a bystander for the next hour as Becky and Larsh chatted away. When it was time for him to leave, Larsh again tipped his hat, and reassured Becky, "It will be a pleasure doing business with you."

Lapsing into the more comfortable Yiddish, Morris asked Becky, "So, what do you think?"

Becky's demeanor was that of a schoolgirl, her raspy voice light and youthful. "Why, Moshe," she said to her husband, "Why did you not tell me what a charming man Larsh was?"

Charming? Morris was not even quite sure what the word meant. Becky read a lot of books—this *charming* must be something she got from one of them.

He hesitated before he replied, "So, this is good, charming? You like him?"

"Yes, yes, Moshe, I like him, it is fine. It is all fine."

Morris beamed a bright smile. He had not seen Becky this happy for a long time. Maybe years. *Yes, definitely years.* He had done something right. *For the first time in years.* And even though he knew it was inadvertent, she was eager to embrace the sound good judgment of Morris Katofsky. *The man the family secretly laughed at.* The relatives might never have gone so far as to think he would do something blatantly mistaken, but they also would never assume he could do something exactly right.

Everything is fine. What could possibly go wrong?

Chapter 24

ESTHER COULDN'T GET PAST THE FACT THAT HAROLD never offered an explanation for his disappearance on the night of Edna's tonsillectomy. *Where could he have vanished to with that old woman?* Not having a clue frightened her and made her think she would have to confront her husband. Esther knew the answer could only come from Harold; Rosie would tell her nothing.

Esther had grown accustomed to unkind treatment from Harold's family. What remained a mystery was the way they treated Edna. Esther assumed that the disdain they exhibited toward her would disappear entirely when it came to a child. But the tightly knit circle in which the Kotkins operated rivaled that of Becky's family, leaving Esther with a misplaced sense of gratitude toward her own parents, aunts, and uncles.

What Esther discovered was that there had been times when Harold or other members of his family had been left alone with Edna and confided in her about inappropriate and bizarre things. Esther became aware of this peculiar behavior by the Kotkins when Edna began asking her mother, "Is it true that one of my uncles has a daughter no one talks about who lives in California?" Esther filed this information about Harold that she gleaned from Edna deep in her memory—afraid even to consider that some of it might indeed be true. Edna said her father once spent an hour talking about a beautiful woman who came into the pharmacy once a week. Esther even asked Edna if he mentioned a name. Edna replied no, just reiterating "Daddy said she was the most beautiful woman he had ever seen."

After much debate, Esther decided not to ask Harold where he had been that night with Aunt Rosie. She was taken by surprise when, four evenings after he had disappeared, and after Edna had gone to bed, he brought up the subject himself.

"So, I guess you want to know where I took Rosie the other night?"

As always, she carefully chose her response to her husband. "Well, yes..."

"You won't believe it. I pick her up and Rosie says to me, 'Hershel, drive to the Flats.' So, I look at her and I say, 'But Aunt Rosie, it's late and...'"

"'You just drive, Hershel, we are going to the Flats. To the Painters Union Hall in the Flats—just drive, Hershel.'"

"So, I'm driving, and it's hard to see, the road is so dark. And I'm thinking, I haven't been here for years. And I'm thinking, what is she up to?"

Esther, who was never curious about the comings and goings of Rosie, was nonetheless intrigued now.

"So," Harold continued, "we pull into the parking lot of the

Union Hall, and Rosie knocks on the door and some guy says, 'Good, Rosie is here.'"

Esther was hanging on every word.

"So," Harold continues, "we walk in, and what do you think is going on?"

"What?" Esther was almost breathless.

"Gambling!" Harold announced. "And the blackjack dealer had finally arrived—none other than Aunt Rosie herself!"

Esther's eyes became huge saucers, riveted on her husband.

"So," Harold continued, "I go to get something to eat. And the food. Man, oh man. I had prime rib with a baked potato. And cheesecake. What a place! What a palace they turned the Union Hall into!"

"Who paid for all the food?"

"Oh, Aunt Rosie paid for everything. She was just glad to have the ride."

"Did you gamble?"

He hesitated before answering. "Rosie gave me fifteen dollars for taking her there."

"So, you didn't lose any of our money?"

"No. No!" He was lying, but she would never know. Harold was eager to tell her more. He settled back into an armchair, having saved the best for last.

"And guess who I saw there?"

Esther couldn't imagine.

"Your Uncle Abe!"

Esther was flabbergasted. "Uncle Abe...why...what was he doing there?"

"Gambling, of course, just like everyone else."

Esther did not know quite what to think, but her inclination was to let her father know. She hastily prepared dinner for Harold and Edna and went downstairs to tell Morris everything.

Harold, satisfied that he had conveyed enough of the story to Esther, started to concentrate on his real problem. If only he had not started gambling after he finished eating at the Union Hall. As he saw it, he had lost almost sixty dollars, which he had "borrowed" from the cash register at work. These were the dollars Hy Zipp had accused him of stealing, that led to Zipp firing him before he could replace them in the register. He intended to replace the money the next morning—he wanted some extra cash in his pocket, because Aunt Rosie had not told him where they were going. And he would have had most of it the next day. He closed his eyes and pictured that night.

The room at the Union Hall was thickly laden with cigarette smoke. Harold constantly removed his glasses, rubbing his eyes. He could barely see Aunt Rosie across the room—she was dealing blackjack. He knew she played poker, but this was beyond anything he could have imagined. He looked around. Everyone seemed the same to him. Were they all trying to make a few bucks—or did they all want to end the evening as big winners? A woman tapped him on the shoulder, offering him a drink. He hesitated—he had a long drive home—but relented and downed the Scotch.

He had chosen to play roulette—his lucky numbers were 6, 24, and 27. After the wheel disappointed him for the fourth time, rapidly chipping away at his gambling allotment, the man standing next to him said, "Why these numbers? They don't seem too lucky to me!"

Harold felt challenged and replied: "These are my birthday numbers, fella. What could be luckier than the day one was born?"

His inebriated roulette mate retorted: "Ya got kids? A wife? Those are the dates you play?"

Harold felt a swell of anger rising. The impertinence of this guy to suggest there was anything unlucky about his numbers. He also felt dismissed—and so turned to the chap and said, "How do you know my birthday is not a lucky day?"

The man reached over and grabbed Harold's shirt collar, but a loud banging on the front door of the Union Hall interrupted him. The occupants ignored the pounding, but the door was shoved open and the police came in.

Everyone remained frozen. Harold's eyes darted around the room, looking for Rosie—who was gone. Within minutes, the officers retrieved his aunt from the back bathroom, handcuffed her, and led her away.

———

As Esther babbled excitedly to her parents about Harold's discovery at the Union Hall, Morris and Becky sat stone-faced, each lost in thought. For Morris, this startling news, that his brother was a gambler, was overshadowed by learning his son-in-law spent the night gambling while his daughter was in the hospital. Inexplicably, Esther was more agitated about Abe than she was about her husband being gone until the wee hours.

Morris wondered if this was what Abe had planned to do with the thousand dollars he had asked for. *Would he gamble it away? And what should Morris do now?*

He thought about getting advice from Larsh, but immediately discarded that idea. Larsh knew Morris to be honest, upright—all the things Morris knew himself to be—why concern his new business partner with this unseemly family problem? *Maybe his sister?* No, Lena also would be no help, and he could not trust her daughter, Frances. *After all, Frances worked for a judge. What would it mean if Abe had somehow broken the law?*

Distraught and confused, Morris glanced at Becky, whose demeanor had changed as Esther's story came to its conclusion. A slight, cruel curl covered Becky's mouth, and her breathing became heavy. What Morris did not know was that before Abe had asked him for money, Abe had made the same request of Becky. Becky, who had some fondness for Abe, had told her brother-in-law, "Ask Moshe, see what he says to you."

Chapter 25

EDNA HAD THE MEASLES, A HIDEOUS RED RASH COVER-
ing her from head to toe. Becky and Esther had decided
it was better to keep her downstairs in Becky's bedroom.
Becky slept in Morris's room, and Morris slept on the living room
couch. They kept the sickroom dimly lit; no sunlight was allowed
to enter.

It was always dark in Becky's back bedroom, even during the
day. In fact, it was always dark everywhere in the house on South
Green Road. At least her grandparents turned on the lamps
during the evening, unlike her father, who rampaged through the
upstairs apartment flipping light switches and yelling, "What's
wrong with everyone up here—do you think I have stock in the
electric company?"

Edna asked her grandmother—for what she thought was at
least the millionth time—if she could have a small portable television set brought into the bedroom. Becky said no. She told Edna
the light was not good for her—that just looking at the television
screen would hurt her eyes. Edna wondered if that meant the mea-

sles could make her blind, but she was mostly upset that every day at five o'clock, she was missing her cartoons—*Heckle and Jeckle* and *Woody Woodpecker*. Edna asked both Ceal and Morris to intervene on her behalf—but Becky could not be moved.

Edna sneaked out of bed at least three times a day—when everyone thought she was asleep—to pull up her pajama top and look at the rash all over her chest. She pressed her face as close to the mirror as possible to examine her scarlet cheeks.

Edna's pediatrician, Dr. Bloomfield, visited twice a week. He assured Edna she would be fine, but she did not believe him. Edna distrusted doctors. *After all, why hadn't Dr. Gold cured Grandma after all his visits?* But Bloomfield seemed nothing like Grandma's doctor. He was a kind man, who always tried to make Edna laugh.

Meanwhile, Ceal understood Morris was distressed that his granddaughter was ill and would not be any help in addressing her preoccupation about what to do about Becky. Ceal was increasingly suspicious that there were things happening that no one knew about and became melancholic remembering the stories of how, growing up, Ben and Bessie had taken her sister to at least three doctors after she'd taxied home from her job at the factory—all of them saying Becky was in perfect health. The solution Ben and Bessie reached was to keep Becky at home. She would cook for the family. She reluctantly agreed to clean as well, although worrying constantly about germs.

Ceal knew it was too late to undo all those years. But Becky seemed to have settled down. *So, what was going on now?*

Ceal thought the rearrangement of the Katofsky household to accommodate Edna's illness was absurd. But neither Becky nor

Esther listened to her protests. Instead, Ceal proceeded like every other family member, paying visits to Edna, who spent two weeks in Becky's huge bed.

Ceal did not share her real anxiety with anyone, not even Al. She was terrified Rosalie would get the measles. She considered keeping Ira home from school, too; the classroom was a breeding ground for the disease. To control her anxiety, Ceal explored all the possibilities. The first had Rosalie getting the measles but recovering. The second, however, had Rosalie contracting measles and dying, or worse: deteriorating into an even more compromised situation than the one she was in.

"The best thing to do, Mrs. Kirstein," Rosalie's doctor said to her, "is to keep her isolated." *Maybe she should tell Al she needed to leave town for a while—with Rosalie—to a warmer climate until this "epidemic" was over.* She knew the doctor thought this was an overreaction.

Despite her fears and the collective family neurosis about illness, Ceal thought locking Edna up for two weeks with the measles was an unacceptable solution.

When Ceal arrived at the house, Becky was reading to Edna— something she did twice a day so Edna would stop complaining about not watching television. Edna's current favorite book was *Melvin the Moose Child*. Becky, an avid reader herself, was also a good storyteller. Around six o'clock every night, Edna asked Becky to tell her a story until it was time to go to sleep. For the entire two weeks, Becky told Edna the same story, one she had invented, with only slight variations.

"Once upon a time, there was a little girl who would never listen to her mother. Whatever the mother told her to do, the little girl simply did not listen or behave. The mother would become angry and punish her. It made no difference. The little girl was stubborn and would not behave."

"What was her name, Grandma?"

"I don't know," Becky replied, and continued, "What the little girl was most stubborn about was cleaning her ears."

This part of the story always fascinated Edna because she hated having her ears cleaned. Edna hated anything that had to do with ears because of the many ear infections she had in the second grade. Nothing Dr. Bloomfield prescribed had made a difference. She especially hated the ear drops—she would run around the room shrieking until her mother held her down, as the warm oozy drops fell from the dropper into each ear. Edna wondered if they forced the nameless little girl in Becky's story to have ear drops as well.

"So, because she was so stubborn, the little girl never cleaned her ears—even though her mother warned her that very soon," Becky paused here for dramatic effect, "very soon, potatoes would start growing out of her ears.

"Sure enough, the little girl woke up one morning, went to the mirror, and saw sprouts coming out of both ears—but did not tell her mother what she saw."

Edna interrupted Becky at this point and asked, "Why didn't the little girl tell her mother, Grandma?"

"I don't know," Becky answered, and she continued the story. "So, the sprouts kept growing, and before you knew it, potatoes were growing out of her ears!"

"But, Grandma," Edna said emphatically, rising straight up

from the two pillows nestled behind her head, "didn't her mother see the potatoes growing out of her ears?"

"Shah, shah, Edna," Becky replied, gently pushing her back onto the pillows. "You need to lie still and listen. You don't want to make yourself sicker by exciting yourself. And no, Edna, her mother did not see the potatoes growing out of her ears."

"But how could that be, Grandma?"

"I don't know." Becky shrugged and continued the story. "So, the little girl went grocery shopping with her mother—and while her mother wasn't looking, she walked over to a big barrel of potatoes in the vegetable aisle of the grocery store."

"Like the potato barrel at Weintraub's?"

"Exactly like the potato barrel at Weintraub's," Becky replied. "So, the little girl was leaning over the barrel of potatoes—and then accidentally fell in. She tried to get out, but only sank deeper into the potato barrel until nothing was showing but her ears. She tried calling for help, but no one heard her. The mother could not find her anywhere—and left the store without her.

"That's the end of the story, Edna—now go to sleep."

Edna had a hard time sleeping the first night she heard the story. By the third rendition, Edna decided none of this could possibly be true—and that Grandma apparently did not know any other stories (she did not ask).

When Libby arrived at the house for another visit, she walked into the back bedroom and handed Edna a slim paper bag. Edna was excited. More paper dolls! The first set was Gisele MacKenzie. Edna had seen Gisele MacKenzie on *The Perry Como Show* and liked her a lot. She then looked at the second set—also Gisele

MacKenzie. Edna turned to Aunt Libby and said, "Aunt Libby, why did you buy me two sets of the same paper dolls?"

The innocent question perturbed Aunt Libby.

"What kind of question is that, Edna?" Aunt Libby replied sharply. "I get no thank you, no 'Thank you for the paper dolls, Aunt Libby?'"

Edna was (as most people were) immediately cowed by Libby and started to cry. Becky, returning from the kitchen where she had gone to get a plate of cookies for Edna, glared at her sister.

Libby, holding a stiff posture, continued her berating. "The reason you got two sets of Gisele MacKenzie, Edna, is because they were on sale. A two-for-one sale, Edna. I have to work, Edna—not like your grandmother. And things are expensive—even paper dolls."

Becky knew better than to challenge her sister when she began a tirade. Instead, she put her arms around Edna and whispered into her ear until she stopped crying. Becky then took her cantankerous sister by the hand and pulled her from the room.

Edna grabbed a cookie, ate half, put it down on the bedspread, and began carefully punching out the cardboard dolls. Aunt Libby returned and silently put some scissors on the bed. Edna cut out the evening gowns first. They were beautiful colors and designs. Pink, green, and yellow, with long flowing skirts. She had a passing thought of taking the scissors and completely cutting up the second set of dolls, beginning with the heads. She decided she would wait until later when she was sure Aunt Libby had left the house.

With Edna preoccupied, Ceal gave Libby "the look," which Libby knew meant some sort of confrontation was about to occur with Becky. The three sisters, now settled at the kitchen table, began gossiping, Libby tapping her foot impatiently. Finally, Ceal pressed her palms on the table, leaned over to Becky, and said, "I want to know—Libby and I want to know—what are these visits from Gold all about?"

Becky responded with the familiar hand on her chest, and replied, "*Meine* heart."

Libby interjected, "There is nothing wrong with your heart, Becky. And what about the thousand dollars you have hidden in the cedar chest in your bedroom?"

Ceal winced, realizing that she and Libby should have coordinated this attack, but before Ceal could speak, Becky replied, "I don't know what you are talking about, Libby. I don't keep any money in the cedar chest."

With that pronouncement, Libby darted to the back bedroom, startling Edna, who shoved the now decapitated paper dolls under her pillow. Ceal and Becky right behind her, Libby threw open the chest, flung the blankets over her head, and stared into an empty drawer.

"All this living with Joe has affected your imagination, Libby," Becky dryly said to her confused sisters. Turning to Edna, Becky said, "Go to sleep now, Edna—you have been up too long," and exited the bedroom, ushering out her sisters and closing the door behind her.

The three women headed back to the kitchen with the exact same thought in their minds: "*I wonder what happened to the money?*" Becky was in a controlled state of panic, trying not to do anything that would indicate this was the first time *she* knew the money was gone.

Edna slipped out of bed, pressing her ear to the bedroom door, confident everyone was occupied in the kitchen. Then, reaching into her grandmother's nightstand, she grabbed the money and put it back into the cedar chest.

With Ceal and Libby gone, and Edna appearing to be sleeping (but having one eye slightly open), Becky reentered the bedroom and dove her thick palm under the blankets in the cedar chest. Feeling the stack of bills, she gently relaxed her sweating hand.

Assuming Edna was asleep, Becky returned to the kitchen and downed several Darvon tablets. Edna, tired and drifting off, reasoned that there was so much money in the drawer, Grandma would never miss the twenty dollars she had taken.

Chapter 26

E DNA WOKE UP IN THE BACK SEAT OF HER PARENTS'
Chevrolet, glad they were almost home. She missed Grandma and Grandpa, and it had been a horrible vacation. She vowed that she would never return to Washington, D.C.

Harold had said he needed a "break," and Esther, reluctant to leave Edna behind, had decided she could easily miss a week of school despite having taken time off for her tonsillectomy and the measles. Esther and Harold began fighting as soon as the car was a short distance from the house—and, of course, it was over something Becky had done. It was about the hard-boiled eggs. Edna loved hard-boiled eggs, and Becky had boiled some—two dozen, to be exact—to take on the trip.

The car was, as Harold had put it, "packed up and ready to go," when Becky had come lumbering out of the house with the eggs tucked in a huge yellow-and-brown checkered cooler. Harold, anxious to start the long drive, had looked at his mother-in-law and remarked, "What the hell is this?" Becky, immune to her son-in-law's animosity, ignored him completely, opened the car's back door, and deposited the cooler on the seat. Harold considered dumping the eggs in the driveway. Instead, he sped away.

Five minutes from the house, Harold had begun screaming at Esther about the cooler in the back seat. As he ranted and raved, Esther lost her composure. She was unable to interject even a syllable into the conversation before Harold cut her off, screaming, "Go to hell, you can just go to hell!"

And then, as always, for some unexplained reason, Harold stopped. Although he could never be described as pleasant, he became relatively quiet for the rest of the drive to Washington. Edna told herself she could not cry during the trip. She was afraid her father would start screaming again. She thought of telling jokes, but instead sank back into the seat and read one of her books for the remainder of the journey.

The family ate in cafeterias for most of the vacation. Edna loved cafeterias. She noticed that her father never questioned how much food she took, and he often ate whatever she did not consume. Harold would tell people, "It's my metabolism, you know? I can eat like a horse, and it doesn't make a difference!" So, Edna experimented, ordering three desserts every night. To her surprise, her father finished them all. He did not once question her judgment, her choices. After the third night, she turned to him and asked, as she put three pieces of apple pie on her tray, "Is this really okay?" Even Esther was wondering how Harold would reply.

"Of course it's okay, Edna," her father answered. "I'm on vacation."

Edna had been looking forward to seeing the sights, but Harold limited their visits to what interested him. Her mother never said a word, and her father met any request to see things not on his list with a sharp rebuke and a stern, "Be quiet." Esther was disappointed as well. She had always wanted to go to Washington, D.C., and longed to be able to see some of the museums she had read or heard about. The Smithsonian—surely Harold would agree to take them all to the Smithsonian. But the mention of anything like that—which Harold characterized as "some stupid cultural stuff"—was met with hostile rejection.

The incident that alarmed Edna the most had taken place in front of the Washington Monument—it was enough to ruin the entire trip. Her parents had argued in the middle of the street, Edna tuning out the caustic words and the frozen, disapproving faces of the people walking past them. She wanted to beg her parents to stop but didn't dare speak. *Was her father going to strike her mother? Would they all wind up in jail?* It was the reactions of the passersby, not Esther, that made her father finally stop screaming. Edna was too frightened to cry. Esther, a vacant look in her eyes, took Edna's hand and solemnly walked behind her husband as they entered the monument.

How to explain to her classmates why she had missed another week of school consumed Edna. They were used to the stories of Edna being ill. They teased her about it. She could hear them now.

"Edna's always sick."

"Edna's sick again."

"What's wrong with you this time, Edna, got the cooties?"

She wanted to tell the truth—*but what if they told the teacher?* And she did not trust the students enough to swear them to secrecy. Edna had not visited one thing on the list she had compiled when Esther had told her they were going to Washington. She had

189

made, she thought, good choices: the Lincoln Memorial, the Jefferson Memorial. But none of that appealed to her father, and she was afraid to make him angrier than he already was.

Harold, with no explanation, had announced the three of them were going to Arlington National Cemetery. Edna was accustomed to cemeteries. Every Mother's Day, Harold took her to visit his mother's grave. They would stand silently for over an hour, and then leave a full bouquet of flowers at Sadie Kotkin's gravestone. On more than one occasion, Edna was certain she detected a tear or two in her father's eyes. Harold would remove his glasses, rub his eyes, and say to her, "Allergies, Edna. It's that damn hay fever. Just hope you never have allergies."

When Edna prodded her mother about her late grandmother, Esther hesitated to say much. The Kotkins spoke of Sadie in quiet tones of reverence—and all agreed, "Nobody fooled with Aunt Sadie." Harold's favorite story about his mother was how, trying to cross a busy street in downtown Cleveland, Sadie finally stepped out in front of an oncoming vehicle, raised her enormous hand, and commanded the automobiles to stop. As cars screeched to abrupt halts, Sadie painstakingly crossed the street, a look of self-satisfaction on her face with every assured step she took.

Finally, the "vacation" came to an end. They were almost home. Esther leaned over into the back seat of the car. "Edna? Are you up?" she asked.

"Yeah, Mom." She rubbed her eyes. "Daddy, can we stop for something to drink? I'm thirsty."

"Hold your horses back there. I'm not stopping for anything now," Harold barked.

"Harold, she's thirs—"

Before Esther could finish her sentence, Harold snarled and said, "Shut up, Esther. The kid's spoiled rotten. Gets everything she wants from your parents. Well, I'm not thirsty, and I'm not stopping. She'll have to wait until we get home. That's it—Fort Pitt!"

Edna was tempted to tell the truth about why she was suddenly so thirsty—she had swiped a small can of peanuts from the hotel gift shop, gone to the ladies' room, and consumed the entire contents. (She was not hungry—they had just finished a large breakfast. Truth was, she was not even overly fond of peanuts.) She was sure the clerk in the store saw her take the nuts and was going to tell her parents. But, to her surprise, the clerk turned his head away, and Edna walked out of the shop with the stolen merchandise tucked into the small pink plastic purse her mother had bought her for the trip.

Edna had two purses—the one from her mother and a small blue plastic purse adorned with a large white daisy, which Aunt Ceal gave her for her ninth birthday. Ceal thought it odd that Edna never used the purse, and asked on many occasions, "Don't you like it, Edna? I will buy you another one if you don't." Edna would smile and reassure Ceal she liked the purse—and feel a slight sense of guilt that she was disappointing her favorite aunt. What no one knew was that the blue plastic purse, carefully concealed in Edna's dresser drawer, contained dollar bills and loose change she swiped from Harold's bedroom dresser. When she examined the coins she had taken, she noticed that one of them seemed odd. It was a nickel, but it did not look like any other nickel she had ever seen. Then she remembered her father collected coins. He kept a box of them

191

in his top drawer. Edna was afraid that, in the act of stealing, she had taken a coin that her father had intended to save and put into his private stash. She recalled the nickel was set apart from the rest of the change—*that must be it, it was one of dad's special coins. Did he know she had taken it? He must. Why didn't he say anything? He was probably waiting until he could catch her stealing something red-handed.*

It was this secret—how she got the money—that prevented her from telling her father that she had stolen the can of peanuts. And so, although she toyed with the idea of being truthful about what happened in the gift shop, she decided to eat the evidence instead. Now she was dying of thirst.

"How far are we from the house?" she asked her father.

"Not far—a few hours," he replied. "Did you have a nice vacation?"

Although she was only ten, her first thought was, *"How could he ask me that question?"* Edna did not understand how he could not comprehend that, as far as she was concerned, this was one of the worst trips she had taken—ever. She paused for a minute, and instead of answering, asked, "Did you have a good time?"

Harold seemed surprised, but then replied, "Yep, of course I did. I always have a good time. I'm the last of the good-time Charlies!"

Edna had no idea what a good-time Charlie was but knew better than to ask. She sank back into her seat and closed her eyes for the remainder of the trip.

Chapter 27

CEAL, MORRIS, AND HAROLD EACH HAD SEPARATE missions. Ceal, after plotting with Libby, was determined to bring this business with Becky, Dr. Gold, and the (now vanished) money to a swift close. Morris, sensing an unusual calm in Becky, who now plodded at an even slower pace than before, was still trying to determine what to do about Abe, who had not paid a visit to the Katofsky household since Harold saw him gambling at the Union Hall. Harold was now working for a much lower salary at Green Drug and was determined to make a "killing" with Rosie at his side. He owed one of his coworkers fifty dollars, money he needed to make a car repair. (Esther had told him to ask Morris for the money, but Harold refused, reminding his wife: "We give the old man too much money for the rent, otherwise we wouldn't be in this situation.")

Harold was the first to act. He left work early, complaining of a toothache, and surprised Esther when he walked in the door at three o'clock. It had been raining heavily. He threw his umbrella to the side as soon as he entered the house and told Esther he was going to talk to Becky.

Alarmed, Esther assumed the two of them were going together, but Harold raised his hand in front of his wife's face and said, "No problem here, everything is copacetic. Just need to ask your mother a few questions. Go do laundry or something, I won't be long."

Esther obediently headed to the basement, and from the second-floor china cabinet Harold removed the package Dr. Gold had given him, slipping it into his pocket.

Becky was sprawled on the living room sofa as Harold entered the room. The plastic furniture covering crackled as she lifted herself to greet her son-in-law, who waved her back down and said, "No need to get up—I'm *gonna* keep this simple." Removing the Demerol packet from his pocket, he handed it to Becky and said, "This is yours—for a hundred bucks. Just between you and me—no questions asked."

Harold had given more thought than usual to the idea of blackmailing his mother-in-law. It would be risky if Esther or Morris found out, but he could handle either one of them—his only real concerns were Ceal and Libby—the uncles would do nothing.

Becky's eyes narrowed as she stared at the vial and syringe in Harold's hand. Pulling herself up, she plodded into her back bedroom, returning with a thick wad of bills which she shoved into her son-in-law's palm. To Harold's surprise, she then rolled up the sleeve of her housedress and motioned him to come over. He paused. He had not anticipated having to administer the Demerol. *Well, no big deal—after all, he had done stuff like this in the Army.*

His mission accomplished, he fanned the money between his fingers. As he proceeded to leave the room, he asked Becky, "So, when do you think the rain will stop? It's been raining for three goddamn days!"

————

Ceal began the morning focused on only one thing—the rain. She had been late to work the entire week. She was determined to be on time today and woke Rosalie up extra early to take her to the sitter. Ira, always self-sufficient, had already gone to school. The only thing left to do was to leave Ben his lunch.

Ben Shafron—*Zaide*—had supported his family by working as a tailor. He kept a sewing machine nearby. Whenever he visited any of the great-grandchildren, he would bring a little something he had made. The last time he went to Becky's, he brought an apron for Edna. It was beautiful, a cheerful print of red and yellow apples, the top bib embellished with scarlet piping. Edna adored it and wore the apron whenever she helped Becky bake.

Although most of his qualities were endearing, the one thing that troubled everyone in the family about Ben was that he smoked. Since the age of thirteen, Ben finished two packs of Camels a day. He spoke only Yiddish, so Edna never had any conversations with him. The aunts and uncles took turns having him stay at their homes, where Ben was content to spend his days watching television. When it had become clear he could no longer live alone, Ceal volunteered to care for him. The brothers and sisters contributed money to the cause.

Watching and being responsible for Ben was a challenge for Ceal—occasionally, a burden. Becky had been upset the last time Ben visited because of what happened with the bowl of fruit. Becky had decorated the coffee table in the living room with the bowl Larsh had given her and filled it with wax fruit. There were purple grapes, bright red apples, perfectly shaped pears, and a bunch of bananas. Becky had asked Esther what she thought of it, and Esther had agreed that it looked real and was colorful on the table. (To Edna, the addition of wax fruit to a home always filled with too much food seemed peculiar.)

Becky had had the centerpiece for only one week when Ceal and Ben came to visit. Ben and Edna were in the living room, Ben smoking and Edna watching *Kukla, Fran and Ollie* on television. Ceal had gone to the bathroom. Becky was in the kitchen making lunch. Suddenly Edna ran into the kitchen, grabbed her hand, and said, "Grandma, come quick."

Becky found Ben desperately trying to pull one of the wax apples out of his mouth. With an exclamation of "*Oy vey*, Pa!" she steadied her father's shoulders and instructed Edna to yank as hard as she could to extract the apple. Edna, certain that she would tear out Ben's teeth, put her small hands on the fruit, closed her eyes, and yanked as hard as she could. On the third try, the apple was dislodged.

Becky, lapsing into Yiddish, asked, "Pa, are you okay?"

Her father did not answer immediately but moved his jaw from side to side to make sure everything was in place. He opened another pack of Camels, Edna went back to watching television, and Becky took the contents of the fruit bowl and threw them into the garbage.

———

With lunch for Ben in the refrigerator, Ceal wrapped herself and Rosalie in heavy raincoats, turned to her father, and said, "Remember, Pa, it's raining. Don't go out today." The last thing she

196

needed was her father traipsing around in the downpour. She was almost out the door when the phone rang. *Who could that be? It was close to eight a.m. She had already spoken to Libby, Becky, and her brothers.* Ira had been instructed to stay in bed for the day, after complaining about a sore throat. As Ceal held the shaking Rosalie, she felt a momentary wave of despair. *This poor sick child, what would become of her? And where would Ira wind up?* Ceal had no illusions about the challenges both Ira and Rosalie faced, and for a second wondered if Ira landed on her doorstep so she could be prepared to meet the rocky road that lay ahead.

She picked up the phone and was not pleased to hear Millie's voice. "I called to tell you that you shouldn't go out today. I'm not letting Arthur go out today."

"What are you talking about?" Ceal asked her sister-in-law. "I'm on my way to work now. Ira is sick. I'm just taking Rosalie to the sitter."

Millie said, "I had a dream last night that someone from the family was—"

Before Millie could finish, Ceal interrupted her. Millie had been having dreams of catastrophes for at least twenty years. When Ceal stopped to think about it, for a woman who was not very bright, Millie did have unusual dreams. Ceal would have been surprised to know that Becky, who was very superstitious, paid attention to every instruction Millie gave her when she called about a dream. Ceal, however, got a headache whenever Millie called, and therefore hung up on her sister-in-law.

It rained all day long. Much like a monsoon, Ceal thought. Exhausted when she got home from work that evening at five o'clock, she was preoccupied with stripping Rosalie out of her wet clothes. She looked at the clock and saw that Al should arrive in another half an hour, then, as she realized Ben was not there, he came walking through the door. He was soaked from head to toe, and Ceal was not happy.

"Pa, where have you been? I told you not to go out in weather like this, and look at you, soaked. Get out of those wet clothes before you catch your death!"

Ben muttered something in Yiddish about going out to get a pack of cigarettes, and, following his daughter's orders, changed into something dry. Al came home on time. They all had dinner, watched *The Milton Berle Show* and the *Texaco Star Theater*, and went to sleep.

By the next morning, the rain had stopped. Ceal got up early, made coffee, and sat down at the kitchen table to read the newspaper. The headline of the *Plain Dealer* read: *OCTOGENARIAN SAVES STRANDED BUS RIDERS*. The article began:

Eighty-five-year-old Ben Shafron rescued seven of his fellow bus riders when the bus they were riding flooded at the bottom of Cedar Hill. The bus, trapped by the torrential rain, began filling with water, and Shafron, apparently the only passenger on board who could swim, guided each of his bus mates to safety until help arrived. The mayor hailed Shafron as a local hero and thanked him on behalf of the City of Cleveland.

Before Ceal could read any further, the phone rang. It was Libby, who had just seen the paper. Ceal told her to call the other brothers and sisters and went to knock on Ben's bedroom door.

"Pa, are you up? I need to talk to you."

Before Ben emerged, the doorbell rang. On the front lawn were three television crews, a reporter for the *Cleveland Press*, and a reporter for the *Cleveland Jewish News*.

Ceal closed the door, went back to her father's room, and said, "Pa, you need to get dressed."

Ceal threw on a housedress. By now, Izzie and Arthur were coming up the front walk. The brothers took over and explained to the crowd that their father spoke no English and then spent the next two hours translating as a subdued Ben emerged and was greeted with a barrage of flashing cameras.

When the crowd had dissipated, the aunts and uncles (save Becky, who was at home with a backache) gathered around the dining room table, with Ben sitting at the head. For the first time ever, they were collectively speechless. They stayed for what seemed an eternity, exchanging silent glances. Finally, Ceal asked the one question Ben was dreading, but that was clearly on everyone's mind: "Pa, why were you on that bus—where were you going?"

Chapter 28

CEAL PLACED BOTH PALMS ON EITHER SIDE OF HER head in a futile attempt to ward off a headache, as a defensive Ben Shafron confessed to his children that he was dating.

"So, Pa, what's she like, this—what did you say her name was?" asked Izzie, trying to suppress the urge to laugh.

Ben hesitated, then, surveying the faces of his disapproving children, replied, "Mrs. Schenker, Sarah Schenker." And before another one of the aunts or uncles could say a word, he added, "It's not like any of you would have said to me, 'Bring her home, Pa, we would like to meet her.' So, we meet downtown and have a cup of coffee."

Libby was about to join the conversation, but a warning glance from Ceal silenced her. To Ben's surprise, Ceal rose from the table and said simply, "Okay, Pa, okay. Next time, just tell us where you are going."

The brothers and sisters exchanged looks. It was unlike Ceal to leave a matter like this without any admonishment, without any firm parameters for future behavior. But the list of things to do regarding the family was out of control, even in the context of the environment they had created for themselves, hopelessly entangled in each other's lives.

It also surprised Ben, who was relieved he would not have to face a lengthy inquisition from the group. As everyone began to leave, Ceal turned to her father and said, "Why don't you bring Sarah with you tomorrow—when we all go to the Smorgasbord?"

Izzie took his cigar from his mouth and was about to speak, but Ceal said, "Shut up, Izzie."

Ceal motioned Libby to follow her into her back bedroom. "I'm headed over to Becky's," Ceal told her sister. "I'm going to tell her I am calling Gold and anyone else I have to call to figure out what is going on. I took the day off from work—I am putting an end to this."

Libby was disappointed. She thought she and Ceal had agreed to do this together. It was something she, Libby, was looking forward to. She had told the office she would only be gone a few hours—there was no way she could change that now. She knew Becky was bound to be unpleasant—she had counted on Becky being unpleasant. *Could Ceal do this without her?* If Ceal were able to end this on her own, it would deny Libby the satisfaction of having reined in her ungrateful sister. *The sister who didn't have to work. The sister who refused to work. The sister who was allowed to stay at home even after she drained the paltry Shafron budget with her taxicab rides.*

Libby had held her tongue all the years their mother was alive. *What had Bessie Shafron known about dealing with Becky?* Besides,

Bessie had been sick. Her devoted mother had had a real heart condition—suffering for years with angina pains. And what could Ben do about Becky at this point? He was a lonely old man—who now apparently was looking for a new companion. *Someone to replace her mother...no, that could not be the reason. To move out of Ceal's house? Where could he go at his age?*

A search for a new companion! How lovely. How about no companion? An even better thought. But—to the matter at hand—Becky. That ungrateful Becky. *Did she know how much aggravation she was causing everyone? And, if so, did she care?* Unlike Ceal, Libby gave not a single thought to how Becky's behavior affected the child in the house—Edna. Children, for the most part, were spoiled. That was how it seemed to Libby.

———

Ceal arrived at 2207 as Mr. Flax, the mailman, was making his delivery. The family was fond of him. It had been an excited Mr. Flax who had delivered the letter to Edna from President Kennedy, to whom Edna had written to tell him how much she liked him as president and how much she liked his family, especially his daughter, Caroline. Mr. Flax had alerted the entire neighborhood about his delivery to 2207. He had even notified the *Cleveland Jewish News*, and they had interviewed Edna by telephone.

The reply, thanking Edna for her good wishes, contained a typographical error. Instead of the phrase "unity in our nation," the letter read "*ubity* in our nation." Harold, excited, without further ado confiscated the letter, stashing it in his upper bureau drawer, convinced it would be "worth a few bucks someday."

Edna, eager to be the center of attention for something like this—a communication from the President—retrieved the note and took it to school. She circulated the letter among her classmates, who returned it to her with peanut butter and jelly stains. Edna tried to remove the stains with water, and then slipped it back into her father's bureau drawer.

After several fitful nights of little sleep, she confessed to Harold what she had done. The uproar she anticipated never materialized. Harold shrugged his shoulders and walked away. She understood this was better than the alternative, and never mentioned the incident again.

"Hello, Mr. Flax," Ceal called out, waving her hand as she went up the front stairs. Before he could deposit the mail, Ceal took the handful of letters, assuring him she would give them to her sister.

"No more letters from the White House?" the gentile postman asked.

"Oh, my niece, Edna. Yes, we are all very proud of her!" Ceal replied.

"Edna and I have great conversations when I deliver the mail on Saturdays," Flax countered.

"Really? What do you talk about?"

"That's the thing with Edna," Flax said. "You never know what's going to come out of her mouth. And what an imagination! She went on and on last week about the doctor who visits her grandmother, poor Mrs. Katofsky, and how he is a really bad man."

Flax had Ceal's attention.

"I asked her, 'What do you mean, Edna?' And she starts telling me all sorts of crazy things, to which I say, 'Edna, what an imagination. You watch too much television.' And she agrees and says to me, 'Mr. Flax, I am just like Mrs. Peel. I am one of the Avengers!'"

A sick feeling overcame Ceal, who smiled and thanked Mr. Flax for the conversation. As the mailman left, Ceal glanced down at the envelopes she held. The first return address said Huron Road Hospital. She thumbed through the letters—all six of them had hospital return addresses. But they were from six different hospitals! And they were all addressed to Ida Koppelman, at 2207 South Green Road. *Was it a coincidence they were sent to the Katofsky house instead of to the Koppelmans?* She tore open each envelope; all the visits were listed for the same day. She read the diagnosis, each the same: back pain. She knew what was going on.

Ceal felt light-headed. *She could not do this without Libby. And she had to tell Morris.* As she entered the house and called out to Becky, she crafted a new plan, to take place on the next day, after the outing to the Smorgasbord.

The entire family was excited about going someplace fancy to eat—The Smorgasbord in Stow, Ohio. Becky, who ordered all her hats and clothes over the phone from Halle's department store, had a new crepe dress. Edna fished into one of the huge, ornate hat boxes that Becky kept in her bedroom closet and donned a black velvet topper with a veil that she intended to wear to Stow. Becky told her to remove it before they left the house.

For the aunts and uncles, outings to Stow, and to Burton for the Apple Butter Festival, were considered trips to "the country." Although Ethel and Millie had fashionable dresses for these events, Ceal and Libby could only afford to accessorize their modest clothing. Ceal always insisted on bringing Rosalie and Ira on these occasions, which was viewed by the family as both an act of bravery and an act of defiance.

The entry lounge to the Smorgasbord had a thick, green velvet carpet, and a small podium where a man wearing a tuxedo—even in the afternoon—held the huge black reservation book. There were several couches and chairs—all in green velvet—and a long table dressed in a crisp white damask tablecloth. On the table was a huge ornate glass bowl filled with a sweet red punch, a huge ladle, and dozens of crystal punch cups. Waiters and waitresses, also in formal attire, passed hors d'oeuvres.

Ceal paid no attention to the whispers and disapproving glances Rosalie and Ira received. As Rosalie sat shaking in her chair, Edna helped fasten her bib and eagerly filled up Rosalie's plate. Rosalie responded with a faint caress of Edna's hand—and a half smile from her quivering lips.

The family attacked the buffet table, diving for the pickled and creamed herring, then immediately headed for the borscht (with sour cream), paying little attention to Ben and Sarah. Edna could not remember seeing so much food on the same table at the same time—even at Grandma's house. There was turkey, roast beef, fish, and a huge honey ham—which they told Edna was *"traif"* and she could not eat. (When Harold and Esther attended these events—they were not there today—Harold would layer huge portions of ham on his plate, making sure he took a seat next to Becky. Morris would utter obscenities in Russian under his breath, as Harold went to great pains to eat everything that was not kosher in front of the family.)

The aunts lamented that the selections on the dessert table left a lot to be desired compared to their European recipes. Edna loved that there were mysterious confections she had never eaten before—Sacher torte, Black Forest cake, and small, sugared fried pastries.

As Becky downed copious portions of sweets and complained about the quality of the baking, Uncle Izzie suggested that she give the Smorgasbord the recipe for their mother's Danish nut horns. The humor escaped Uncle Joe and Uncle Al, but Uncle Arthur jumped right into the conversation and said, "He's just *zetzing* you, Becky."

Arthur shot his brother a withering look. Arthur did not pay all this money for Sunday dinner to spend the afternoon listening to the inevitable pastry debate that would follow had Izzie's remark been taken seriously. Instead, Arthur engaged Uncle Al in a discussion about the new car Al had just bought, even though he knew the conversation rankled Ceal, who lost every battle she waged with her husband about this one extravagance. Izzie, whenever he was in the mood to tease Ceal, would interject, "Let's face it, Ceal, the only thing Al loves more than you is his car."

But the talk of Al's latest automobile went right over Ceal's head today. Confident that everyone was immersed in the meal, she motioned Libby to join her in the ladies' room.

Ceal pulled the crumpled hospital bills out of her purse and gave them to Libby.

"So that's what she is doing!" Libby said triumphantly.

Just then, Edna walked into the room.

"Aunt Ceal," said Edna, "Ira needs help with Rosalie."

Ceal left to attend to Rosalie, and Libby, determined not to be excluded from the drama of Becky's demise, returned to the dining room and asked Morris to join her outside. Handing the bills to a perplexed Morris, Libby assured her brother-in-law that she and Ceal would put an end to all of this.

Morris, however, had a different plan. He was going to give the hospital bills to Becky to pay as soon as they got home. He had no time for this nonsense with the aunts—or with the uncles either. Tomorrow was a big day at the Katofsky household—it was Becky's first monthly meeting to go over the books with Larsh. Whatever the aunts had in mind would have to wait until after that.

Things were going so well with Larsh. Becky, too, seemed calmer than she had ever been. She was even getting along with Harold. The aunts—they meant well, he knew that. But *tsores* was their middle name. Ceal, he decided, was overly excitable—*didn't he have a new kitchen door to prove that?* And Libby—well, Libby enjoyed trouble.

If they wanted to help him, maybe they could figure out the real problem—what was going on with Abe? *Was the incident Esther told them about—the night at the Union Hall—a one-time thing? After all, he wasn't arrested like Rosie. And so, his brother gambled a little— and maybe drank a little—was that so bad?*

Chapter 29

ORRIS PRESENTED BECKY WITH THE CRUMPLED PILE of hospital bills Libby had given him and babbled in Yiddish, "Libby was worried...Ceal was worried," until Becky raised her hand and stopped him with a command. "Stop talking, Moshe. I will pay the bills. Now, I have to get ready for Larsh coming tomorrow."

Becky was seething. *These no-good hospitals—so what if I gave them Ida's name, I gave them the right address to send the bills to, didn't I? I was going to pay them, wasn't I? Well, I'll have to change my plans for next week's visit to—now, where was it?* Her mind was having troubling placing the name of the hospital. *South Euclid? Shaker Heights? Well, it doesn't matter—I wrote it in my notebook.* And now she was going to have to give them another address. *It would be their problem, not mine. They asked for it, being so difficult.*

She changed her outfit three times in anticipation of her meeting with Larsh. And baked extra. She would show him how good a bookkeeper she was. Larsh would know—really know—that Becky Katofsky could be trusted, counted on to help run the business. She removed the large green ledger from the top drawer of the dining room buffet, sharpened several pencils, and began making notes for her meeting with—yes, he was hers as well—her business partner.

Morris could not do this without Becky. She knew that...*but did he?* Of course, he was responsible for all the physical labor—that is what Morris would tell everyone was the hard work. But keeping George and Willie happy and a tight rein on the checkbook, that is what made Morris successful. Larsh, she assumed, would see that distinction immediately. *And what would the aunts and uncles say when they—the Katofskys—announced their business deal with Larsh?*

The brothers would have a new admiration for her. Libby would—well, who knew what Libby would say about all of this. And Ceal would be jealous. Jealous of her poor, sick, uneducated sister Becky, who could have her clothes delivered to the house. Who could throw away sour milk at a moment's notice. Who could take taxicabs all over Cleveland if she decided to—all day long, to any hospital she chose to visit. That was success.

While Becky made her preparations for the meeting with Larsh, her father, Ben, was at his usual place, the Hebrew Home, and today he was winning big. No one in the family gave much thought to what Ben did on a regular basis. They knew he played cards every day, maybe cheated when Ceal could not monitor him, and ate an extra Danish or two, and maybe stayed a while after poker with his *lantsmen.*

Ben looked forward to his weekly game at the Hebrew Home, not only because he had a chance to spend time and *kibitz,* but also because, aside from being an excellent tailor, he was an extraordinary card player. While other kids had been learning hopscotch and hide-and-seek, Ben's offspring were busy learning the difference between a full house and a royal flush. Although he never bet much money, his ability to play hand after hand while maintaining a stoic expression gave him great satisfaction. He loved to bluff, and it was not unusual for him to win a round holding only a meager single pair.

Today was a good day. He was up three dollars, and he had been at the card table for only an hour. It was two o'clock. Al would not be by until 4:30 to take him home. Ceal insisted that Ben be back at the house by the time she arrived from work. He would deposit his winnings in the tin Ceal kept in the kitchen and then watch some television before dinner.

He was close to running out of Camels, which irritated him. He smoked incessantly while he played, and on the day of a game went through three packs instead of his usual two. He and the four men he was with had finished a round, and Ben, whose long legs always felt cramped under the table, decided to get up and stretch. He took three drags of his cigarette, thought about what Ceal was making for dinner and whether Rosalie was having a good day, and dropped dead.

Ben sprawled out on the floor, a single Camel still smoking in his right hand. One of the nurses gently stepped over him, retrieved the cigarette, and snubbed it out in the ashtray on the poker table. His fellow cardplayers gathered around him and in muted tones began murmuring "stroke" and "heart attack." Sol Sokowitz, who knew Ben for thirty years, felt a tear trickle down his cheek. Who would tell his lady friend, Sarah? Although Ben was eighty-six years old, his contemporaries considered him young. His youthful aura arose not only from his skills at the card table, but also from the fastidious attention he paid to the comings and goings of his cronies and the way he regaled them with detailed stories of his children and grandchildren. As his friends stood sadly around his still body, they knew that he would be much missed (although some admitted to each other later that they glanced at their watches to see if the afternoon snack of Danish and coffee would still be on time).

The Hebrew Home reached Ceal at work, and she called Al to pick her up at once. Back at the house, she instructed Ira to take care of Rosalie while she called her brothers and sisters. First, Izzie.

Ceal's voice on the phone was shrill and agitated. "Get Ethel and come over now," she commanded her brother. "Pa's dead."

"Dead?" answered Izzie, incredulous. "How...where..." His voice trailed off.

"At the Home...about an hour ago...playing poker...we'll talk later," barked Ceal. "Just get Ethel and come!"

Izzie was silent for a moment, and then asked, "Was he ahead?"

"Was he *what?*" Ceal shot back. "What is this *mischegas*, was he *what?*"

"Was he winning?" Izzie repeated calmly. "Was Pa winning when he died?"

Ceal contemplated hanging up the phone and moving on to call the others, but instead modulated her voice to a deep, dull tone and asked, "Izzie, what difference does it make?"

"I just want to know if Pa died winning or losing at poker."

Ceal hung up and dialed Libby. Then she called Esther and

212

told her to tell her parents and come over with Edna.

All the aunts and uncles headed for Ceal's house, except for Becky, who began complaining of chest pains and put in a call to Dr. Gold.

The aunts and uncles collectively had fourteen children. Out of all of Esther's first cousins, she was the only one who was bereft at the death of her grandfather. She called Harold at work immediately after hearing from Ceal. The only condolence he offered was, "He was an old man, Esther, old people die."

Uncle Izzie and Aunt Ethel picked up Esther and Edna. The four of them rode silently to Ceal's house, Esther continually wiping her tears. Morris was still at work.

In keeping with tradition, they had scheduled the funeral for the next day, and a big discussion began as to which rabbi should officiate. Ben was not a religious man, and, along with his children, only went to synagogue in the fall on the three High Holy Days. Esther, usually timid in the presence of the aunts and uncles, surprised them all by saying, "I think it should be someone who has some connection to the family—someone we can tell about *Zaide* and who will say nice things about him."

Aunt Libby was the first to respond. "It should be Philip Horowitz. He buried Ma, and they should be buried by the same rabbi."

Esther looked around the room and saw the aunts and uncles nodding in agreement. Determined to secure a meaningful eulogy for her grandfather, she turned to Aunt Libby and said, "Maybe that's a good idea, Aunt Libby." The aunts and uncles, unaccustomed to Esther asserting herself, shifted their attention in her direction.

"But I think it should be someone we are close to. Are you close to Rabbi Horowitz, Aunt Libby?"

Libby, annoyed by her niece interjecting herself into the discussion, turned to Esther and said sarcastically, "Yeah, real close. He calls me Libby. And I call him Rabbi!"

Esther, not in the mood for her aunt's sharp tongue, excused herself and left the room. The brothers and sisters, having no better suggestions than Libby's, placed a call to Rabbi Horowitz and made the arrangements.

———

The memorial service was held at the Berkowitz and Kumin Funeral Home. All the Shafron children (except for Becky, who claimed her heart was too weak for her to attend her father's funeral), their children, and the friends of Ben Shafron were in attendance as Phillip Horowitz gave his familiar eulogy about a man who was devoted to his family. One other mourner, Ben's lady friend, Sarah, sat quietly in the back of the chapel. The congregation for the most part remained composed, apart from Esther, who sobbed the entire time the rabbi spoke.

While the service proceeded inside the funeral home, the weather outside turned foul. When Rabbi Horowitz was finished, under black skies and in a heavy downpour, the Shafron family gathered and proceeded to the cemetery.

Harold had begrudgingly taken time off from work for what to him was a nonevent. He was the only family member who refused to put on a suit, and, as they lowered Ben Shafron into the ground, he stood at the gravesite jiggling his keys. This did not go unnoticed by the aunts and uncles, who each decided privately they would deal with Harold later.

Shortly after noon, the family regrouped along with the rabbi at Aunt Ceal's to begin sitting *shiva*. Esther had grown more distraught, and now, seated between Aunt Millie and the rabbi at the dining room table, was completely inconsolable. The requisite customary bowl of hard-boiled eggs made its way around the table. Aunt Millie took one, and then handed the bowl to Esther.

"No, Aunt Millie, I can't. I can't eat. I don't want one," Esther said, her chest heaving heavily and her sobs continuing.

"You have to, Esther," said her aunt. "It's tradition—it's the symbol of life. You have to."

"No, please. I can't. I can't." Her words were barely audible.

Embarrassed and annoyed, Millie leaned close to Esther's ear, and tersely said, "You must! You're sitting next to the rabbi—eat the egg!"

Esther reluctantly took an egg and, choking on each bite, retrieved the bowl from Millie's hands and offered the eggs to the rabbi. Without an instant's hesitation, Rabbi Horowitz courteously said, "No, thank you," and sent the bowl on its way to the next family member.

Edna was fixated on watching Ira attempt to feed Rosalie one of the eggs. Ira had cut the egg into several pieces, gently nudging each segment into Rosalie's mouth. Ira patiently wiped the yolk from around Rosalie's lips, each time cooing and caressing the invalid. Edna felt a tear trickle down her cheek, which she later attributed to an allergy.

The relatives stayed until after dinner. The only thing left for the aunts to do was to help Ceal clean up. The immediate family had decided, in accordance with Jewish law, to sit *shiva* the entire week, and they all planned to be back early in the morning.

Edna, experiencing her first funeral, was upset most by her mother's behavior. Edna had never seen her so sad. By day's end, Esther finally stopped crying, but settled into a deep state of depression. Harold drove Morris, Esther, and Edna back to South Green Road. Morris was not eager to see his wife. The aunts and uncles, too angry about Becky's decision not to attend her own father's funeral, had not mentioned her once the entire day.

No one had to tell Morris that Becky had called Dr. Gold. When they arrived at the apartment, they found her dreamy-eyed, sitting at the kitchen table having cake and tea. She greeted no one. She asked no questions about the funeral. She expressed no grief.

————

The next day, everyone planned to go about their usual routine and then arrive at Ceal's either in the late afternoon or after work. Esther picked up Edna at the school bus stop, and then went home to wait for Morris to take them to Ceal's. Harold announced that he had already been to the funeral—that was enough. The family, still remembering his behavior at the gravesite, was inclined to agree.

Morris came home early from work, determined to arrive at Ceal's before the others and fill the void Becky created. With Esther and Edna in the DeSoto, he was almost at Ceal's when a car driven by Bobbi and Flossie—Libby and Joe's two daughters— raced down the street and cut him off. The car jumped the curb and landed on the sidewalk as Bobbi and Flossie, without bothering to close the doors, ran across the front lawn into the house.

Uncle Arthur hurried toward the DeSoto. He leaned into Esther's window and said, "Don't bring Edna into the house. It's Joe—it's Joe."

Uncle Joe was dead.

Chapter 30

AS SHE WAITED ON CEAL'S FRONT LAWN FOR THE hearse to come to collect Uncle Joe, Edna began to get hungry. Everyone was running in and out of the house. In a way, it was exciting—some of the people were cousins she saw only on special occasions. Actually, this *was* a special occasion. She did not know anyone at school who could match this story—a great-grandfather and an uncle dying in the same week...they might accuse her of lying. She knew her classmates were already angry that, when they had a break to use the restrooms during a standardized test last week, she did not give out any answers.

Edna wondered if she could stop someone to ask them to bring her something to eat. Or maybe she could go inside and get something herself. But before she was through the front door, one of the cousins took her hand, turned her around, and admonished, "This is no place for you, Edna."

She was disappointed because she was curious to see Uncle Joe's dead body. She wondered if he looked happier dead than when he was alive. If that was true, she assumed that it was probably only true in Uncle Joe's case. She mentioned that to one of the many cousins, who reproached her, "Now really, Edna! What a thing to say."

She saw Izzie, his false leg leading the way and his arm resting on his trusty cane, emerge from the house to flick the ashes from his huge cigar onto the front stoop. If she could not go inside, at least, she was hoping, someone would tell her what had happened.

The scene in Ceal's living room, where Joe Warhaft breathed his last breath, had been chaotic. Lunch had been in the process of being served to those who were sitting *shiva* with Ceal, when, after consuming his usual Swiss cheese sandwich, Joe closed his eyes for the last time. It was only after Ceal, wiping her hands on her apron, had taken a seat beside her brother-in-law that anyone knew something was amiss.

"Joe," Ceal had asked, "how was the sandwich?"

Joe had not replied. Libby, who had been engrossed in conversation with Izzie, had turned toward her husband. Ceal at that point was shaking Joe by the shoulders, and Joe's head had slumped over into his lap. Ceal said to her sister, "Libby, I think he's dead."

Uncle Joe, indeed, was dead. With Ceal's pronouncement, the few non-family visitors paying *shiva* calls had gathered their things and left. Libby got up from the small *shiva* stool she'd been sitting on, went into the kitchen, and called her daughters. As she calmly spoke on the telephone, the rest of the family sat in stunned silence around the late Joe Warhaft.

Ceal was the first to break out of their shared stupor. She had begun shaking. She ran into the kitchen where Libby sat motionless at the table. As Ceal moved toward her sister, Libby turned and said, "It's all for the best." She paused for a moment, and then added, "I suppose we will have to call Berkowitz."

"Yes, of course," Ceal replied.

Libby decided not to remind the family that she had announced several years ago that she, Libby Warhaft, would never use the services of the Berkowitz and Kumin Funeral Home. She had once been running errands on a calm spring day and bumped into Mr. Berkowitz as he emerged from Corky & Lenny's Delicatessen.

"How are you, Mr. Berkowitz?" Libby had asked the undertaker.

"Well, thank you," the slight man had replied. "Business is good."

Business is good? That man makes money burying his own kind, and business is good? When my time comes, he won't get my business!

Yet now, met with the job of removing Joe from Ceal's house, Berkowitz was the only reasonable choice.

Izzie, Arthur, Millie, and Ethel were left sitting in the living room waiting for the hearse. Arthur was in a controlled state of distress. Ethel kept muttering under her breath, "Oh dear, oh dear, poor Joe..." Millie sat stock still, her hands folded in her lap, a wide grin frozen on her face. The remaining aunts and uncles were growing fidgety.

Suddenly Arthur bellowed for Ceal and Libby to come in from the kitchen, and they obliged. Izzie announced he was going to give a speech. He cleared his throat, lit a fresh cigar, and began to speak. "Four men are playing gin rummy and, at the end of a few hands, one of them has lost two hundred dollars. The man gets up from the table, says he is going to get a glass of water, and immediately drops dead. The other three men continue playing, and when they are done, draw straws to see who is going to tell the unsuspecting wife that her husband is dead.

"The loser of the draw goes to the wife's house and rings the doorbell. She answers. He tells her, 'Your husband just lost two hundred dollars playing gin rummy.'

"The wife screeches, 'He should drop dead!'

"The man replies, 'He did!'"

Arthur tried hard to keep from laughing but could not control himself. Ceal was flabbergasted, while Ethel began giggling, and Millie sat unmoved and still grinning.

Libby tapped Izzie on the shoulder and said, "Sounds like something Joe would do, lose two hundred dollars playing gin," and retreated into the kitchen.

———

After the hearse appeared from Berkowitz and Kumin and the remains of Joe Warhaft were collected, Edna was allowed into the house. *(Finally.)* She purposely and strategically positioned herself in the kitchen, as Joe's daughters wept (quite loudly, Edna noticed) and Aunt Libby sat calmly (which Edna noticed as well).

The Warhaft daughters collected their mother, leaving Edna alone in the kitchen with Ceal.

"You must be upset, Edna," her great-aunt said.

Edna was not sure but nodded yes. "Why doesn't Aunt Libby seem sad?" Edna asked.

Unprepared for the question, Ceal thought a moment and replied, "She is sad, Edna, she just doesn't show her sadness like everyone else."

Edna nodded again. "Why does everyone die?"

Ceal often wondered that herself and had no ready answer. "I don't know, Edna, they just do." Edna sat motionless, and Ceal felt helpless. *What must this child think? About everything? Her grandmother? Her father and mother? And now this? Was it too much for a small child?* She knew it had become almost too much for her.

Ceal looked around the kitchen, littered with paper plates and empty soda bottles. She found a garbage bag and handed it to Edna, instructing her to help her clean up. As they tidied the kitchen, Edna said, "Do you think Aunt Libby would let me put something in Uncle Joe's coffin?"

"Why, Edna," a startled Ceal replied, "what would you want to put in?"

"Oh, I don't know," Edna demurred. But that was not true. She had decided she was going to draw a picture for Joe. In the picture, Joe would be sitting all alone at the counter at White Castle, surrounded by everything Aunt Libby would not allow him to eat. And he would be smiling—something Edna realized she never saw Uncle Joe do. A happy picture—Uncle Joe—dead, but finally in a happy picture.

Ceal took Edna's hand. "I'm sure Aunt Libby would think that was very nice," Ceal assured her. "Just give it to me, and I will take care of it."

Esther came into the kitchen, her fingers tightly interlocked, overwhelmed by what had transpired, and told Edna it was time for them to leave. Morris joined her, wondering how Becky would take the news that Joe was dead—two deaths in one week was a lot, even for him. He considered not telling Becky, but Esther looked

223

him squarely in the eyes and said, "You have got to be kidding, Pa!" Morris acknowledged that Esther made sense but wondered if he would have to reschedule the business meeting with Larsh yet again.

With all that had happened, the conversation about what to tell Becky—or not to tell Becky—became overwhelming for Ceal. She was about to offer her opinion, but, uncharacteristically, said nothing. She wanted everyone to leave as soon as possible. It had been a terrible week, becoming more surreal with each passing minute. She toyed with the idea of throwing Izzie and Ethel out of the house.

Pa was dead. Poor, miserable Joe Warhaft was now in the same place, wherever that was. She was depressed. And she was overwhelmingly discouraged about Becky. *What to do?*

Rosalie came slowly into the kitchen, taking painful, unsteady steps. Al never wanted to talk about it, *but what would happen to Rosalie when they both were gone? There wasn't enough money—and there never would be enough money—for good private care.* Al had suggested they ask Arthur or Izzie for help.

Izzie, maybe. Ceal knew Millie would tell Arthur no, eliminating that option. *Did Becky and Morris have enough to help them?* There was too much unresolved, too much she did not know, and it weighed heavily on her.

As she prepared to take the last bag of garbage out of the house, it overflowed, splattering the kitchen floor. Disgusted, Ceal scooped up wads of sticky paper napkins and crumpled paper plates. While she did this, she noticed a tube protruding from the bag. Always curious, Ceal pulled out the tube—it was not familiar to her. *What was it?*

2207 South Green Road

Turning it over in her palm, she read the label: Rat Poison. Ceal's knees buckled, landing her squarely on the floor. *Rat poison? Who in her house had rat poison?* And then she remembered the story of Joe and Edna and the rats and squirrels. *But...was this possible?* Earlier that day Libby had taken Joe's sandwich into the kitchen for a minute. Ceal had asked her what she was doing, and Libby replied, "Joe wants lettuce." Ceal left her sister in the kitchen, but had wondered if there was any lettuce in the house. It was hard to know since so many people had brought food, but she didn't think so.

Was it possible? Did Libby poison Joe?

Chapter 31

T HE AUNTS AND UNCLES SPENT EVERY HOLIDAY TOGETHER
no matter how unpleasant the previous one had been, and so
each produced new, major, unresolved conflicts. The Fourth
of July crisis erupted the year Libby, told to bring hot dog and hamburger buns, arrived an hour late with frankfurter buns only. Izzie
was the first one to point out that, while one could conceivably put
a hot dog on a hamburger bun, the prospect of eating a hamburger on a frankfurter bun was an unpleasant thought indeed. Libby
insisted that she brought what she was told. Because everyone was
crammed uncomfortably into the Katofskys' backyard, three of the
cousins volunteered to go down the street to Weintraub's Grocery
to buy the missing bread, only to find Mrs. Weintraub locking the
door to head out to her own holiday celebration.

The Fourth of July contentiousness carried over to Rosh Ha-
shanah and Yom Kippur, where a heated discussion ensued as to
what it "really" meant to fast. Ethel insisted, "If you get a headache, God wants you to eat, because now it is a question of your
health, but it is still considered fasting." Millie disputed this the-

ory, reasoning, "God wants you to suffer, so it makes sense to get a headache when fasting." Neither woman raised her voice, but Millie and Ethel stopped speaking for at least two weeks, and Izzie and Arthur did not encourage any resolution between them. Becky, who always lied about fasting anyway, went about her usual routine. Ceal, unable to answer any of Edna's questions about the matter, told her, "God has more important things to worry about."

Thanksgiving always took two weeks to plan, even though each aunt and uncle had the same assignment every year. Edna loved Thanksgiving—especially because she did not have to tell her classmates, "We don't celebrate Thanksgiving, we're Jewish."

The last Thanksgiving before the deaths of Ben and Joe, Aunt Ceal had been tasked with making Russian tea biscuits. Although there were several good Jewish bakeries in University and Cleveland Heights, according to the aunts, they could not duplicate authentic Russian tea biscuits. This was, to a certain degree, true. And Russian tea biscuits were the one pastry that Aunt Ceal baked to perfection.

No one ever knew the entire truth of what happened that year—but Edna's recollection was the most vivid. Edna understood, from overheard conversations, that Aunt Ceal had been exhausted. *Zaide* and Rosalie had both been sick, and Ceal had been unable to take any time off from work. The aunts told Ceal not to bother to bring the tea biscuits. Grandma Becky had even offered to make them herself. It was that offer, Edna learned later, that, according to the aunts, had led Ceal down the path of deceit.

Edna heard Libby launch into a lengthy soliloquy, telling the rest of the aunts, "Ceal thought she had the perfect plan. Lox and

Mandel Bakery made delicious tea biscuits. If you ate an Aunt Ceal tea biscuit, and then ate another from Lox and Mandel, most palates, but especially those of non-Jews, would not detect any difference. Everyone knew how tight money was for Ceal and Al— especially because of Rosalie. No one would ever believe she would buy three dozen tea biscuits—the price was prohibitive."

The Thanksgiving of the tea biscuit incident, Becky had stuffed a goose—a disappointment for Edna who loved turkey. It had disappointed the rest of the family as well, because none of them was overly fond of goose. Becky had proudly presented the fat-laden bird on a huge white ceramic platter, surrounded by plumped apricots and prunes. The one benefit of the oily bird was that the vegetable stuffing, which was delicious, had stayed incredibly moist.

Edna questioned the wisdom of the goose selection from the start. Lugging her huge Merriam-Webster dictionary downstairs, she informed her grandmother, who was dressing the bird, that a goose was "a large waterfowl with a long neck, feathered lores, and reticulate tarsi." Before Becky, staring at her granddaughter, could respond, Edna added, "It doesn't sound like something we should eat!"

Unmoved, Becky told Edna to go watch television.

When dinner was ready, the family, never health conscious, had done the best they could to find edible meat within the noxious layers of fat. The silence around the table had been the initial indicator that the entrée was not well received. Izzie had acted first, taking his dinner into the kitchen and scraping the goose into the garbage. He then filled his plate with the other offering— brisket—and made a sarcastic remark about how he had not intended to eat brisket and stuffing for Thanksgiving. Joe immediately asked for a glass of Alka-Seltzer, providing entertainment for Edna, who loved dropping the white tablets into the water to watch them fizz. The rest of the family dove into the brisket, which for some reason they served as a side dish at every holiday meal. The mood at the table had been one of consternation, rather than hunger; there was so much food that the goose was irrelevant anyway. However, the aunts and uncles' annoyance primed everyone for the dessert incident.

In most households, the tea biscuits would have gone unnoticed, because, according to the count Edna made that night, there were eight other desserts. Edna had asked Becky to please make a pumpkin pie, but Becky had said, "Pumpkin pie is something that the goyim eat for Thanksgiving." Edna had done everything she could do to persuade her grandmother. She had checked out a book from the school library that portrayed the first Thanksgiving dinner, only to be told that the Pilgrims and Indians were goyim as well.

The uncles, with huge pastry-laden plates, had not detected anything amiss, but all the aunts knew, after the first bite, that Ceal had not made the tea biscuits. Becky, Libby, Ethel, and even Millie tried to determine where Ceal got the pastry. If they had been able to read each other's thoughts (which Edna maintained they could), they would have pieced together the clues: the size of the raisins, the flavor of the jam, the texture of the dough. These were the forensics of baking. And the aunts were all first-rate detectives.

Unfortunately for her, Aunt Millie had decided to speak first, and said, "These are delicious, Ceal—better than yours. Where did you buy them, Lox and Mandel?"

———————

For months, the family disputed who said what next, and what they did. One version had Ceal, Al, and Rosalie, and Ira departing immediately, with Arthur and Millie close behind them, carrying a huge plate of the tea biscuits. Ceal said Millie had the nerve to corner her in the driveway to ask how much the pastry cost. Uncle Joe swore he never ate a single biscuit because he still had gas from the goose, but Libby said she was watching him out of the corner of her eye, and he had consumed at least two. Aunt Ethel claimed she was in the kitchen the entire time, but Becky and Libby maintained Ethel was standing next to Millie when she made the awful pronouncement. Harold and Esther initially claimed to be having an argument at one end of the living room and therefore knew nothing, although Esther later changed her version to having heard "something."

———————

Edna came to miss those days when the family disputed things like store-bought tea biscuits, the quality of rye bread, and the merits of opioids. With Joe's death, the family socializing seemed to stop. Even the Saturday night poker games. Becky could no longer keep track of how many different emergency rooms she had visited. After being turned away from Suburban Hospital ("You were just here last Tuesday, Mrs. Schwartz, we gave you enough pills for two weeks.") Becky decided it made sense to limit her list to only three hospitals she could depend on to medicate her appropriately. Three emergency rooms that did not ask many questions, understood her dilemma, and gave her the drugs she required.

Initially resentful that she had to go to these lengths to get the treatment she deserved, Becky began to view the problem as a challenge, a game, a sport—like playing cards. And she *always* knew which cards to play.

At first, she was reluctant to say anything when the nurses or doctors tried to engage her about the details of her personal life. She knew they would not understand the truth. But after a while, she decided it made sense to give them a little information— enough so she could count on them to dispense the medicine.

People liked being appreciated. Becky knew that George and Willie felt appreciated. Lurlene felt appreciated. She was convinced Larsh, whom she barely knew, both appreciated her and understood Morris could not run the business without her. And, Ira, she sensed, felt appreciated, given how easily the aunts and uncles let her blend into the family.

So, Becky began by complimenting each nurse who saw her in the emergency room, telling the hospital personnel how grateful she was for the attention they were paying her (even though, in her opinion, they were only adequate at their jobs). She then launched into a sad tale of her circumstances—a poor widow, all alone in the world, no husband, no family—absolutely no one from whom she could seek help. The more she told this story, the more she believed it was true.

She failed to notice that her only protector—Ceal—had stopped "bothering" her. In fact, Ceal seemed to Becky to be upset about something ever since Joe died. And Ceal and Libby did not seem to be spending much time together.

Ceal had not told Becky about the conversation she had with Libby following Joe's funeral. Anxious to interrogate her sister, Ceal had promised Libby she would help clean Joe's things out of the house. Joe had only been dead a week, but Libby seemed unusually calm. She had gone back to work. She was, according to Izzie, "serene."

Ceal arrived at the Warhaft house as Libby was stuffing Joe's few belongings into large trash bags.

"So, Libby, how are you?"

"Me? I'm fine, Ceal. Why do you ask?"

"I ask because—well, Libby, Joe has only been gone a week and—"

Libby interrupted her younger sister. "To tell the truth, Ceal, we didn't have much of a marriage. But you knew that. And then there was the time he sent me...sent me to the hospital. All in all, I can't tell you I'm sorry he is gone."

Ceal, methodically bagged a few more items before she confronted Libby. "I found something strange in the trash the night Joe died. Rat poison—a tube of rat poison."

Libby did not reply.

Flustered, Ceal demanded, "Libby, did you poison Joe?"

A cruel smile danced over Libby's lips. "I'm going to get some more bags, Ceal." As her sister left the room, Ceal was shaking. It was the last time they ever spoke about Joe Warhaft.

Had Becky been privy to Ceal and Libby's conversation about Joe's death, she would have advised Ceal to leave it alone. After all, she would have reasoned, Joe was hard to live with—not a bad person, but hard to live with. But even the suspicious death of Joe would not have distracted Becky from her current situation with Harold, who had stopped paying rent. Becky knew this was the cost of Harold's silence.

At least Larsh and Morris seemed content with her now. There was, however, a slight problem with Edna. Although her family, of course, did not celebrate Christmas like her classmates' families, she did not mind the holiday because it came with things she was able to enjoy. This Thanksgiving, however, was a huge disappointment.

After years of trying, Edna had finally convinced Becky to make a pumpkin pie. Edna was busy planning Thanksgiving decorations—papier-mâché turkeys, carved pumpkins—her grandmother nodding yes to each request. And then Becky announced no one was coming for Thanksgiving. It would just be Edna and her parents.

"What do you mean...Grandma...?" Edna stammered, "What do you mean! I planned all these things. You said I could have them..."

Becky raised a firm hand in front of Edna's face.

"No more talking. This is how it will be."

Edna's distress was met with no real explanation. Thanksgiving Day was quiet. Edna watched the Macy's Parade in the downstairs apartment. She could not quite make out, from the snatches of conversation she overheard, what had prompted this unusual break in tradition. She decided not to press the issue because Becky did fulfill the one commitment she had made: the pumpkin pie. Edna ate three pieces.

Edna decided to focus on Christmas, but uncharacteristically threw a temper tantrum when Becky told her she did not have time to take her downtown to Halle's Department Store to visit Mr. Jingeling.

Mr. Jingeling was a fixture in Cleveland and, for Edna, the highlight of December. The seventh floor of Halle's Department Store was decorated with snow and sparkly trees, angels, reindeer, and candy canes. Halle's pseudo-Santa asked everyone what they wanted for Christmas. Not a substitute for Santa, Mr. Jingeling was a bald elf, who, as one of Santa's helpers, carried a huge set of keys he said opened the door to Santa's workshop. Each year, Edna patiently informed him that the gifts would have to arrive for Chanukah—for eight consecutive nights—and that was okay with Mr. Jingeling. She even memorized the Mr. Jingeling song:

Mister Jingeling/How You Tingeling/Keeper of the Keys

On Halle's Seventh Floor/We'll be Looking for/You to Turn the Keys

He Keeps Track/Of Santa's Sack/And Treasure House of Toys

With Wind Up Things/That Santa Brings/To All Good Girls and Boys

When Becky informed Edna she did not have time to take her to Halle's this year, Edna became so difficult that Becky called Ceal, who agreed to take Edna on Saturday when she did not have to work. Al promised Edna they would also take her, along with Rosalie and Ira, to see the Christmas lights at Nela Park. This pacified Edna somewhat—the lights at Nela Park were splendid. But Edna ended up in the principal's office that week when she informed her classmates at Belvoir Elementary that the Santa Claus that visited them was really the school janitor.

Although snow-covered, with a touch of winter glisten, the homes on South Green Road exhibited no Christmas finery—most families on the tiny block were Jewish, except, of course, for *those* tenants of the Frankels. Becky glared at Dorothy Frankel every time she saw her leave the house. Although the Christophers generally kept to themselves, and no one made any overtures toward them, their Christmas lights were visible, flickering through their living room window. To Esther, the lights brought comfort, reminding her of the Cafferellis of her youth. However, the glow from the tree next door added to Becky's chest pain.

The single acknowledgment Becky gave to the Christmas season was to please Larsh. She adored everything about him. When he came to the Katofsky house on Christmas Eve laden with brightly wrapped packages, Becky could not turn him away. There was a new Barbie doll for Edna, complete with several sets of clothes and a Barbie car, and a stylish hat for Becky. Larsh, ever the gentleman and politician, had red-ribbon-wrapped trays of Polish pastry—which Becky only admitted to herself were as good as anything produced in the Katofsky kitchen.

After tending to the broken arm she imagined Barbie had, Edna fell asleep around ten o'clock that night. Sirens next door awakened her—it was two a.m. She pulled her bedroom window shade up and was immediately confused. *Why were all the lights on at the Frankel house?* People were coming in and out, and Edna saw Dorothy Frankel running through the upstairs apartment, holding both sides of her head. It looked like she was screaming.

She heard her parents' bedroom door open but was too frightened to go into the hallway. It took her over an hour to fall asleep because she could not get the image of Dorothy Frankel out of her head.

Their bedroom was empty when Edna woke up the next morning. She went into the kitchen, heard voices downstairs, and ran to her grandparents' apartment. Harold was sitting at Becky's kitchen table, Esther beside him, wringing her hands, and a sleepy Edna tuned into her father's voice. "A stroke. How do you like that! Dorothy had a stroke! A young woman like her." Turning to his mother-in-law, Harold taunted, "I guess you never know when something like that is going to happen, do you Becky?"

Becky sent Harold a withering look, and Edna, standing in the kitchen, asked, "Is Ricky's mother dead?"

Esther answered. "Yes, Edna, Mrs. Frankel died last night."

"But who was that woman running through the apartment?"

"Her sister, that was Mrs. Frankel's sister."

Edna sat down on the kitchen floor. She did not know Mrs. Frankel had a sister. She also did not know what a stroke was and was about to ask when she heard a car pulling into the Frankel's driveway. Edna went to the Katofsky dining room window and saw Mort and Ricky Frankel, neither wearing boots, climb out of Mort's car. Mort looked tired. Ricky looked like he had been crying.

Ricky glanced up, saw Edna, and waved. Edna waved back, ran into the kitchen, and asked the group, "Ricky and his dad are home, can I go over there now?"

Esther responded, "No, Edna, not now. Now is not the time." Edna turned her face toward her grandmother, who had become pale. She did not answer.

Harold continued his monologue of disbelief. "I just saw Dorothy two days ago. And then, poof." He flailed his arms for empha-
sis. "Poof, she's gone. How do you like them apples?"

Becky could not tolerate a minute more of this conversation.
She began breathing heavily and headed to her back bedroom.

Edna was frightened. What she had never told anyone was that,
on a daily basis, she was afraid that Becky was going to die. She
could not bear the thought. Grandma was a little crazy—everyone
knew that—but Edna loved her. Really loved her. And now, with
Zaide, Uncle Joe, and Mrs. Frankel gone, she began to think that
could happen to her grandmother. *After all, Mrs. Frankel wasn't
even sick, and Grandma has a terrible heart condition.*

Edna sat quietly on the kitchen floor, listening to her parents
discussing Dorothy's demise. Grandpa had gone to work. Ceal
pulled into the driveway. She headed over to the Katofskys right
after that morning's "What's new?" report broadcast Dorothy's
death. Edna noticed Aunt Ceal looked pale as well, even though
she was sure her aunt did not know Mrs. Frankel. After hearing
Becky had retreated to the back bedroom, Ceal took Edna by
the hand, walked into the living room, and snuggled Edna on
her lap.

Although the death of such a young woman had jolted all the
aunts and uncles, Ceal was particularly upset. She had planned to
share some news of her own, then changed her mind, deciding she
would seek the counsel of her siblings right after the New Year, but
the frightened look on Edna's face caused her to rethink. Well, she
had Al as a confidant. That would have to be enough. *And everyone
has tsores, don't they?*

She absentmindedly surveyed the garish trappings of the Ka-tofsky living room while rocking Edna in her lap. She was mustering the strength to enter Becky's bedroom and listen to the litany of imagined illnesses. For a moment, Ceal wished she could trade places with her drug-addicted, hypochondriacal sister, then caught herself. *No, of course, I don't want to do that.*

She and Al had been through much worse than what was down the road for them now. At first, she thought the doctor's diagnosis was some sort of a sick joke. He must have somehow heard about Becky—or maybe he and Dr. Gold were secret confidants. But it was no joke—it was real. Even Al could not believe it when she told him she had a serious heart condition, and open-heart surgery was on the horizon.

Chapter 32

EVERYTHING WAS OUT OF SYNC, ROUTINES ABANDONED. Abe's Sunday appearances at the Katofskys were erratic as well. Morris was reluctant to tell his brother he and Becky knew he was a gambler. Becky promised Morris she would not mention it to Abe, which Morris interpreted as a gracious, yet uncharacteristic, gesture from his wife.

In truth, Becky could not be bothered by what was happening to Abe. If it occupied Morris and distracted him from her visits from Dr. Gold, all the better. If Morris no longer wondered if she stayed home all day or not—although she believed he had no idea she left the house for long periods of time—that was fine, too. Abe had demonstrated himself to be a liar—totally untrustworthy. And he had tried to take money from them both—so a *goniff* as well. If Abe had gambling debts, well, *he took after Morris, didn't he? Morris couldn't play cards either.*

She purposely did not tell Morris about the phone calls she was receiving from Frances, who told Becky she was worried that Abe seemed to be neither at home nor at work most of the time. "I even made a point of going to the candy store, Aunt Becky," Frances told her. "And they told me they had not seen Abe for days. He had left them strict instructions about opening and closing the shop and told them he could not be reached."

Becky was barely listening as Frances droned on, "I went to Abe's apartment, and Aunt Becky, I'm telling you, it looked like he had been gone for weeks."

This last piece of news sparked Becky's interest. "You went inside his apartment?"

Frances hesitated. "Yes, I did. I went inside. I have the keys."

You have the keys. She was not eager to become entangled in anything Frances was doing. As Ceal admonished her long ago, following Esther's wedding, "You have now learned your lesson concerning your niece Frances Black." It was years before the family said anything positive about her, always warning against any interaction with Morris's niece. Libby was fond of saying when things were not going well, "It could be worse, Frances Black could be here."

Becky was now focused, determined to discover what Abe was hiding from them, so she told Morris to get in touch with Frances.

"Prepare yourself, Uncle Moshe," Frances warned as Morris followed her into Abe's apartment. Morris winced as he walked through the door. The kitchen sink was piled high with dirty dishes. There was trash all over the small one-bedroom. On the kitchen counter, was a mason jar that Abe had cracked open. Morris found a single penny from the jar beside the sink.

Loose change? Morris wondered. *Why would Abe smash open a glass jar full of change?* Frances lunged for Abe's closet—most of his clothes were gone. By the telephone was a small pad of paper, with a series of phone numbers. Morris handed the pad to Frances, who shrugged her shoulders. With no explanation, Morris opened the freezer. The only contents were several trays of ice, and Morris noticed there were plastic figures encased in the cubes. The first tray held replicas of Hawaiian hula dancers and women's legs with frilly garters. The second tray contained large, buxom women, their huge breasts taking up most of the available space in the cubes. Morris handed the trays to Frances, who wrinkled her nose and ran the ice immediately under hot water, watching the hula girls' bare breasts slide down the drain.

There were several empty cartons of Chinese food. Morris did not know Abe ate Chinese food. In fact, the only person *he* knew who ate Chinese food was George. On occasions, when George decided to buy lunch, he would seek out the closest Chinese "hole in the wall," as George described it. He once brought an eggroll back for the boss, which Morris discarded when George wasn't looking.

Morris sank into an overstuffed green corduroy chair, the only thing he recognized in the apartment. Becky had given it to Abe when she replaced some furniture, and Abe had thanked her profusely for the gift. His eyes now moist, Morris looked around the room several times. He noticed a small overflowing trashcan, with something protruding from the top.

He motioned to Frances to bring the can over. He pulled out the contents—empty matchbooks from places Morris had never heard of. And a map. Morris unfolded it.

"What is this?" he asked his niece.

Frances frowned. "It's a map of Florida, Uncle Moshe."

Why would Abe have a map of Florida, with various points circled? Only one way to find out. He had to go to Florida to search for his brother.

––––––––

Abe barely had enough money left to get back home, when the man at the window said to him, "Go take a look at the flamingoes, buddy." At first, he thought it was a joke. The odd birds he had only seen as plastic reproductions in his brother's yard were walking in front of him as he stood, anxiety ridden, in the hot sun. Staring at Abe, one of the flamingoes honked, causing him to lose his balance.

Brushing the gravel from his pants, it all seemed like a bad dream. A nightmare. He had lost several hundred more dollars in the last couple of days. He had taken the loan from Frances, paid the debt, and made a little money at home at the track. But now he was gambling it away. The Florida sun was no longer soothing against his unshaven face—instead, it had a searing, metallic feel. Although he had successfully pushed all thoughts of family out of his head for days (and he had no friends), he found himself becoming sentimental and melancholic, thinking about Morris.

Maybe it was time to tell Moshe the truth. Like the gawkish birds standing in front of him, he had managed to create a comfortable sense of mystery about his life and proclivities. He would miss that. And unless he was forthcoming, no one ever had to know about this. *Ever.*

While he had several imaginary conversations with Morris, confessing his visits to Thistledown and Randall Raceways, this trip to Hialeah Racetrack would be hard to explain. Even he did not understand why he decided to go. Or how he had lost so much money once he got here. Or why he could not stop. He did not understand at all why he could not end it.

The bird honked again, *like a goose,* Abe thought. He had several hours before the first leg of his bus trip home. He was thankful he still had the crumpled, Greyhound ticket in his pocket. *And I can get by for a few more weeks on my own once I'm back in Cleveland, then, maybe, I can ask Frances for more help.*

Three hundred miles north, with the motor sputtering, Morris, exhausted and somewhat confused, pulled into the parking lot of the Fountain of Youth in St. Augustine, Florida. Becky had agreed to his trip to look for Abe on one condition—that Morris bring her back a bottle of water from this hallowed spring. Leaving the dusty, dry parking lot, Morris became wide-eyed at the sight of several peacocks walking alongside him. Suddenly, one fanned its enormous tail. Morris stopped, unable to take his eyes off the strange bird. He blinked, and thought the bird blinked back. "Too much sun..." he said to himself.

Morris wandered through the park, beginning to feel melancholic. After encounters with several individuals, using his fragmented English to try to explain where he was headed, he found the famous springs. The first taste of the water was repugnant. *Becky would never drink this.* He glanced at his watch—he was so tired. *And what was he doing? Why did he decide to go all the way to Florida to find Abe? Did Frances talk him into it? He could not remember.* He thought he made the decision on his own, but he'd thought Frances would tell him, "Wait, Uncle Moshe. I'm sure Abe will come home soon, wherever he is." But she didn't say that. The cranky niece not only encouraged this adventure, she offered to go with him. That's right—offered to go with him! Or did she? His memory was cloudy.

"No, no," he had told her, "you need to stay here and take care of your mother." *But why had Becky agreed to let him go? Did these people suddenly have faith in him? Morris, who never did anything right?* He was emboldened now. He had a mission, and he would not fail. He never had to admit to anyone the difficulty he had figuring out where Florida was.

Chapter 33

BECKY WAS IN A PANIC. EVERYONE WAS DYING—DORO-
thy Frankel, her father, Joe—she was convinced she would
be next. *And where was Abe? He was probably dead, too.* She
had to devise a plan to save herself, to protect herself. She was
confident the family was distracted. *And they didn't care about her
anyway, did they?*

Morris was still on some crazy mission to find Abe in Florida. The welfare of his brother was obviously more important to
him than the reality that his wife's health placed her in constant
peril. *And, really, when did he ever inquire about her health? Only
to question her calls to Gold.* She was convinced he must be angry
about the doctor bills. *But how could it be about the bills—she kept
the books—Morris didn't even know how much money they had. And
Morris was never angry.*

The rest of the family—all they cared about was themselves.
Izzie and Arthur kept making more and more money and never
asked her once, "How are you feeling today, Becky?" Esther was
useless—she could barely do the few things Becky asked of her.

She was pleased that she had that bastard Harold under control—as long as she slipped him money, he kept quiet about the Demerol that Gold left for her. *Maybe she could bribe Harold to steal some drugs from the pharmacy. Why hadn't she thought of that before?* But she could not depend on that, which was the problem.

Before *Zaide's* death, Becky might have trusted Ceal or Libby. But Ceal was behaving oddly—appearing more distraught about Joe's demise than Libby. And Libby—now that Libby was a widow, she probably needed money. *Well, she won't be getting it from me!*

There was no one, she concluded, whom she could depend on but herself. The anxiety from the responsibility made her chest pains unusually strong. She downed a Percocet, a Darvon, and several swigs of paregoric. She had to act fast—and tomorrow would be the perfect opportunity. Esther would be gone for the day, and although she had agreed to watch Edna, that would not be a problem. Edna was a good child. There were times she sensed her granddaughter would even understand Becky's problems, if she chose to confide in her. *However, Edna could not be trusted to keep a secret.* Edna had too close a relationship with Ceal, and that prying Ceal could eventually coax any information she wanted out of the child.

Becky suspected Edna was confiding in Ira as well. Becky told Ceal she was "surprised how smart Ira was," which only elicited a prolonged lecture from Ceal. She assumed Ceal only told Ira negative things about her—so who was to say what Ira really knew and thought about all this? *How bizarre was that—a Negro Jewish member of the family? Well, it must have been the stress of Rosalie. Ceal went mad. Insane. If Becky had time after she took care of herself, she would have to reassert her position in the family hierarchy and put all of them back in their places. Especially Ceal.*

The real enemy was time. Time ran out for Zaide. He was eighty-six, but still his time did run out. And Joe. She assumed Joe would live forever—just to spite Libby. Becky tried to clear her mind of Dorothy Frankel. *And if that son of a bitch Harold said to her one more time, "Here today, gone tomorrow," well, she could not predict how she would respond.*

They could all go to hell. She knew what she needed to do. She picked up the phone and began making calls. Everything could be put into place by tomorrow.

———

Esther woke up not quite believing that she was going to be out of the house for the entire day. She was so surprised when Izzie's wife, Ethel, invited her downtown for lunch and a movie. She loved the Old Mill Restaurant—it was the best cafeteria she had ever been to. She would wear her one good dress. They were going to see *El Cid*, and she loved Charlton Heston movies. Edna, as always, would be fine with Becky.

Esther had not anticipated having an argument with her daughter before she left. When she told Edna she was disposing of her tile collection, the child went ballistic, alarming Esther. Construction on the back lots of South Green Road was dormant for the winter, yet Esther had discovered Edna was now adding nails to the bucket that held her tile collection.

"Edna," Esther said to her daughter, "you can keep collecting tile if you promise me you will not pick up any nails. You could get tetanus."

Edna was indignant. "But I need them," she protested, "and I'm going to keep collecting them."

"No, you are not," her mother said, taking the bucket away from her. "And I am going to have your father get rid of all this stuff over the weekend."

Edna knew her mother never invoked Harold's name unless she was serious.

As soon as Esther left with Ethel, an enraged Edna headed to the basement—a place that held a strange attraction for her. There was a finished recreation room, but no one ever used it. In that room, there was a tiny closet. Edna told her mother on numerous occasions that she thought the closet was haunted. Esther dismissed these fears, saying, "Really, Edna some of the things you imagine." The tiny room had a peculiar design, with a sloping ceiling, like an attic. Edna sometimes convinced herself that she heard voices coming from the miniscule closet, only to realize she was listening to echoes from the upstairs kitchen.

She finally shared her fears with Ceal: the ghost of Joe Warhaft haunted the closet. Edna had given Ceal a drawing to put in Uncle Joe's casket, and she had included a sealed note to Uncle Joe as well.

Ceal had initially wanted to ask Edna what she had written to Joe, and then changed her mind. She hesitated at the funeral home before placing the note alongside her brother-in-law, and for a moment thought perhaps she should read what Edna had written. But, knowing how odd Edna could be, and still shaken by her conversation with Libby, Ceal decided against tearing open the envelope.

Edna had invited Uncle Joe to come back and visit her—as a ghost—and asked him to meet her in the closet in the basement. At first, Edna thought this was a good idea—poor Uncle Joe might be as miserably lonely dead as he had been when he was alive. But, upon reflection, Edna thought perhaps this invitation to her late great-uncle was a mistake. She did accept Aunt Ceal's explanation that the voices she heard downstairs in the basement were mere echoes from the kitchen above, but that did not mean that Uncle Joe hadn't taken her up on her invitation.

Most probably, he was hiding in the closet. Silent. Just as he was when he was alive. Waiting for someone to acknowledge him and talk to him. That made perfect sense to Edna, and she dreaded finding out if her theory was indeed true.

Focused on her mission to retrieve her tile bucket, she searched the entire rec room before realizing it must be in the closet.

That's where my bucket must be. Mommy knows I won't go in there.

Edna stood staring at the closet door. Maybe she could ask Joe to push the bucket out of the closet. *Would he do that? For her? He must know from the picture and invitation that even if no one else was sorry he was gone, she was.* She opened her mouth but paused. A lot was at stake here. And then, inhaling deeply, her eyes squinting, she yanked open the door. The closet was empty. She decided to retrace her steps.

She moved to the part of the basement that housed Morris's sanding equipment, an extra refrigerator and freezer, and the entrance to a locker. She opened the freezer—no bucket in there. Her last hope was the locker. She never went into the locker—and she knew that was something else her mother counted on. She assumed it was where the family was going to hide during a nuclear war, which was a better idea than under her desk at school.

She opened the creaking locker door and tugged on the dusty cord attached to a lone light bulb. She jumped when she saw several spiders crawl across the concrete floor. She looked up.

There, on the highest shelf, was her bucket of tiles.

The DeSoto sputtered from exhaustion as Morris pulled into the parking lot at the Hialeah Park Race Track. The attendant gave him an unusual look, then a lengthy explanation of how he would have to purchase a ticket to gain entry. Katofsky was confused, and the attendant finally said, "Do you speak English, buddy?"

Morris replied, "No cowabunga!"

The attendant began gesturing to explain what he needed to do, and finally a beleaguered Morris rolled into the racetrack.

He was overwhelmed. *How am I going to get Abe out of all this trouble and deal with Becky at the same time? And what if Abe isn't here? And how am I going to find my way back to Ohio?*

Abe must be here. Frances would not have sent Morris all the way to Florida for no reason. What did she say? "I'm sure it is not a wild goose chase, Uncle Moshe!" What did that mean, anyway? Even in Yiddish? What was Frances talking about—oily, greasy geese?

He wanted to ask Ceal for help, but for some reason, she seemed distraught over something else. *Anyway, first things first. He was convinced he would find Abe at Hialeah because that was the only thing that made sense. Abe was a gambler. Always talked about how much he liked horse races. Hialeah, where else could he be?*

Slamming the door of the DeSoto, he began wandering around the racetrack. He did not have to go far. Lying on a bench, a crumpled newspaper and empty beer can beside him, was his brother.

Abe, without a dime to his name, had fallen asleep on a bench. His brown sport jacket was laced with bird residue. He was filthy. His few wisps of graying hair were matted on his perspiring, bald head. He was snoring heavily. Morris was about to shake his sleeping sibling, when Abe opened his eyes.

At first, Abe thought he must be dreaming. Then, in halting Yiddish, he asked, "Moshe, is that you?"

Morris walked silently to his brother, extending his hand. Both men began to cry. There was no need to speak. Abe knew it was time to go home, and he was relieved that Moshe had come for him. Abe struggled to his feet. Morris asked him when he had last had something to eat. Abe shrugged his shoulders, and Morris said they should buy some sandwiches.

Oblivious to the whispers of passersby about the two strange old men wandering through the park, the Katofsky brothers, armed with cheese sandwiches, sat down in front of the flamingoes to have lunch. Morris began to laugh uncontrollably. Turning to his brother, he said, "They are real!"

"Yes," Abe said, laughing too, "they are real."

The two men continued laughing, swigging bottles of Coca-Cola, neither of them sure why this all seemed so terribly funny.

With Abe safely passed out in the back seat of the car, Morris turned his thoughts to Becky. Something had to be done. *Well, there is plenty of time to take care of all of that once I get Abe home and settled.* The return to Ohio would take several days, but the good news was that everything was okay—he had his brother. He would make sure Abe was rested, showered, and had clean clothes. Then they would talk about Abe's future. *Maybe Abe could stay with Becky and him while they worked things out. And maybe Larsh could help. The two men—Morris and Larsh—understood each other. They were lantsmen. And you always helped a lantsman.*

As with most everything else in Morris's life, he was unprepared for what he found when he finally arrived at the house on South Green Road.

———

Edna left the basement and ran back upstairs. Activity at 2207 had increased. People were carrying things in and out of the house. Edna waited until she was sure Becky was paying absolutely no attention to her. There were numerous trucks pulling up to 2207. More people were coming and going. Edna had no idea what was happening. Lurlene seemed upset. Grandma stayed in her back bedroom.

She paused for a moment. *Why was Lurlene so upset?* She saw a strange woman go into Morris's bedroom. *Who was that? What was that all about?* Well, there would be an explanation of some sort. Or maybe no explanation at all. But it wasn't the first time that events turned suddenly strange at Grandma's.

She could not waste any more time. She had a plan. She knew her tile fragments were soon to meet the same fate as her tonsils. Edna returned to the basement and went straight for the locker. She stacked milk crates and anything else she could grab to build a ladder that would enable her to rescue her tile bucket. She found a small pile of bricks and began layering them between the crates.

She climbed carefully, hesitating when she felt her construction wobble beneath her feet. Soon she was within reach—her outstretched arm mere inches from the shelf and the bucket. She could see there were more tiles in the bucket than she remembered and decided she would have to stand on tiptoe. She tugged the bucket's handle and felt herself turning sideways.

As if in slow motion, she tried to grab onto something as the crates gave way, but she could not stop or break her fall. Covered with fragments of porcelain and rusty nails, her head bleeding, Edna lay unconscious on the basement floor.

Chapter 34

BEFORE HE LEFT TO RETRIEVE HIS BROTHER, MORRIS had Becky give George and Willie each a week's pay. Willie was glad to have the time off. He did not know where the old man was going, or why, and he found himself doing the same thing that Becky had done for all these years—seeking answers to things he knew were none of his business.

Edna was disappointed when Willie told her he would be off for a week because he had promised to sneak her some baseball cards. Edna told him she was not allowed to have them—they cost too much. Her father prohibited them. Willie was disgusted. *Harold wasn't even conniving enough to use the bubble gum as an excuse. Amazing. A guy like that—a pharmacist—could not even spring a nickel to give his kid some baseball cards.*

He hated himself for becoming sentimental about Edna. *What good would that do anyone? But maybe the one aunt, Mrs. Katofsky's sister Ceal, the one Edna talked about all the time, maybe Ceal would wind up doing some good for the child.*

Well, at least he could drop the cards off at the house. He and

Edna had agreed on a secret place, behind the bushes in the front yard. Willie promised to seal the cards in a plastic bag and leave them in a cigar box she had given him—Dutch Masters—the one gift she got from Harold were empty cigar boxes from the pharmacy.

As Willie approached the house at 2207, he was alarmed by the level of activity. Maybe Mrs. Katofsky was in some sort of trouble again? He pulled into the driveway and ran inside.

Willie and Lurlene almost collided as he sprang through the side door of the Katofsky house. In a stream-of-consciousness flow, the distraught maid told him what was going on. He knew immediately this was not a place he wanted to be—or to be found. He abandoned any thought of leaving the baseball cards for Edna. He even wondered if Morris was ever returning to 2207.

He let Lurlene calm down and then left the Katofsky home. He got halfway down South Green Road when he decided to turn around and head back to 2207. Although everyone inquired later—more than once—Willie did not know what made him return to ask Lurlene where Edna was.

Lurlene became hysterical again. "The child—Edna—that's right, where is Edna?" the frantic maid said aloud. Huffing and puffing, her wide frame almost making the stairwell impassable, Lurlene, as quickly as she could, darted upstairs to the second floor. Nothing seemed out of place. The apartment appeared empty, but Lurlene knew Edna had a hiding place—in her bedroom closet—and she yanked open the door. Neatly arranged in the closet were a group of dolls and a small pile of twigs Edna had collected from the neighbors' yards.

Willie realized this was the only time he had ever been on the second floor of 2207. He knew Becky never ventured upstairs—she had made that clear in one of her rambling, prying conversations with him. On a few occasions, he had heard Morris call up to Edna from the small landing that led to the second-floor stairs. *"Yenta Telebente!"* he would bellow, and Edna would come bouncing down to see him. Willie had no idea what the Yiddish meant, and was surprised to learn from Edna that she did not know either.

He surveyed the small bedroom. *Not exactly a little girl's bedroom.* On her bed was a baseball mitt. The wall was adorned with several Cleveland Indians posters. No wonder she wants the baseball cards. She had never told him she was an Indians fan. He glanced back at the closet, at the dolls and the twigs. *What a strange child.* His thoughts kept wandering until Lurlene shook his shoulder. "Edna," she said plaintively, "we have to keep looking for Edna."

Willie commanded Lurlene to head for the basement and the two ran downstairs. They were going room to room, when Willie noticed a small hand protruding from the locker. He gently pushed the door back and saw Edna's tiny frame on the cement floor. He picked her up—she was barely breathing. Lurlene screamed. Willie removed his shirt and wrapped it around Edna's head to try to stop the bleeding. He instructed Lurlene to call the telephone operator for help as he tried to perform CPR which he'd recently read about in a magazine.

Lurlene shot up the stairs and phoned an ambulance. Then she called Ceal, but there was no answer at the Kirstein house.

Ceal was already on her way to the Katofskys—she had arranged with Ethel to get Esther out of the house so she could have

259

a talk with Becky. *A talk.* It was intended to be a talk. She promised Al it was going to be just a talk. But Ceal knew it was going to be a confrontation—and potentially a nasty one. She was determined not to tell Becky the unexpected news about her own health. That part would be easy—not telling. But Ceal was apprehensive that years of frustration, resentment, and disappointment with Becky would cause her to begin spewing in every direction.

Al tried coaxing her into a different mindset. "Your sister is mentally ill, Ceal. You are the educated one. She needs help. I don't know what kind of help we can get her—but she needs it."

"And," Al had admonished her, "the real issue at this point is Edna. No child belongs in that house, what with all that is going on. The real problem is Edna." Ceal knew he was right.

As the taxi approached 2207, Ceal was distracted by the assortment of vehicles parked outside. *What on earth is going on here now?* Before she was even able to exit the cab, she heard the faint sound of sirens. Then, in disbelief, she saw the ambulance roar into the driveway, blaring at the taxi to get out of the way.

With her heart beginning to beat rapidly—*breathe slowly, remember what the doctor told you,* she reminded herself—she ran through the front door, pushing her way past a group of men who were unloading medical equipment from a large truck parked behind the ambulance, and entered her sister's bedroom.

Becky's bedroom at South Green Road could only be described now as "state of the art." There was a hospital bed, an additional oxygen tank, a heart monitor, and about every form of emergency equipment one could imagine. Becky, from her bed, turned toward Ceal, and then turned away.

Ceal began walking backward when she saw a woman she did not recognize unpacking a suitcase in Morris's bedroom. "Who are you?" Ceal demanded of the stranger. The woman matter-of-factly informed her she was the nurse who was moving in "to take care of Mrs. Katofsky." Ceal felt nauseated. She wobbled into the kitchen, then out the side door where she was shocked to see ambulance attendants strapping a seemingly lifeless Edna, covered in blood, to a stretcher. By Edna's side was Willie, shirtless, holding the child's hand. In the driveway, Lurlene sat hunched over, sobbing.

Ceal started to scream, caught herself, and then, along with Willie, climbed into the ambulance.

Ceal asked the ambulance attendant for the third time, "Is she still alive?" The attendant assured Ceal she was, but said he had to concentrate on monitoring Edna's shallow breathing. Ceal was too frightened to cry. She held Edna's limp hand, rubbing her small forearm as if to will consciousness back into the tiny body. They arrived at Huron Road Hospital, and Edna was carried away. Willie asked Ceal what calls he should make. She knew she could not reach Al. She instructed Willie to call Izzie and Arthur and to tell Izzie to find Ethel and Esther and bring them to the hospital.

A doctor came out and informed Ceal they were taking Edna into surgery. Willie returned and told Ceal her brothers were on the way.

"Should I call Edna's father?" Willie asked the shaking Ceal.

"No, I will—I mean—where is the pay phone, Willie?"

Harold picked up the pharmacy phone on the third ring, and for the first time in Ceal's memory, without question, dropped everything he was doing and headed to the hospital.

Willie asked Ceal if he could stay and wait with her.

"Yes, of course," she told him. Then, she added, "And thank you, Willie."

He nodded.

Edna thought she was dreaming. She remembered hearing Aunt Ceal's voice, but it sounded far away. She felt several arms under her body, moving her. It seemed like she was on a cold bed. She wanted to open her eyes—but could not. Two thoughts went through her mind: "Please don't cry, Willie" and "Please don't cry, Aunt Ceal."

Then there were no thoughts at all.

Chapter 35

MORRIS SAT ON A LAWN CHAIR IN THE BACKYARD OF the house on South Green Road as he moved Edna's teeter-totter up and down with one hand. He closed his eyes so he could picture his granddaughter on the swing set—jumping off at whatever she thought was the "right moment," and running around collecting flowers. He remembered last spring when, armed with a broomstick, he spent an hour waving away the birds that were attacking his cherry trees, with Edna by his side, yelling, "Get them, Grandpa! Get them!" He walked to the side of the garage and the overgrown lilies. He would ask Koppelman to tear them all out—as a favor to him. Maybe he would plant something in their place. Or maybe he would not plant anything at all.

He returned to the green-and-white lawn chair, repositioning himself by the teeter-totter. He had always been afraid Edna would fall off and hurt herself—she would go up and down so quickly with the boy from next door. He caught himself in a half-laugh that he suppressed, almost gagging. *This is what you thought was dangerous, Moshe?* He felt another wave of anxiety and tried to control his breathing.

Edna's bike remained in the garage—he would get rid of it eventually. The locker had been cleaned out, although it had been harder than he anticipated to remove the bloodstains from the cement. George suggested he use one of the sanders, but Morris knew the weight of the machines would crack the surface. Koppelman told him he first needed to scrub the stains with a strong bristle brush to remove any dried blood. Then, Koppelman advised him, pouring hydrogen peroxide on the stains should remove them completely. But Morris froze when he went into the basement, so Larsh removed the dark red blotches for him.

"It is not for you to do, Morris," Larsh had assured him. "This whole business is...was...I will do it for you." His friend put his hand on Katofsky's shoulder for the first time.

He caught the teeter-totter and carefully rested it on the ground. Ceal was right, he supposed. *It was everyone's fault—not his alone. They all saw—but did not see. They all knew—but did not know.* He heard the screen door at the side of the house slam shut.

He went back inside where he could hear Becky calling for the new nurse, Louise, to straighten her pillows and bedcovers, and then change the channel on the television. He wandered into the living room, where bedsheets and blankets had been neatly arranged on the sofa for him. His first instinct, months ago, had been to remove the plastic from the couch before spreading out the sheets to make his bed, but he stopped himself when he realized that no one had ever removed the plastic. Not even once.

Ceal had told him the psychiatric hospital said Esther was doing as well as could be expected. She still was not talking. She was something Ceal called "catatonic." She had been that way ever since the moment the doctor told her about Edna. They might have to give Esther something called "shock therapy." He was afraid to ask Ceal exactly what that was. Harold, though, was visiting Esther every day. At least that was some good news. Morris wanted to tell Becky, but Louise insisted his wife was not interested in seeing anyone. And Becky did not inquire about anybody or anything.

Abe suggested Morris come live with him. Just until everyone was better—Becky, Esther. When everyone was okay again, Morris could move back into the house. Frances urged him to accept Abe's offer, saying, "After all, Uncle Moshe, things are so unsettled now. Just until things get better." *Did Abe and Frances believe things would eventually be better? Was Abe better?* Abe was now coming to the house every Sunday again—with Frances and Lena. Frances brought along the cake and coffee that Becky used to provide for the gathering.

Morris only briefly considered staying with Abe. He was reluctant to leave 2207 South Green Road now that things had been turned upside down. *Maybe none of this would have happened if he had not gone to Florida.* Ceal told him it would have eventually happened anyway—she was right, somehow Ceal was always right.

At least business was going well—and it was a good suggestion that Ceal had about letting Willie do the books. Larsh was thrilled with the idea and told Morris, "I was about to suggest the same thing myself." Morris admitted to himself that he liked Willie. Larsh liked Willie, too. Ceal had told him Willie had been wonderful during the emergency—and Morris knew he should be grateful for that.

For Willie, doing the books was a form of restitution. Becky had come close to unmasking him—at least in his mind. *What would they think if they found out he had gone to jail for embezzlement, only to be released later when it was discovered another teller at the bank had taken the money? Would they have kept him employed?* That was a question that would never surface now, Willie was convinced. He was respectable again—the business manager for Katofsky & Larsh.

Business was better than ever for Morris. They were about to hire three more people. *A good thing, too. Becky's equipment and nurses were expensive.* Morris wandered for a few minutes in the living room, and then put on one of the records he used to listen to with Edna in his lap. Absent tears, he slipped into his now-daily dull feeling, closing his eyes as he thought about his granddaughter.

———

Fifteen minutes away from 2207 South Green Road, in Cleveland Heights, Ira came home early from school to help Ceal straighten the house and get things ready. She was excited. She knew Ceal was excited, too. She helped Rosalie put on a new outfit and spent twenty minutes brushing Rosalie's hair.

A car pulled slowly into Ceal's driveway and the passenger door of the Chevy opened. Ira ran out and Harold handed her a suitcase. A few steps behind Ira was Ceal, who walked more slowly since the heart surgery. She reached into the automobile and took Edna by the hand as she slid out of the front seat, limping slightly. Harold gave Edna her silver walker.

"Are you going to go see Esther now?" Ceal asked Harold.

"Yes, yes, of course," Harold replied.

"How is she?"

Harold saw Edna studying his face, waiting to hear his answer. "She is going to be okay—it will take some time. But everything will be okay again soon—just like it was before."

He leaned over to Edna, handing her a packet of baseball cards and comic books. Edna hesitated. She pulled the top comic out of the bag—her favorite, *Lois Lane*.

Slightly apprehensive, she looked at her father and said, "I don't know when I will be able to give them back."

Harold paused, and then said, "You don't have to give them back. They are yours to keep."

Edna, a bit confused, took the package. "The baseball cards, too?"

"Yes," Harold replied, "the baseball cards, too. See you later, alligator."

Edna broke into a smile and replied, "After a while, crocodile."

Tightly gripping her great-aunt's hand, she walked up the front stairs to Ceal's porch, paused, and turned around. The huge smile still on her face, she waved goodbye to her father.

Harold waved back as Edna and Ceal entered the house and closed the door.

Acknowledgments

Thanks to Alice Peck, Duane Stapp, and Ruth Mullen for making it happen.

Special thanks to Carole for putting the pieces together.